A Pinch of Coriander

Available Now

A Pinch of Coriander:
Book One
Time Will Tell

A Pinch of Coriander:
Book Two
The Truth About Secrets

A Pinch of Coriander:
Book Three
Long Way Home

A Pinch of Coriander

Book Two:
The Truth About Secrets

Loretta Gatto-White

Loretta Gatto-White, Publisher: https://gattowhitewrites.com

Cover designed by Kate Cowan

ISBN 978-1-7750341-2-4 (Paperback edition)
ISBN 978-1-7750341-3-1 (eBook edition)

Print Edition

Chapter One

WINTER

A POST CHRISTMAS PACKAGE

IT WAS AFTER New Year's and Nick was experiencing some holiday remorse, as he sat at the edge of the bed struggling with his socks, groaning with the effort to pull them on.

"Oh god, looks like I'll have to take Pickles speed-walking now to lose this Christmas package. And I think we'll be eating less carbs too."

"Fine by me. Look, I can't even do up the top button on my new suede slacks, which isn't fair, as I've been abstemious, haven't even had much of an appetite…damn, I wanted to wear them today. Guess I'm bloated. Oh well, I'm just going to the doctor's, I think stretchy jeans and a loose pullover will do."

She held-up her black jeans against a new plum cashmere turtleneck, a present from Jesse. "Now, some silver earrings and the vintage mother of pearl pin you got me, and I'm set." Lidia turned, smiling at Nick, who was buttoning his shirt.

"Lovely bella, as usual. But why are you going to the doctor? You've had your flu shot already, haven't you?" Nick asked, straightening the pillows on his side of the bed.

"Oh yes, before Christmas. I'm due for my cervical exam, stress test, mammogram, and blood work. I decided to get it all done in one go, then forget about it for the rest of the year.

"I booked the day off, but if I get an early start, I can get the mammogram without much waiting, see Dr. Avery for the poke and probe, blood work requisition, then I'm almost home free. Should be back by three."

Lidia gave Nick a peck on the cheek, as he fastened his watch strap, ready for his first day back at the college, and the new year staff meeting.

"Good, then perhaps a nosh at ComPanis later?" Nick said.

"Aren't we watching our carbs?" Lidia reproached.

"Domani." Nick waved his hand, dismissing her objection.

JUST AS LIDIA predicted, she got her mammogram with less than a thirty-minute wait, then got in to see

Dr. Avery early, as luckily, he had a cancellation.

"Well Lidia, did you have a nice Christmas?" Dr. Avery asked his long-time patient as he prepared for her examination.

"Lovely, doctor. Although Nick and my father are a bit blue. Jesse's announced she's flying the coop to nest with her boyfriend. As for me though, it couldn't have come at a better time. I can use her apartment as an office, now that my superior has decided that hot-desking is the next strategy in her austerity plan. I can easily work a few days a week from home, I actually welcome it... Ugh!" Lidia's chatter was interrupted by the intrusion of her doctor's cold clamp.

"And Nick, how is he? You two have been active lately? Taking precautions?" Dr. Avery asked pointedly.

"Well, yes and no. Yes, we've been active, quite active actually and mainly rely on withdrawal. Lately my cycle's been erratic. It's not unusual for me to skip two months; I think I might be peri menopausal. I've gained some weight too, but I'll drop it," Lidia said confidently.

Dr. Avery pulled-off his gloves and examined Lidia's breasts.

"What's wrong? I've just come from my mammogram and everything seemed ok." Lidia said, a little anxious.

"Dress, and I'll be back shortly." With that he left the room, closing the door behind him.

A LILTING WIND propelled the snow in pillowing drifts against the figure on the stone bench in the cemetery's glade, the private sanctuary where Lidia reposed shivering in the twilight. This was her retreat, where the shadows spoke to her of dark secrets, of Pluto lurking in the underworld, waiting for the Sun to pass into Aries, the herald of spring.

Mount Pleasant Cemetery was one of Toronto's oldest and finest repositories, situated just beyond an eighteenth-century city boundary, called Gallows' Hill. Lidia's mother was buried here, but she wasn't visiting her grave today. No, instead she sought the unlikely crypt of a tragic socialite, a lovely young woman who passed too soon, leaving a grieving, broken husband, and several motherless children.

It was to her shrine Lidia was drawn, a gothic tribute to the woman's last day on earth. Her antique dressing table was just as she left it, the whole a gloomy vignette of this woman's private, intimate space. But no trace of her private, intimate self. Which made it all the sadder and gloomier.

I am such a fool.... I don't want this, dear god, I

don't want this. Maybe I shouldn't tell Nick, deal with it alone…tell me what to do…give me a sign at least…please," Lidia implored.

Her invocation was suddenly interrupted by a muffled ring. She brushed the snow from her purse and dug for her phone, "Yes? Oh, it's you. No, I don't know what time it is. I'm at the cemetery… Because I needed to talk to someone here. Yes, I'm ok, I'm cold. What? No. I need…I need you to come and get me, Nick. Would you please come and get me?"

Then rising stiffly, she walked towards the cemetery entrance, where Nick would pick her up and take her safely home.

"CAN'T YOU MANAGE a little more passatelli? The broth is still warm and mmm, just smell the coriander," Nick said, holding-up the bowl, tempting Lidia to eat. "You haven't had anything all day and you're still shivering. I'm sure you've caught a chill."

Nick took the dinner tray away then tucked an extra blanket around his pale, shaking wife. He sat on the edge of the bed and took her hands in his. "Please tell me what's happened, no matter what it is, we'll deal with it. Your silence is scaring me… Lidia, do you have cancer? Just tell me, do you?"

"NO! I'm pregnant," Lidia wailed.

Nick incredulous, demanded, "How pregnant?"

"About five weeks… I need an ultrasound to be sure, but five weeks sounds about right." Lidia blew her nose loudly and wiped her eyes. "I don't want this Nick, I don't want to be pregnant, raise another child, not at my age. I'm going to be forty-two, this is a high-risk pregnancy," Lidia twisted a tissue in her hand and looked desperately frightened.

"Is that what Dr. Avery said? I mean, you are a healthy woman, you've never even had your tonsils out…and you rarely get sick," Nick rationalized to quell her fear.

"Doesn't matter, Nick. I'm frightened – Dr. Avery and I discussed termination. But that has to be done soon, within a few weeks." Lidia looked down at the bed, then up at her husband.

"Termination? Is that what you want?"

Clutching his hand tightly, she cried-out, "That's not fair…I'm still trying to take this all in. Nick, I need more time."

Nick rose abruptly, grabbed the dinner tray, rattling the cups, slopping the soup over. Retreating, he paused to say, "These things need clearing, you need to rest. Please try to rest. I'll be back soon."

Not waiting for a response, he hurried downstairs, propelled by a sudden stab of fear.

FORGIVE ME FATHER, for I have sinned." Lidia crossed herself, whispering into the grail separating penitent from confessor.

"Lidia?" Frank asked of the supplicant, ignoring the knot forming in his gut. "What's the matter?"

"I wished for the death of my child…I wanted to be rid of the life I'm carrying. I'm afraid now that it may die because I wished it…can that happen?" Lidia cried, desperate for a negative answer.

"No, no. That's just 'magical thinking'," he assured.

"I'm so afraid for us both and that even if we're healthy, I won't cope well with mothering this child. Part of me screams out that I don't want it and I'm ashamed of myself," she responded.

"Shame is of no use to us now, is it? You can't help the present by damning the past. And what about Nick? Are you sure about Nick?" Frank asked, emphatically.

"Yes. Well, as sure as I can be," Lidia responded tentatively. "He's confused, and emotional. To be fair, he knows ultimately the decision is mine, but I don't know what to do. Please, just tell me what I should do, and I'll do it," Lidia pleaded.

"Lidia, I can't do that, no matter my feelings and you don't need me to tell you chapter and verse what your faith says about termination. What you need is assurance, not absolution. Let's talk outside the confessional, alright?" Frank said calmly.

"Alright," came the timorous response.

They sat in the empty church, side by side, at the end of the pew, eyes fixed on the altar. Frank spoke first, "Ever since you told me, Lidia, I've wanted to reach out, but you cut me off. Still, I'm glad you've come to me at last. I prayed you would.

He continued, "Your fear troubles me, as decisions taken out of fear are often regretted. You know the doctrine of your Church on this matter, but you also know that you have free will. No one can make this decision for you, but you must make it in a peaceful state.

"Now, I want you to let go of your fears, put yourself in the hands of the Holy Spirit, only then can you be in touch with your inner guide. Let it speak to you in truth. I want you to pray to the Holy Spirit for peace and wisdom," he said, pressing his simple, worn rosary into her hands.

Frank's voice was warm and soothing. "I will pray with you for a little while, then I will leave you alone."

Lidia dropped to the worn leather kneeler, enveloped by the faint scents of candles and incense. Closing her eyes, she began to pray, fingering the smooth wooden beads, she felt lightness, a sense of comfort wash over her, as she was dimly aware of the solemn incantations of her confessor.

When he felt her breathing deep and slow, she was beyond his call and in communion with the Holy Spirit. Frank rose, mouthed a silent benediction, then making the sign of the cross, left Lidia to her prayers.

NICK, IRASCIBLE, STRUGGLED to liberate a cart from the line at Coletto's Fine Foods. "Damn you stupid…"

"Can I help you, sir?" asked the clerk. Nick stepped aside, as with ease, the youth pulled-out a cart. Embarrassed, Nick grabbed the handle and quickly pushed-off to his destination; the magic forest of post-Christmas, marked-down panettone, where the iconic festive Italian cakes, in their brightly colored packages, still hung from the ceiling on shiny red ribbons.

These were truly magic cakes as it was a mystery to Nick how they could travel from the bakeries of Italy to the supermarkets of Canada, cello-sealed within their fancy boxes, remaining moist and edible for months. He refused to read the ingredients label, deciding it was better not to know.

Nick chose the classic candied fruit version, then decided on a luscious almond custard, he reached for a tempting apricot one he hadn't tried before. Then as he was about to exit the panettone forest and head to the cash, he reversed, swung around, and grabbed two more, a Grand Chocolate and a Sorrento Lemon.

"Hmm, *somebody* certainly likes their cake," the pale, thin man ahead of him in the check-out quietly sneered to his wife.

The bloody nerve. Who's he calling a 'mangia cake'? thought an incensed Nick. *Just look at their basket…boneless skinless chicken breasts and organic chicken broth? Boneless, skinless idiots! If they knew anything about cooking, they would know that buying a whole organic chicken is cheaper, cut off the back and wings to make a wonderful stock. Oh, I just knew it, gluten-free pasta. I guess that's for their fat-free, flavour-free joyless dinner, probably drink de-alcoholised wine too.*

"Sorry," Nick apologized with a smirk as he 'accidentally on purpose', nudged the man ahead of him with his cart…*take that, you skinny prick.*

The man grimaced, as if reading Nick's mind.

NICK STOOD IN the middle of the parking lot, bewildered, trying to keep a grip on several plastic bags of panettone. "I don't believe this. Where's the blasted car? Ah, I remember. Just hope that pink Cadillac is still there." He shifted to the left and craned his neck. "Yes! Thank-you Mary Kay."

Nick strode confidently to his destination, placed his packages on the roof of his car, and prepared to head home, when an insistent knock on his window halted his progress.

"What?" he said with annoyance to the young woman holding-up several shopping bags.

"I think you forgot these," she responded with a bemused smile.

"Oops,…guess I did, thanks."

She smiled again at him, then turned to go.

Is she flirting with me? "I'm married," Nick blurted.

"What?" said the young woman, taken aback.

"Nothing, nothing, thank-you!" Nick waved out the window as he pulled-out of his spot.

I am an idiot! What's wrong with me? That poor girl, she's old enough to be...oh, old enough to be my daughter. Maybe even has a baby old enough to be my grandchild. Nick suddenly felt sad and wanted more than anything to just get home.

"WHAT'S ALL THIS, Nick? I thought you were going on a diet," Aldo said, surveying the kitchen where his son-in-law lined-up his impulsive purchases.

"I'm going to make us some much-needed comfort food, panettone and butter pudding, to be exact." Nick chewed a fingernail as he scanned them, trying to decide which one to use.

"You can be as exact as you like, but Lidia won't like this one little bit, she's trying to lose weight," Aldo advised, folding his arms across his chest.

"What? Are you saying Lidia's fat? She's not you know, women should carry a little extra weight, it's healthier for the baby, er body. It's healthier for their body. Now leave me alone to organize myself," Nick said, choosing the Grand Chocolate, stashing the rest of the selection away.

Aldo, undeterred replied, "Okay buddy, on your head be it. Anyway, how much of this you makin'? Can I have some to take to Voula's tonight?"

"Lots. And yes, I'll make a pan for you and Voula, okay? Now stop pestering me, I have work to do." Nick turned his back on Aldo and set about organizing his mis-en-place.

Satisfied, Aldo grabbed a beer from the fridge and headed for his room.

Nick turned on the jazz station, tied-on his pristine, white apron and prepared to create. But before he could, Pickles made an appearance, hearing the fridge door open, he anticipated a treat.

"Hello buddy, looking for something?" Nick bent down to scratch behind his companion's ears and pat his back. Pickles wagged his tail energetically.

"Here you go." Nick offered him four bread and butter pickles, Pickles gobbled them appreciatively, then retreated to his favorite spot beneath the kitchen table where he could watch and comment on the unfolding action. Nick washed his hands, then got into his culinary groove.

Hmm, Grand Chocolate bread and butter pudding cries-out for, lemme see, ah! Just enough Nutella left to whip into the butter spread. Leftover chocolate truffles, chop-up and sprinkle over the hot pud. Then... I think some orange, just to lift the heavy chocolate. Oh, here it is. Nick reached for the large, ornate tin perched above the fridge, a tin of French glacé fruits from Javi. He shook it, then selected a few sticky, glistening orange slices to accent his luscious chocolate masterpiece.

"She's gonna love this, Pickles. Yes, chocolate is just what the doctor orders! So glad she doesn't have morning sickness, we're lucky that way. Didn't have any with Jesse either… that's one less drama to cope with." Nick looked over his shoulder to where the dog was lying, yawning, and stretching, nestling his head between his paws.

As Nat King Cole crooned about craving, 'The frim-fram sauce with ausenfay and chafafa on the side', Nick buttered his pans, cut-up the cake, whisked together the eggs and cream, while ruminating on his dilemma.

"Well Pickles, I hope she's willing to talk when she gets home. We really need to talk. I hate being shut-out like this, after all it's my life too and my baby too."

Pickles acknowledged with a yelp.

"Women can be so tough on us, they think we don't have feelings, just urges. Oh no! Only they have feelings. Well, I'm having it out with her when she gets back from the ob-gyn. I have rights and feelings…"

The dog let out a low growl.

"Who're you talking to? And who's got feelings?" Lidia interrupted Nick's diatribe.

"AAH! – Oh, it's you. You shouldn't sneak up on me like that," Nick said, breathing heavily. "I nearly dropped my pudding."

"I wasn't sneaking. Who were you talking about anyway?" Lidia laughed. "Sounds like you were yelling at the dog."

"No. No. Just working something out." He turned to put the pudding in the oven. "So, how'd it go at the ob-gyn?" Nick tried to sound casual.

"Alright, quite good actually. How about I make us some tea and we can chat in the living room," Lidia said brightly.

"Alright, yeah. Sounds good." Nick nervously struggled to untie the knot in his apron, Lidia gave him a hand, then shooed him out.

"Well?" Nick looked-up expectantly at Lidia as she poured their tea.

"Well." Lidia paused, blowing on her hot tea. "Nick, I think we can do this."

She regarded her husband for a reaction; he nodded quietly wanting her to continue. "I've worried over it-mainly the health issues, prayed over it, and discussed it with Dr. Chen who helped me put my fears into perspective," Lidia said, taking a sip from her dainty cup.

"Oh, what did she say?" Nick asked calmly, struggling to contain his relief.

"That I'm an extremely healthy woman, who having had one normal, healthy pregnancy, is a candidate for a positive outcome, all things being equal. Which means there's still a risk of delivering a child which may have health issues because of our ages.

"However, they can give me a triple screen test in the sixteenth week, to see if amniocentesis is warranted, or I can opt for amniocentesis as early as eleven weeks. It's my call."

"I see. Look, although I'm still concerned for you and the baby, I can't pretend that I'm not really happy." Nick reached out to embrace and kiss his wife.

"Thanks for backing-off; giving me time to work this out for myself. I know that was hard for you love, but it was the right thing to do." Lidia kissed him back and smiled. "But let's wait until after the tests to announce our news, okay?"

"Definitely, mum's the word, 'til then." Nick smiled as Lidia groaned at his corny pun.

Now that the tension and suspense were over, at least for now, Nick felt free to gush forth about his plans re: prospective fatherhood. "I've been looking into a few things though, like parental leave from the college, which is six months, then maybe go part-time, just until he's four, ready for Junior Kindergarten.

"Hopefully, we can get a sitter in the neighborhood who's a stay-at-home parent, to mind him while I'm at work. And we could rent the basement suite to cover costs." Nick looked to Lidia for approval.

"Yeah, sure. It's a bit 'jumping the gun' but doesn't hurt to be prepared. Uh, why do you keep saying, 'he' Nick? It might be a girl; odds are even it will be." Lidia looked at him mischievously.

"I just think we'll have a boy. I don't know why, I just do, okay?"

"Okay, but I think this one's another girl, so there."

Nick relaxed, spreading his arms along the sofa back. "D'ya know what this makes me, Lidia?"

"A dad?"

"Ah, but not just any dad, I'm going to be an S.O.D.!" Nick smiled broadly.

"So, you're going to be a 'sod' and you're happy about that?"

"Yes, a Start Over Dad, like Mick Jagger, he just had a baby at seventy-two," Nick said smugly.

"No Nick, his nubile girlfriend had a baby at twenty-nine, Mick just stood around handing out cigars," Lidia snickered.

"C'mon, you know what I mean. Anyway, I've noticed at the park, there are several mature dads, spryly running after toddlers, swinging on swings, grappling with the monkey bars. You know, I'm thinking of taking yoga class. If you don't stretch it Lidia, you lose it," Nick advised.

"Uh huh…I think you've been spending too much time in the park, Nick."

HOME AWAY FROM HOME

IT WAS FRIDAY night, the evening when the seniors gathered at the Italian Social Club in Little Italy to play bocce, billiards or cards, gossip, eat and drink. And in more liberal times, smoke.

Aside from the church, clubs like these were an important part of the cultural and social fabric of Italian life across the country. Whether they settled in a small town or a big city, once established, Italian immigrants pooled their resources, bought a property and formed a club. Some were regional, founded by immigrants from areas like Lazio, Calabria, Friulano and others were generically 'Italian'.

The clubs were indispensable in helping the recent immigrant feel at home, where they could be connected to a social network, to get advice, find work and even a spouse. It was a place that would embrace and feed you as you are.

However, the new culture for the *straniero*, the foreigner, is a place where one must find opportunity amongst prejudice, a potential banquet without and with reservations. Work hard and smart enough and you could earn a seat at that table. And Aldo did, with the support of this network; he got his first job, met his wife, and formed enduring friendships.

The Italian Social Club to which he and Cheech belonged was founded in 1950 and the game room's interior hadn't changed much since. The knotty pine panelled walls, red leatherette upholstery, wagon wheel chandeliers and Formica-topped bar evoked the ambience of a mid-century suburban 'rec room'.

Aldo and Cheech were at their usual table, playing cribbage and drinking beer. Cheech laid out his hand, pegging-out his score on the board accordingly, "I got fifteen-two, fifteen-four, and the rest don't score, so drinks are on you, paesan."

Aldo just stared silent into the distance.

"Eh! What's the matter with you? We've played three hands, all of which I won, and you haven't even given me an argument. Didn't you notice I cheated on that last hand's count?" Cheech tried to get a rise out of his companion.

"Yeah, I noticed, but I have bigger things on my mind than keeping you honest," Aldo said glumly.

"Like what?"

"Like Voula's leaving for Arizona in March," Aldo answered, annoyed.

"For a vacation?"

"No, for good," Aldo grimaced.

"What about her business, and what's she wanna' go to Arizona for anyway?"

"Voula's selling the business to her niece, so she can go to Sedona and study astrology with her 'guru'."

"Guru, eh? What's that about, are they…close?" Cheech raised an eyebrow.

"Dunno, maybe. I'm not really sure, but something tells me it's not on the up and up. Anyway, it's all moot as she and I are finito." Aldo slapped the table.

"Finito, why? You give up too easy, as that Beyoncé says, you want it, put a ring on it!"

"I tried that Mr. Hippity-hop and she turned me down," Aldo raised his voice, jutting out his jaw.

"Okay then, what's your next move?" Cheech asked, assuming Aldo had a Plan B.

"Nothing. Unlike you, I don't have another card

up my sleeve." Aldo shrugged.

Cheech got them some more beer, and offered one to Aldo with this consolation:

"Listen paesan, don't feel so bad. You had a good time and have some nice memories. After all, as my Carmela used to say, just because it wasn't forever good, don't mean it was never good. So, be happy with that, can't you?" He grinned and snapped the cap off his beer.

"Ha, easy for you to say. You and Siu-Mee are alright, pretty cozy lately, aren't you?" Aldo said as if accusing his friend of a betrayal.

"Yeah, she's a real gem…cooks like a dream, steamed dumplings light as a feather, moves like one too; I like graceful women. Her barbequed duck though, too salty and fatty for my taste. Otherwise, it's all good.

"Hey, maybe you should join our Tai Chi class. There's some real nice ladies. Widows, well provided for, if you know what I mean." Cheech winked at Aldo, who just shook his head and sighed.

NURSING HER SECOND cup of cappuccino, Jesse

looked out the bay window of her new second floor flat, watching Hermann salting the steps of the variety store below. It was nine o'clock on a slushy Valentine's Sunday morning. Most of the regulars hadn't been in yet for their last-minute greeting cards, box of requisite Valentines' chocolates and single cello-wrapped red rose, *Hmm, guess they're sleeping-off Saturday night,* thought Jesse, as she turned towards the kitchen where Josh was sautéing, chopping and banging pots around, preparing her birthday lunch. Deeming it best to leave him to it, she decided to call her grandfather.

"Hi nonno, it's Jesse."

"Of course, it's Jesse, d'ya think I'm so blind I can't read the call display?" Aldo kidded.

"Okay smarty pants. I hear you have a cold and won't be coming over to celebrate my twenty-one glorious years on planet earth. Are you sure you can't come? You don't sound that sick to me. Josh is making your cioppino arrabbiata, smells fantastic," Jesse said, inhaling deeply.

"Oh, I only wish I could," Aldo said coughing, his voice suddenly becoming thick and scratchy. "But I'm sending my birthday greetings along with your present, in case that's what you're really worried about." Aldo sat down in his easy chair, turned the TV on to the racing, muting the volume.

"No, that isn't what I'm worried about nonno. I'm worried about you. I heard that you and Voula broke-up; are you sure this 'cold' isn't just a heartbreak sulk? I know it's Valentine's Day and everything, but I can't help when I was born," Jesse scolded.

"Well, maybe I do feel a little down, not very celebratory. I wouldn't be good company, Jess."

"So, what's new?" Jesse teased, trying to lighten his mood. "I want you to come, nonno. It'll be good to be with people. C'mon, you can't miss this opportunity to tell Josh how he screwed-up your cioppino, now can you?"

"Anybody else invited besides me and your parents?"

"Just Josh's folks, Kate and Lucinda," Jesse said.

"Lucinda, eh? She's a real firecracker, I like her. She's a good kid, means well, if a little clumsy. I'm glad you're taking her under your wing. I think she needs to feel part of a family."

"I like her too, nonno. It's never dull when she's around, and I kinda' feel like she's the little sister I never had."

"Alright then, I'll come, but don't expect me to be happy about it."

"Oh no, heaven forbid!" Jesse exclaimed. Then laughing, she said, "Bye nonno, love you."

"Love you too pussycat, and I'll be pleased to help you celebrate your birthday," Aldo replied, returning to his racing.

Jesse joined Josh in the kitchen where he stood stirring the sauce. Putting down his spoon, he asked, "Well, is he coming, or not?"

"Yes, finally. He's worse than a teenager," Jesse chuckled.

"Okay then, I'd better get started on this stuff if we're gonna' have it in time for lunch."

Josh pulled on some rubber gloves and started to clean and prep the mound of seafood in the sink.

"Wow Josh! That's a lotta shellfish, are you sure we need all this? Here, let me help." Jesse went to put on her apron.

"It's fine, I'm sure people'll want seconds and no, you can't help. Just relax and go do something nice for yourself. This is your day, sugar puff." Josh grabbed her apron.

The entry buzzer interrupted their kiss. "Uh-oh that must be 'S&M', early as usual. I'll let them in, but *please* entertain them while I get lunch going?" Josh asked, as he hurried to answer the door.

"Yeah sure, thanks a lot Josh, I thought this was supposed to be my day!" Jesse shouted at an enterprising lobster making its way out of the sink. She shoved it back with a ladle and gave it a smack on its back for good measure.

Josh got his parents settled on the sofa, when Jesse, resolved to playing gracious host, made her appearance bearing a tray of hot tea and biscuits.

"Lovely Jenny! We are positively parched, aren't we Sudhi?" Miriam beamed at Jesse as she poured their tea.

"Miriam, I believe the young lady's name is Jesse, isn't that right?" Sudhi looked to his hostess for confirmation.

"Yes, that's right, Mr. Patel. My name is Jesse."

"Mom, it bewilders me how you can be so successful in retail yet be so bad with names." Josh shook his head laughing.

"Well, all I can say is it's a good thing we only had one child, as remembering two names would've been two challenges too many. Do you know what cognitive brain theory has to say about your condition, Miriam?" Sudhi asked archly.

"Not especially, dear. Would you like to know what Emily Post has to say about your lack of gallantry?" Miriam flashed her husband an acid smile.

Before his father could respond, Josh jumped-in, "C'mon you two, this is Jesse's birthday and the first time you're meeting her parents, so best behaviour please." Josh looked to them both for assent.

"Certainly Joshy. I'll keep an eye on your father," Miriam said, as she reached down into her bag. "Happy birthday, Jesse!" She handed her a silver box tied with a sumptuous pink velvet bow.

"Oh, wow! Thanks so much you two. It's absolutely gorgeous," Jesse said as she pulled out a floral Prada pashmina.

"Do you like it on me Josh?" Jesse modelled the shawl, pirouetting prettily.

"I love it on you sugar puff." Josh blushed as he realized he'd used her pet name.

"Sugar puff, eh? Well, my boy, you certainly are a romantic. You get that from me." Miriam smiled, satisfied.

"What do you mean, my lady? I am a very romantic person," Sudhi huffed.

"Oh really? And what romantic gift did you present me with last Valentine's? Snow tires!" Miriam scoffed, turning away.

"They were Pirelli's, the best!" Sudhi said, agitated. "There is just no pleasing this woman." He bit down angrily on a biscuit.

"Uh, speaking of which. No one'll be pleased if lunch ends-up turning into dinner, will they Jess? So, I'll just leave you three to get better acquainted, while I get on with the cooking." Josh made a dash for the kitchen before Jesse could protest.

As Josh's parents were finally quiet, drinking their tea and eating their biscuits, Jesse racked her brain for neutral conversation.

"So, Mr. Patel, Josh tells me you've come from Montreal for a wedding."

"Yes, that's right Jesse and please, call me Doctor Patel." Sudhi held out his cup for a refill.

"Nonsense," Miriam retorted, "we are Sudhi and Miriam, dear. After all, Sudhi, she's like family, isn't that right, Jenny?

"Um, well thanks, Miriam. You seem just like family to me too." It was all Jesse could do to keep from giggling, recalling her constantly bickering great aunt and uncle.

Miriam smiled benignly, "As you say, we attended the wedding of a dear friend's daughter, who is also like family to us. Isn't that right Sudhi?" Miriam nudged her husband, shaking his third biscuit from his hand.

"Yes, Jasmine has grown from a precocious child into a lovely woman. A credit to her parents, Dr. Rajeev Kumar and his wife, Justice Sonja Preem. Both of them distinguished in their fields and now little Jasmine has added to the family honour. She has won a top zoological prize for the discovery of a new species of Gastrocopta," Sudhi announced proudly.

"Gastrocopta? What kind of animal is that?" Jesse asked.

"A giant snail!" Sudhi and Miriam both answered enthusiastically.

"Ugh, yuck…" was all Jesse could say.

"No, not at all, young lady. The giant cave-dwelling snail is a fascinating species." Sudhi nodded taking a sip of his tea.

"Oh yes, they've even named her discovery, Gastrocopta Jasmineae. Imagine having a giant snail named after you," Miriam rolled her eyes in wonder.

"Yeah, just imagine." Jesse put her tea down, suddenly feeling desperate for a glass of wine.

"And to top it all off, she just wed a distinguished proctologist! You know, there was a time when we hoped our Joshy and Jasmine might find their way down the aisle together," Miriam sighed.

"Oh, is that right?" Jesse said, annoyed.

"Ha! Fine mess he made of that opportunity. Your son thinks he's such a rugged outdoorsman but frightens like a little girl at some deep spelunking and the grasp of a giant snail. Ran-off screaming, with the torch, leaving poor Jasmine in the dark to break her ankle. Disgraceful. Set her research back by months," Sudhi recounted indignantly.

"Such a shame, but if you'd only spent more time bonding with him Sudhi, a boy needs his father's attention," Miriam scolded.

Before another round of bickering could break-out, Jesse hopped-up declaring, "I'll just see if Josh needs a hand, and maybe it's time for a little bubbly?"

Before she could get to the kitchen, the buzzer rang again, insistently; the rest of the company had arrived.

AFTER KISSES WERE exchanged and the guests relieved of their coats and presents, Jesse showed them into the living room where introductions were made, and Josh was pouring-out the prosecco. He gave them each a flute and a welcome greeting to he and Jesse's first home together.

Lidia passed her glass to Nick, then looked down to admire the vibrant colors and motifs in the large Indian rug, centre stage in the living-room. "What a gorgeous rug, where did you get it, Josh?"

"That came from Josh's great grandfather Azir, a rug merchant from Amritsar," Sudhi…

"I do love it, even though it's seen better days and has had a few repairs." Josh stooped to show where the colors were mismatched.

"Still, this is quite a valuable piece. The colors are so vivid. The pattern looks like it has a colonial influence," Lidia observed.

"Very likely, Azir traded in antique as well as new rugs. I have a beautiful collection of smaller silk ones I've had vacuum packed. When Josh marries, they'll be passed-on to him," Sudhi said, taking a sip of prosecco.

"Yes, they're Josh's dowry," Jesse chuckled, hugging him.

"Oh really? Well, what do I get from you, except a bigger grocery bill?"

"Why my beauteous self Mr. Patel and isn't that enough?" teased Jesse.

"Absolutely. Everyone, a toast to Jesse; happy birthday Jess!" Josh raised his glass as everyone joined him in the toast.

"C'mon mom, I want to show you my studio," Jesse grabbed Lidia's hand in her excitement to show off the new space.

"Wow, it's really bright and spacious," Lidia remarked, scanning the room.

"Yeah, faces south and even has skylights, we didn't have to touch a thing. And look there's a built-in laundry closet with a sink, in the hallway, so I don't have to go far to do clean-up. You know mom, even though I'm going to teach, I'm determined not to give up my art practice."

"Good for you, Jess. No reason to lose your talent, or your passion. I'm very proud of you," Lidia gave her daughter a hug.

Jesse blushed. "What's brought this on, mom?"

"Oh nothing, just the day, I guess. We should have a proper girly lunch next week at the Four Seasons, on me. I'm free Saturday, what d'ya say?" Lidia smiled at her daughter.

"Sure, that'd be great." Jesse had a feeling her mother had something else on her mind.

Just then, a new voice came from the living room, Jesse and Lidia went out, curious to see who had arrived.

"AAAH, there's the birthday girl!" Athina opened her arms and rushed towards Jesse.

"Oh my god, Athina!" Jesse hugged her friend tightly, then stood back to appraise her. "You look fabulous, so healthy," Jesse exclaimed. "I can't believe you're here. Josh said you'd be tied-up in Montreal until April."

"Well Ainsworth will be. I have to get back in two weeks, but I couldn't let my best friend celebrate her birthday without me. And I really wanted to see my folks now they're back from Greece."

"That's great you get to spend time with them…

and me!" Jesse hugged Athina again, "Oh, I'm just so glad you came," she said, a little teary now.

"Lunch is served," Josh summoned everyone to the table, ushering them into their seats, setting an extra place for Athina.

As the salad and focaccia were passed around, the wine poured and another toast proposed, Lucinda observed, "Must be a bit of a bummer Jess, having a birthday on Valentine's. You're just like Jesus."

"What? How's Jesse just like Jesus?" Miriam asked.

"Well, Jesus' birthday is on Christmas, so he must've been well cheated on the birthday bling. Jess's is on Valentines, so it's like here's some crummy chocolates, oh and by the way, happy birthday too!" Lucinda replied indignant.

Everyone at the table, except Miriam broke-up laughing. "Huh, I gave her a Prada pashmina…" she grumbled into her salad.

After the first course was cleared, the cioppino ladled out, Josh turned, wine bottle in hand to Athina, "Yes?" indicating her glass.

She quickly put her hand over her barely touched glass, "No, thanks Josh, I'm good."

"Is there something wrong with the wine? I'd really like your opinion as an aspiring sommelier."

"The wine's fine, Josh, I had a few sips. It's just that I can't really drink right now."

"Oh, why's that? Are you on antibiotics?" Jesse asked.

"Um no… Well, I might as well tell you… I'm pregnant," Athina announced, grinning.

Jesse's eyes widened, she was dumb-founded.

Then Nick, excitedly blurted-out, "Fantastic! So are we! Isn't that great?"

He beamed, looking from stunned speechless face to stunned speechless face. Lidia gave his shin a sharp kick.

"*WHAAT*?" exclaimed those regaining their senses.

Lidia took the lead in handling damage control, "I'm so sorry Jess. This isn't the way we wanted to announce our news…is it, Nick?" She gave him another jab.

"Ow! Uh no, I'm sorry, so sorry." He took a gulp of wine. "Like Lidia says, we wanted to do this privately, as a family. Guess I blew it. So sorry," he said, squeezing Lidia's hand, "So happy, I just got carried away."

"Ha, ha, Nick, looks like you got carried away with the coriander too!" Aldo chided lewdly, his daughter giving him a poisonous look.

Well, doesn't that just take the cake? Glad I didn't

miss this party." Aldo, ignoring Lidia's disapproval, grinned to himself, as from beneath the table's edge, everyone else was busy texting the news.

Josh's father looked to his wife and observed dryly, "Just like family, Miriam?"

POST-PARTY BLUES

"WELL, DIDN'T THAT just blow-out my birthday candles," Jesse said as she poured herself a glass of wine, passing the bottle to Kate, who had stayed behind for the debriefing.

"Oh yeah, that's an understatement." Kate handed the now empty bottle to Josh who rose to open another.

"Honestly, I'd rather've been bashed on the head with a pumpkin," Jesse said, glumly.

"Squash," Josh interjected.

"What?" Jesse held out her glass for a top-up.

"Your dad was hit by a Hubbard squash his last birthday, not a pumpkin," Josh corrected.

"Oh thanks, professor. Anyway, it's preferable to the big headache of learning your middle-aged parents have been at it like rabbits and with as much protection." Jesse pouted.

"So, you don't think this pregnancy was planned?" asked Josh.

Kate and Jesse, both shot him an arch look, then broke-up laughing, sputtering-out their wine.

"Okay, okay, that may sound stupid, but not entirely beyond the realm of possibility," Josh said, trying to save face.

"Oh, it *so* is beyond that realm. I mean, what? Do you really think my mom wants to waddle around in elasticized pants, tee shirts like tents, nipples down to her knees, stretch marks like the Grand Canyon and endure it all sober for nine miserable months?" Jesse was close to shouting now.

"Then once the demon's hatched there's the poopy diapers, late night screeching, constant wiff of 'eau de colique' on your shirt and the vicious horror of piles," Kate added, recalling her mom's version of her last pregnancy.

"Anyway, I'm not worried about mom, she made her playpen, and she can lie in it. There'll be no babysitting from me." Jesse drained her glass and held it out for more.

"Ah c'mon now Jess, you're gonna' adore the new baby. I think it's great that after all these years you won't be an only child. I only wish I had a little brother or sister." Josh smiled winsomely, pouring each of them more wine.

"Yeah, if only to be a buffer between you and your dad," Jesse scoffed.

"Well guys, losing your 'only child' status is no laughing matter in these hard economic times," Kate advised.

"Why? What's the economy have to do with it?" Josh asked.

"Think of your parents' present assets as your future wealth. Now do either of you, after putting in so much time and hard work on them, really want to see a 'Junior come lately' drop in and take half of it, maybe more as the youngest kid is often spoiled rotten?"

Josh and Jesse listened intently and shook their heads.

Kate continued, "I didn't think so. Look at me. I have two younger, greedy siblings to compete with, who are now on daddy's payroll. So, to make things equitable, I'm living in the family home rent-free for as long as I can. And driving the company car."

"Ah-ha," Jesse and Josh both nodded.

"And another issue is my parents' potential divorce, they can be killer on the aggregate value of family assets."

Josh said, "I know what you mean, divorce is expensive. I think that's why my parents stay together, always having their eyes on the bottom line."

Jesse added, "That, and it'd be a shame to spoil *two* houses. But there's nothing you can do about your parents' split, Kate. Your mom seems determined to go her separate way."

Kate laughed, "You think so? I don't. During our cozy family time in The Townships this Christmas, mom was getting pretty affectionate. Trust me, it's only a matter of time 'til they fall back into their old familiar pattern. Older folks think they want adventure, but what they really want is comfort. They're creatures of habit. And this is one habit I'm doing my best to encourage; especially now that mom has new value to bring to the party."

Jesse nodded her head sagely, "You mean the travel agency? Just beware though, with what my parents have been up to, you don't want your folks following suit, peer pressure and all that, and your mom's younger than mine. Consider the ferocious make-up sex they'll be having."

"Oh right, hadn't thought of that. That's a tough one. Hmm, how to bring them together, yet keep them apart?" Kate looked thoughtful. "Think my dad's had a vasectomy?"

"Well ladies, I can't think anymore 'cause I'm starving. Anyone for a curry?" Josh asked, opening-up a take-out menu.

"Okay, now Mrs. Ponti I'd like you to take a deep breath in, when I say 'in', then release it when I say 'out', alright?" the technician asked as she peered intently at the monitor. In her right hand was the ultrasound, held firmly over Lidia's navel, in her left the amniocentesis needle.

Lidia responded, "Ready when you are."

Nick held her hand as she obeyed the commands, and the needle was inserted, first through her abdomen, then into her uterus and the amniotic sac, where the fetus floated as an alien astronaut oblivious of the invading universe above it.

"Ach!" she felt a sharp jab on exhalation and struggled to keep from peeing as her bladder was very full.

"Not much longer now Mrs. Ponti, you're doing really well," the technician smiled down at her reassuringly, "Would you like to know the sex?"

Lidia looked at Nick, "Sure," he said.

The technician withdrew the needle, and as if pulling a rabbit out of a hat, declared, "It's a boy!"

"Ha! I knew it, I just knew it!" Nick gave Lidia a

loud, sloppy kiss.

"Great Nick, but this means you just won the midnight feedings. Now help me off this gurney and into the washroom before I burst," said Lidia feeling a little non-plussed; *A boy! God, I just hope he doesn't want to play hockey...chess yes, hockey, no. I'm putting my foot down on that one.*

IT TOOK TWO weeks for the results to come in; Dr. Chen reported they were negative; the mother was fine and so far, baby was too. Lidia was surprised at the relief she felt upon hearing the news despite feeling optimistic. It was like the sudden relief of a chronic pain, and the realization of how much energy it had absorbed.

For the first time in months, she felt carefree, and to celebrate decided to go shopping for the nursery furniture and even some clothes. Nick had assiduously researched the latest cribs, bottle sterilizers, strollers and bassinettes for the best designed and safest products. Armed with this formidable arsenal of consumer-tested data he sallied forth into the department store's nursery furniture section. Lidia headed for the 'Yummy Mummy' boutique, agreeing to meet Nick in baby clothes later.

As she perused the racks of stylish dresses, shirts and trousers, jeans and sweaters, Lidia couldn't help but admire how far society and fashion had come in accepting, even celebrating the voluptuous proportions of a burgeoning mother-to-be. Even if now, she felt heavy, she could at least look fashionable, even sexy…if she chose. Today, she was searching for a comfortable, practical set of pieces to get her through the work week, and some things for the weekend too.

"Would you like to try those on?" A young sales associate asked her, eyeing the pile of garments slung over Lidia's arm. She loathed trying-on clothes at the store, usually shopping at a few select boutiques between her home and work, so if a return was necessary, it wasn't a bother. Usually though, Lidia was spot on with just holding the garment up to herself in a mirror.

"No thanks, I'm sure they'll be fine. Anyway, they're all stretch fabrics, right?" Lidia said, moving over to search the sales rack.

The associate seemed disappointed, "Yes, they stretch somewhat, but you're looking at size ten, when really size twelve is likely what you're going to need," she said, looking Lidia up and down.

"I know what size I need, thank-you," Lidia responded peevishly, then handing her the clothes said, "Now, you can take these to the cash for me and

I'll be along shortly, alright?" Hoping the woman would take the hint and leave Lidia in peace to get on with her search.

After a little while, having exhausted the possibilities of the sales racks, Lidia decided to check-out.

"Did you find everything you were looking for?" asked the associate as she took the security tags off the clothes.

"Yes, thanks. I did take your advice and got a few things in twelve, just in case, but it's only three more months," Lidia lied.

"You're due in three months?"

"Oh yes, I can hardly wait. I've gained so much!" Lidia said, rubbing her modest bump.

"Wow, you don't seem big enough to be nearing your third trimester. You must be very disciplined. Is this your first child?" the associate asked, furrowing her brow.

"First? Oh god, no. It's my third and fourth. I'm having twins!" Lidia said, deciding to have some fun.

"Your third and fourth? If you don't mind me asking, how old are you?"

"I'm thirty-eight, and an only child, but I always knew I wanted a big family. Serafina, our oldest, is eight, then Felicia, six and Blake, five.

"Six and five? Your last two are only a year apart," the woman remarked, carefully folding each garment in white tissue.

"Yep, proof you *can* get pregnant while breast-feeding." Lidia sighed. "Do you have kids?"

"No, not yet."

"You know, if you have a bigger family, close together, they practically raise each other. Piece o' cake." Lidia could barely contain her amusement.

"Really? I think you're amazing," the associate replied, handing Lidia her purchases with a certain reverence.

"Oh, it's nothing, you'll find out. Like I said, piece o' cake!" Lidia left, happily swinging her parcels, deciding not to share her fictional expansion of their family with Nick.

Chapter Two

SPRING

MYSTIC PIZZA REVELATIONS

T HE LATE MARCH sun caught Nick in the eyes, blinding him for a moment as he crossed the busy thoroughfare. He'd made this journey many times before in pursuit of cold beer and hot pizza at his favorite trattoria.

Shit, he cursed silently as he slipped on a patch of ice lurking in the shade beneath the stoop. Holding the door handle, he quickly regained his balance. Upon entering the comfort of ComPanis, the aromas of parmesan, garlic, tomato sauce and yeast embraced him, rousing a lurking hunger.

Not bothering to look for the waiter, likely having a smoke break after the lunch rush, Nick hung his coat and scarf on the rack. The place was nearly empty, and he could see his three friends, already served with beer, seated at their usual table. Nick hoped that Javi and Paul were going to be, if not on really friendly terms, then at least congenial. They had after all, invited him to this late lunch to celebrate his imminent fatherhood.

"Hi daddy!" Paul grinned mischievously at his friend. "You're late, but we've managed to amuse ourselves anyway."

"Yes, I see that," Nick said, pulling up a seat, looking expectantly at the assembled.

"Barry," Javi shouted, "a Stella for our friend, if you please."

The waiter appeared and hurried over, bearing a glass and a frosty bottle. Nick drank appreciatively while his friends surveyed the menu board.

"Hey, that looks interesting," said Paul. "Mystic Pizza. Hmm, pizza with arugula, cuttle fish, white anchovies and bottarga. What's bottarga?"

Nick explained, "Bottarga's Italian caviar, it's the cured roe of grey mullet or blue fin tuna. I've had it in Sardinia on pasta, but never on pizza. It has a fairly distinctive taste and a price tag to match, no wonder the pizza's thirty bucks."

"Pass, make mine a 'mangia cake'," said Paul, indicating the pedestrian option of salami, olives, onion, and cheese.

"Well, I think I'll go with the Mystic Pizza, just for the novelty of it," Frank addressed the waiter.

"And me," said Nick. "But I'd like a little pepperoncino too."

"No problem," the waiter assured him, then looked to Javi for his order.

"I'll have the pizza bianca alla vongole," Javi said, ordering the house specialty, pizza with clams.

"Well, well, Nero. You certainly were aptly named, being such a dark horse, eh?" Javi laughed, giving Nick the elbow. Nick looked down, a little flushed and laughed.

"Ha! You're one to talk, Javi. Having a teenage daughter tucked-away in the family closet. Kate tells me she's pretty precocious too, likes playing with fire. Like father, like daughter, eh?" Paul laughed loudly, looking sideways at Nick for approval. Nick didn't join in as he feared Paul's teasing might escalate into an outright argument.

"And you're a saint, Paul? In grade twelve you were selling bootleg booze from your home still," Frank recalled.

"Until Father Ignatius got wind of it and you had to explain to your mom why all your friends were visiting the back shed to see your 'science lab'," Nick laughed.

"Yeah, they shut me down. Then old 'feely Phelan' would only give me a D in chemistry, the prick," Paul scoffed, taking a swig of his beer.

"I remember you wanted him to accept it as your independent study project. Ah well, never mind

Paul. At least you passed." Frank mocked, patting Paul's hand as if consoling a child.

"To hell with the past. Let's salute the future. Here's to Nick and his impending fatherhood." Javi raised his glass and the others joined in.

Just then the pizzas arrived, more beer was ordered, and the men diverted their attention to devouring the warm, delicious feast. Nick offered Javi a slice of his pizza. "Well, what do you think? Too salty?" Nick asked.

Javi chewed thoughtfully, "No, I wouldn't say so, but then I like salty things. I think the white anchovies are a nice touch."

"I agree," said Frank, "Maybe we could make it sometime, only several small ones as an appetizer?"

"That's a pretty expensive appetizer," Paul observed.

"I think I can source some bottarga wholesale, the anchovies too. We wouldn't need much, only a few ounces," Javi added.

"Well pricey or not, that was good, thank-you gentlemen," Nick patted his stomach, "I could eat another one, but I think I'll save room for dessert and espresso. Shall we have our usual, the cannoli and biscotti selection?"

It was agreed and Nick placed their order. While they waited for dessert and coffee, Nick's friends presented him with their gifts.

"Oh, I didn't expect gifts guys, just the meal is enough. But thank-you," Nick said as he reached into Frank's gift bag. "Ah, how interesting," he said turning a book in his hands, not quite sure what to make of it, "*The Post-Millennial Baby Brain*, well I'll be. Didn't realize there was one." Nick smiled at Frank.

"Oh yes, research shows that with each generation there are subtle changes in our brains. They're constantly evolving in response to new challenges and stimuli in our environment. It is crucial to understand the cognitive differences between your generation and the one you will be raising, genetics notwithstanding," Frank said earnestly, pushing his glasses up on his nose.

"Really? Perhaps that accounts for the apparent cognitive dissonance between my curriculum and some of my students' brains," Nick dead-panned.

"Oh, very likely." Frank nodded soberly.

"I was kidding, Frank," Nick shook his head.

"Oh sorry, I thought you meant that your difficulty with – oh never mind," Frank said, taking a big bite of biscotti, deciding to eat his dessert and be quiet.

Paul asked, sitting back, "So, if 'Millennials' are Gen-Z, right? Then what's the generation that baby

Ponti belongs to? We've run out of the alphabet. That was bad planning on Coupland's part. I mean did he think, like the Mayan calendar, that the world would end before we needed any more letters to name our disaffected youth?"

"Good question. Maybe we should call this cohort Gen-A, beginning of a new paradigm," Javi offered.

"Sounds good to me, we certainly need one," Nick agreed, as he pulled a wireless baby monitor and another book from Paul's package. "*Stop the Crying!* Wow, I'd actually forgotten about that." Nick looked thoughtful.

"Take it from me Nick, the first is reasonable, the second's a howler and the third's a sulker. Ask my niece, she's just had her second, calls him 'The Banshee', howls all night, just will not go down. She suggested the book," Paul said, reaching for his second cannoli.

"Thanks, but this is one book I hope not to have to read," Nick laughed.

Javi reached from beneath the table and presented his gift.

"A back-pack?" Nick held up the orange and blue object from which dangled a bewildering array of Velcro belts, straps and toggles.

"No, it's a baby carrier. Give it here, I'll show

you." Javi stood-up and proceeded to model his gift, as Paul took a sneaky snap. "This is the new Superio 180. It is ergonomically correct, supporting your back with two-way adjustable waistband and cushioned straps, four interchangeable carrying positions, like this one." Javi fiddled with the straps turning the carrier to face him. "Which is indispensable for breast-feeding."

"Thanks, I'll keep that in mind," Nick said, as the others laughed.

"Oh, and it has a retractable sun hood and removable storage pouch too," Javi added as he sat down.

"I think you've got a future on The Shopping Channel," Frank said, as they all slow-clapped.

As a second round of espresso, accompanied by equal measures of grappa were served, and dessert consumed, the four men settled into a leisurely post-prandial chat.

"This is nice," Paul said, sitting back, stretching his arms. "We should do this more often. Take a break from all the bullshit on the Saturday to-do list, half of which can wait 'til Monday anyway, relax and have a boozy late lunch with friends."

"I know. Why does it have to be such an effort to get face-time with people nowadays?" Frank asked.

"Like Paul says, we distract ourselves with a lot of

bullshit, buying into unfounded fear that all of it's urgent," Javi said, taking another sip of grappa.

"Right, well I guess it's easy for us to philosophize on prioritizing our time, but Nick here is set to go into a very busy, 'no time for it!' mode," Frank warned.

Nick looked up from his cannoli, surprised, "Oh c'mon, I'll still have time for my friends. We can still do our farmers' market and dinner thing and late lunches too, right?" he looked from face to face for affirmation.

"You're dreaming chum." Paul laughed. "First, you've forgotten that it's impossible to have a decent meal or conversation with a baby, much less, a toddler around. Second, do you really think Lidia's gonna let you swan off to the market or a long lunch after she's put in a hard week's work at the magazine?"

Nick felt defensive. "Our marriage isn't like that," he sniffed.

His friends laughed.

"Oh, it is so like that," Javi said.

Nick frowned and thought, *Huh, this is a revelation, I never thought they saw me as pussy whipped.*

"Speaking of work, are you gonna be a stay-at-home dad?" Paul asked.

"Well yeah, I plan on taking a six-month paternity leave, after Lidia's had her mat-leave, then teach part-time until he's four."

"Oh boy, you're gonna have to give up the idea of 'freedom sixty', as that'll put a dent in your pension," Paul observed.

Javi added, "Yep, you'll have to kiss good-by to that retirement year in Tuscany, where you planned to do some writing. The unfinished novel and cookbook'll just have to wait."

Nick, feeling a little surly, ordered another grappa.

"It's not that bad though, when you consider that Lidia's younger, so she can work longer too, but unlike you, without feeling burnt-out, right?" Frank smiled, happy with his conciliatory point.

Nick knocked-back his grappa and suddenly realized why he didn't do this more often.

THE IDES OF MARCH

"SURPRISE!" TOO MANY of Lidia's colleagues shouted as she entered Shelton's living room. *Rats, I told Shelton I didn't want a party…*Lidia tried to act happy and surprised but felt uneasy instead.

She was late and it seemed the company was

already in high spirits. "Oh, thank-you sweetie." She kissed Shelton on the cheek as he handed her a Shirley Temple and sat her down on a cushy antique Bergeron. "The place of honour, well don't I feel like a queen." Lidia held up her glass in mock salutation. She took a sip of the colorful concoction, then set it aside.

Seeing the opportunity for attention a pair of empty hands and a vacant lap presented, Beelzebub, one of Shelton's cats, leapt onto Lidia where he nestled in for the duration.

"Oh shoo, you wicked creature." Clive swatted at the cat with a napkin. "Don't give him any attention Lidia, then he'll go away. He doesn't take notice of me I'm afraid, neither does his brother Barney, the vicious thug." Clive sat down on the sofa beside his guest.

"He doesn't bother me, Clive. Beelzebub's really quite an attractive cat," she said, stroking his sleek fur from head to tail.

"Yes, isn't he, Siamese-tabby. Not a purebred of course, not like my little Pickles." Clive smiled winsomely.

"Oh, we just adore Pickles. Nick spoils him, makes him a special jar of bread and butter pickles with extra coriander and woe betides anyone who nips them. You must miss him, come by some time and visit," Lidia offered.

"It's alright, I knew he'd be going to a good home. He's a shihtzu you know, they're highly intelligent and loyal."

"Well, he certainly seems devoted to Nick, although that may just be on account of the pickles," Lidia said, taking another sip of her drink.

"Men and dogs, the way to their hearts is usually through their stomachs. Well, I shouldn't monopolize the guest of honor; I think Siobhan would like to have a word."

Clive got up to give Shelton a hand passing around the rice paper rolls and satays, when Siobhan slid over to take his place.

"Well, my girl, Santa certainly surprised you, eh? Must've been nice and naughty!" She nudged her friend and laughed.

"Okay, get all the corny jokes over with now, Siobhan. But just know I'm sober, so I won't forget." Lidia fixed her with a mock searing glare.

"Oh alright, just havin' a laugh. Do you know in France doctors *prescribe* a daily glass of red wine for expectant mothers and Irish mothers drink Guinness to help their milk?" Siobhan took another sip of wine.

"Yes, but those are civilized wine and beer producing nations trying to balance their GDP," Lidia snickered. "Still, I wish my ob-gyn was that open-minded."

"When're you due, mid-August is it?"

"Yes, that's right. And August can't come too soon, even though I'm not feeling very preggers yet, not too much of a bump," Lidia sighed, hand on her tummy.

"Don't worry, it'll come too soon." Siobhan leaned in closely, "Speaking of which, have you thought about who might replace you during mat-leave?"

"Not really, haven't had time to give it much thought."

Lidia was a little surprised at the prescience of the question. "But it seems you have," she observed, raising an eyebrow.

"Ah well, yes. I mean, not just me, Lidia. Now don't be upset, but Brunhilde, you know how organized she is…" Siobhan coughed, "called me in yesterday, to have a little chat about my thoughts on that very subject."

Siobhan took another sip of wine and steeled herself for Lidia's response.

"Oh really. And you didn't even think to confer with me in advance?" Lidia straightened her back and gave her friend her most withering look.

"Brunhilde gave me strict instructions not to. I

guess she was just feeling out my willingness to assume the mantle in your absence, no need to involve you if I wasn't interested." Siobhan shrugged, trying to seem casual.

"No, no need to involve me at all! So, I assume you want the position?"

"Well yes, I do. And I was hoping that you, being such a good friend and so loyal to your readers, would help make this a smooth transition. When the time comes, obviously." Siobhan gave a little light-hearted laugh.

"Yeah, obviously."

"Oh, and before I forget, since she couldn't be here, she asked me to give you this." Siobhan handed Lidia a gift bag clumsily stuffed with stereotypical blue and pink tissue. Lidia dug into the bag to withdraw Brunhilde's gift.

"Ye gods! It's a breast pump," Lidia's intern declared, looking at it in horror, the other women tittered.

Lidia dropped the object into the bag, pushed Beelzebub off her lap. "Excuse me ladies, I need the restroom."

Rigid with fury, Lidia marched to the kitchen to find Clive. He had arranged more satays on a platter and was just topping-up the tamarind sauce when she cornered him. "Funny, but when I read my horoscope this morning Clive, it didn't say, 'Beware the Ides of March!'"

"Ah, Siobhan has told you then? Well good, I'm sure you two consummate professionals can make this a smooth transition," Clive said over-brightly, parroting the party line, nervous of confronting the obvious issue.

"The transition? The transition, Clive? Ha! Don't you mean the coup-d'état?" Lidia shouted uncomfortably close to Clive's face; hands firmly planted on her hips.

"What coup? What's going on?" Shelton bustled-in bearing several empty wine bottles.

"Your 'loyal and loving partner' here has been colluding with Brunhilde to shoe-in Siobhan as acting editor of *The Good Life* during my leave, and who knows, maybe even beyond!" Lidia's face was livid as she glared at Clive.

"WHAT!" Shelton nearly dropped his bottles. "Why didn't you tell me? You knew I wanted to throw my hat in the ring."

"I think you're over-reacting, you both know very well Brunhilde isn't one to make decisions collegially, her management style's more, 'unilateral'." Clive decided to diffuse the drama, acting the voice of reason. Then he tossed-in a dampener. "Anyway, it may be moot as she's set her sights on a potential executive vacancy opening in the publisher's office."

Fearing he'd said too much, Clive grabbed the tray and made for the living-room, pushing past Shelton who shouted bitterly, "Brutus!"

"The little weasel. That's why he kept her plans secret; he wants to make sure he follows her upstairs." Lidia smirked.

"Honestly, I feel like stabbing him with one of his satay skewers, then plunging him in peanut sauce," Shelton muttered, as he angrily pulled the cork from another bottle of wine.

"And what good would that do?" Lidia sighed.

"Clive's deathly allergic to peanuts," Shelton answered.

"I'll keep that in mind," Lidia said, crossing her arms.

AFTER ALL THE gifts were opened, all the wine and food devoured, the shower was finally over and Siobhan offered Lidia a ride, an offer she accepted reluctantly, out of fatigue and practicality, needing help to manage her loot.

"Look Lidia, I really didn't have much choice in the matter and no, I did not make the first approach.

I really was going to ask you what you thought of me offering my services, but Brunhilde gazumped me," Siobhan said earnestly, looking away from the road for a second to make eye contact with her friend.

"I know, I know Siobhan, our fearless leader is nothing if not strategic, the alacrity with which she moves to retain her control over everything never fails to amaze, and this time, blind-side me. I should'a seen it comin'." Lidia pulled-up her collar huddling into her shearling coat.

"So, are we still friends?"

"Yes Siobhan, we're still friends," Lidia assured her in a dull voice thinking; *Like Machiavelli says, keep your friends close, your enemies even closer.*

"GOD, I WISH I was drunk," Lidia moaned as she kicked-off her shoes, undid her bra from beneath her sweater, rotating her shoulders in blessed release.

"The lunch was that good, eh?" Nick looked-up at her from the divan where he'd been half-snoozing, half-watching his *Medici* boxset. Lidia sat down on the edge of the divan facing Nick, picked-up the remote and paused the show.

"I've had way too many surprises today, Nick. First, it wasn't just an intimate lunch but a surprise baby shower with most of the women at the office present."

"What's wrong with that? Your friends going to extra fuss and bother to celebrate your pregnancy and give you gifts, what's not to like?" Nick scoffed.

"You know I don't like surprises."

"Could'a fooled me. My last birthday, despite my wish not to, you threw me a party, a surprise party no less."

"I love throwing them, for other people. I just don't like them thrown at me. Anyway, that's the least of it. I felt like Caesar in the Forum, because Brunhilde has already unilaterally appointed my replacement, Siobhan. And with Clive's knowledge and collusion, she sprang this on me in absentia, during the shower – never even deigned to show-up. Instead, she sent a very shabbily wrapped breast pump! How's that for being treated like a valued part of the team," Lidia said, reaching for a hug.

"There, there." Nick, hugging her close, gently rubbed her back. "It'll only be for a short while, then you'll be on your high horse, back in the saddle again. Right?" He looked to her for a smile.

"It might not play out that way, Nick. Maybe Brunhilde, true to form, sees this as an opportunity to replace me permanently. I mean, Siobhan's ten years younger than me and has just launched the second edition of her cookbook."

"Yes, but she doesn't have your experience or your creative track record for coming-up with fresh ideas, season after season." Nick was reaching for consolations.

"After my mat leave is over, she'll have four seasons of editorial experience. And I know she, like our publisher, is big on internet presence. Siobhan has an award-winning food blog and her podcasts are popular on the magazine's channel. And she just has that 'Irish thing'," Lidia said annoyed.

"What 'Irish thing'?"

"You know Nick; the charm, gift of the gab, ironic humor, twinkle in the eye, to say nothing of that dopey accent. I'm sure she exaggerates it. I haven't got a chance. I'm doomed," Lidia said, throwing her hands up and listlessly flopping on the bed. Burrowing under the duvet, she lay there, glumly staring into space.

Nick guessed this was not the best time to seek assurance that his social life wouldn't end with the baby's arrival.

THE LATE-SPRING SUN streamed through the large warehouse windows separating the terrace from the chic interior of Javi's downtown loft conversion.

"I think we need some shade," Javi said, pointing the remote at the invisible blinds. "We don't want to cook our guest too, now do we?" He looked to his daughter, who was busy arranging a mass of brightly colored Gerbera daisies in a tall green glass vase.

"I know, I can barely see, dad. The sun's great on the terrace, but we fry in here in the afternoon," Lucinda said, putting her creation in pride of place on the immaculately set, round glass table resting on a raw-wood pedestal.

"And please stop messing around with those napkins Martha, I folded them just like you showed me, okay? Go sharpen your cocktail skewers or polish the olives, or something." Lucinda waved him off, bemused at her father's apprehension over impressing their brunch guest.

The entrance console lit-up, "Oh she's here, Fernand just let her in," Javi sprang to the door; he could hear the elevator opening. "Ah! Bella, come in, come in." Javi kissed her on both cheeks, too late to check his greeting, remembering that she hated him calling her 'bella', said it was condescending.

Javi stood by to take her jacket. Wriggling her arms free, she stepped forward and surveyed the room.

"What a beautiful job you've done with the place, Javi. I love those Riopelles, perfect for this expansive wall, gives them lots of room to breathe." Then handing her wine gift to Lucinda said, "You must be Javi's daughter."

"Yes, this is Lucinda Correia-Ortiz, my daughter. Lucinda, meet Rebecca Deauville, Kate's mom."

"Pleased to meet you Rebecca," Lucinda extended her hand.

"Please call me Becky. Kate speaks highly of you, and I can see why. You're quite a striking girl Lucinda, not surprising though, as you have a handsome father." Becky was in fine form, warm and charming.

Lucinda responded, liking her immediately, "Oh, don't say that about dad, his head's already big enough. But you can keep on flattering me.

"I love your hair, all the silver and platinum hi-lites woven through the lavender, it seems to shimmer. Where'd you have it done?" Becky asked.

"In London originally, but I've had it touched-up here. I'm thinking of going ginger this summer, maybe with some gold," Lucinda said, ruffling her hair.

Javi, feeling side-lined, interjected, "Given the amount you spend on that mop, it may as well be done in gold, 24carat." He led them into the open-concept dining area, where they perched on trendy chrome and faux pony-hide bar stools.

"Well ladies what's your pleasure? Perhaps a Bloody Caesar, Becky?" Javi asked.

"Sure, that sounds good. Just an ounce of vodka, please."

"Me too, dad. Only I'll have the works, two ounces, one cube."

"Ah, you'll have a virgin Caesar with two cubes and like it," Javi said, taking down three chunky highball glasses.

"Gee dad, you should'a stuck around Argentina, you would've done a great job as dictator, put Peron to shame." Lucinda and Becky laughed.

Javi felt obliged to offer a pithy riposte, "Well, don't cry for me Ms. Argentina, 'cause I've done pretty well for myself right here." He grinned, handing Becky and Lucinda their drinks, "Cin-cin ladies."

While Javi was whisking-up the eggs for the crab and asparagus omelettes, Lucinda passed around the shrimp cocktail shooters, jumbo shrimps perched on the rims of jewel-colored shot glasses with a spicy tahini dip at the bottom.

She felt quite grown-up playing chatelaine for her father; it made her feel in-synch with him as they coordinated their hospitality. They made a good team in this regard. Javi was quietly pleased with Lucinda's comportment and admitted to a certain pride when Becky complimented her.

Like the food, the lunch time banter was light and agreeable, grazing topics such as Becky's travel agency venture, Javi's new wine imports, and Lucinda's birthday gift from Javi, an Appaloosa pony she named Frida, after her favorite artist, Frida Kahlo.

She was bonding with the mare, who was young, a bit temperamental at times, but Lucinda, being a competitive and skilled horseman, was bringing her under control. They tacitly avoided Becky's domestic issues and Lidia's mid-life pregnancy; those would have to wait for grown-up ears only.

While Javi was setting-out the dessert of petits fours and chocolate-dipped strawberries, Lucinda finished clearing, when her phone beeped.

"Oh, I can't do dessert dad. Gotta' meet my tutor in twenty," she declared, making a beeline for the door, grabbing her school bag, stopping by the mirror to check her hair, pull-on her jacket and dash on some lipstick. "Nice meeting you Becky. I'll be home around nine, dad. I'm meeting Charlotte for a movie after, we'll grab something there, okay?" Lucinda shouted over shoulder.

"Okay, see you later," Javi responded, setting down the sweets tray, as Becky seemed about to say something. "Oh, don't say you're deserting me too? C'mon Becky I slaved for hours icing these teeny tiny cakey things," he laughed miming the action.

"Yeah, I'll bet. Okay, I've got some time…It was really nice to meet Lucinda. You're coping well with full-time fatherhood, although I admit to having my doubts when Lidia told me about it," Becky said.

"I know, I doubted if I was up to the job. But Lidia pointed out that her acting-out was understandable, I needed to listen to her more.

"Adolescence is a time when kids need to feel unconditionally loved, not unwanted if they fail our expectations. That touched a chord in me, I resolved that if nothing else, she wouldn't experience more rejection. I know how that feels, to be rejected," Javi said with a tinge of bitterness, looking intensely at Becky.

"I guess I own that one. Breaking-up with you wasn't easy for me either. I know I come-off as tough, unfeeling even. That's because my early life made me be tough, hold everything in just to get through my father's binges, my mother's depression, pregnancies, producing children she was too poor to feed and too exhausted to love.

"That was my childhood. So no, I don't do well with 'feelings', mine or other people's, but that doesn't mean I don't have feelings, or that I don't love," Becky said softly, meeting his gaze.

Javi reached over and stroked her cheek, then ran his thumb across her lips, they parted and met his in a light, lingering kiss.

CAPPUCCINO CONFIDENTIAL

"WE REALLY NEED to talk…*please*. I know you're busy, but can you just meet me for coffee? I'm around the corner. Usual place? Okay then, see you in twenty." Becky exhaled deeply and leaned, eyes closed, against the headrest.

This was going to be tough, but she needed to unburden. Pausing to compose herself, her inner coach advised; *explain without blaming, be truthful, respect the verdict whether you like it or not, after all you asked for it.* Feeling ready, she locked the car and quickly made her way to the cafe.

"Well, hello you!" Lidia exclaimed exchanging kisses on both cheeks, then settling into her chair, "So, what's the big emergency?"

Before Becky could answer, the waiter interrupted, handing them each a frothy cappuccino with almond cantucci.

Stirring her coffee thoughtfully, Becky admitted, "I did it again."

"Okay Britney, care to elaborate? What did you do again?" Lidia asked, looking intently at her friend. "No. Oh no!" Lidia's eyes widened as she suddenly realized what Becky had been up to.

"Oh yes, oh yes! And I have the shame and remorse to prove it," Becky said with a sigh.

"But why, Beck? I thought you had all that under control, drama done, boundaries drawn, life goes on. Why screw it up?" Lidia said a little sternly.

"Yeah, 'screw' being the operative word here. Oh god Lidia, I just don't know. We were having a nice, 'meet the daughter' brunch, when suddenly we were alone discussing *feelings*, no good ever comes of that with an ex. Then we discovered we still had some for each other, sexual ones anyway. Or so I thought." Becky stirred her coffee energetically, adding two packets of sugar, without yet taking a sip.

"What do you mean 'so I thought'?"

"I thought it was just a strong sexual chemistry between us, but Javi's in deeper than that. Since our 'encounter' he has sent me no less than three extravagant bouquets, begging to meet again, so I did, just to put an end to it." Becky took a sip from her now cold, over-sweetened coffee, grimaced and set it aside.

"And did you put an end to it?" Lidia challenged.

Becky laughed cynically, "No. He asked me to marry him, so I stalled, and we ended-up in bed again. Help me Lidia, please!" Becky pleaded reaching out for her friend's arm.

Lidia paused, deep in thought, then spoke, "Are you *sure* the attraction's only sexual for you? If it is, then why did you accept the brunch invite, why didn't you leave before things got steamy, eh? …Ha!" Lidia slapped the table declaring, "I think that you, Becky, are in denial. You, my friend, are as in love with Javi as he is with you, but just won't admit it." Lidia sat back smiling, triumphant, like a lawyer after a brilliant cross-examination.

"Ouch! Is that what you think? I've never really thought about us, beyond the bedroom, which is magic, I admit. I'm so confused, Lidia. During the family holiday, I had the old familiar yearnings for Paul as well, but didn't act on them – thank god. Was that just sexual too?" Becky asked, furrowing her brow in consternation.

"That's a whole 'nother ball o'cookie dough, tied-up with Christmas tinsel, sentimental memories, and kids.

"I think you'd better explore your feelings about Javi, be open to the possibility that you are in love. Silence your inner Judge Judy and her wagging finger. Be honest with yourself, then you can be honest with Javi.

"You don't have to love everyone who says they love you," Lidia said reassuringly, "but you do have to respect their feelings."

Becky was quiet for a moment, taking in her friend's advice.

"Huh, in love with Javi. I guess it's worth considering, he has matured, seeing him with his daughter is touching. There's a side of him I didn't know, maybe that's why…anyway, I'm worried about Paul, he's still so fragile." Becky bit her lip, resting her head on her hand.

"Oh, don't worry about him. He's moved on, been dating that Ramona now for a quite a while," Lidia said, taking a last sip of coffee and checking her texts. "Sorry kiddo, must dash. Keep me posted, okay?" Lidia gave her friend a kiss as she got up hastily to leave.

Becky sat dumb founded, *why didn't my kids tell me about, 'Ramona', who the hell is this Ramona? Sounds like a cheesy salsa queen.* She paid the cheque, leaving the cafe with more than just advice.

A ZEPHYR OF warm air, the scent of fresh earth and lilacs, blew through the house on this warm Sunday in May, when Nick was busy assembling equipment for Jesse's next culinary lesson. She had mastered three iconic dishes each of fish, meat, poultry, and pasta. Next was desserts.

He thought a citrus theme was in order. Starting with a simple lemon gelato would be good, especially since he had optimistically made a quantity of limoncello liqueur a few years ago after a Sicilian sojourn, realizing too late that everything you loved eating and drinking abroad loses its charm at home.

After the lemon gelato, they'd progress to a raspberry and lemon semi-freddo; a good excuse to use up the Sorrento lemon panettone and splash around more limoncello. The amounts of liqueur in each recipe, considered in portions per person, were negligible and could safely be consumed by a pregnant Lidia, who loved lemon and wouldn't feel deprived.

As he prepped, Nick sang along in his scratchy tenor to Pavarotti's Rigoletto; *'la donn'e mobile, qual pium'al vento, muta d'accento, ento di pensier'*, just as the maestro hit and sustained the high notes of '*eee di pensier, eeeee di pensier'*, Nick's voice broke. He humbly bowed to the forgiving audience, waving his dish towel in gratitude, then mopping his brow, imitating his idol, Pickles barked appreciatively. Taking another deep bow, he threw the towel triumphantly into the cheering crowd.

It landed at Aldo's feet as he walked-in bearing several bunches of flowers bought at his club's Daffodil Cancer fundraiser.

"Hey Luciano, if you can tear yourself away from the paparazzi, I'd appreciate a hand with these," Aldo said, passing the flowers to Nick, who placed them in the sink, then got out some vases, as Pickles snuck his tea towel trophy beneath the kitchen table, where he set about carefully pulling it to pieces.

Filling each vase with warm water, Nick remarked, "You must be in a generous spirit today, you've ten bunches here, either that or there's a funeral you're planning to attend."

"No, no funeral. I just thought I'd take some to Filly's grave tomorrow. Haven't been for awhile and I'm sure it needs tidying. The rest'll brighten up the house," Aldo sighed.

"Oh sorry, Aldo. That was tactless of me. It seems it's more than just the house that needs brightening-up though." Nick turned the radio off and sat down opposite his father-in-law.

"I've noticed you're a little down in the dumps lately. It can't be the February blahs, we're way past that, it's spring now, a renewal, a new bright season to look forward to, so cheer-up, eh?" Nick patted Aldo's shoulder.

"It could still snow," Aldo said flatly.

"Yes, this is Canada after all, so I'm aware of the very freak chance of that. I'm also aware that you miss Voula."

"Not just her, Jesse too. The house seems empty."

"Gee thanks. Then I guess Lidia and I are mere spectres?" Nick laughed. "Have you heard from Voula lately?"

"Yeah, she keeps in touch. Skypes me once in a while, though I wish she wouldn't," Aldo said, looking away.

"Oh? And why's that?"

"I don't really want to see her tanned arms, her sun-bleached hair, her blue eyes light up when she tells me about her guru, and the cute little freckles dance across her nose. Did you notice her little freckles, Nick?" Aldo's eyes looked far away.

"No, can't say that I did. But I'm sure they're cute." Nick was reaching for something of consolation to offer. "Anyway, the house won't seem too empty today. Stick around, Jesse's coming over for her cooking lesson. You can sit by, have a beer and give us some pointers. We're doing gelato today, okay?"

"I don't wanna' just sit by," Aldo said glumly, then asked, "Nick, do you think I'm boring?"

"Why no. In fact, you never cease to surprise me… what you really need, is an adventure!" Nick said inspired.

"Voula was my adventure, now she has her own 'adventure'. I've got some stuff to do, I'm going to my room." He rose stiffly and shuffled-off.

He's depressed again, just like last year, before Voula. Then, he suddenly sprang to life, was ten years younger, now he's twenty years older. Maybe the baby'll lift him out of this mood. But that's not until August, three and a half months away, too long a time to be hounded by that black dog, Nick worried as he finished with the flowers.

Jesse hollered from the front hall, "Hi dad! It's me," as she dumped her purse on the bench, and took her offering of discounted vintage pinot noir to the kitchen.

Nick gave her a peck on the cheek, handed her a vase, "Would you take this to Aldo's room, but knock first."

He took the other two off to the living and dining

rooms, as Jesse knocked a few times on her nonno's door, getting no answer. Assuming he was asleep, she returned the flowers to the kitchen island, where she found the recipes she and Nick would make that afternoon.

"This looks easy, dad. I thought making gelato was a big production," Jesse observed, as she scanned the recipe for limoncello gelato.

"It usually is. Here, have a drop of my limoncello, see what you think," Nick said pouring her a half-shot.

"Mmm, that's good, very lemony, a little tart beneath the sweetness and something else, I can't put my finger on. What is that flavour?"

"I infused the lemon syrup with coriander seeds. I think it does add a subtle dimension," Nick said, licking a drop from his finger.

Picking up the recipe, Nick continued, "I chose this one because it's easy, but just so you know, traditionally, gelato's a bit more complicated. Since we're using mascarpone and condensed milk, we don't need to make a rinforzato, a base of cornstarch and scalded milk. The French ice cream, the one most North Americans eat, has a custard base of milk and eggs. But I like this for a beginner; it still produces a rich, smooth texture while being quick. You can use this base to add any number of ingredients and flavours as long as you keep in mind that adding more alcohol or sugar will yield a softer texture, pureed fruits will add an icy, almost granita consistency, right?"

"Right. But can we add some candied fruit to this, like ginger?"

"Good idea. Get that tin down from top of the fridge, pick-out a couple of small pieces of candied fruit, I'm sure there's some lemon peel too."

As the cooking lesson progressed, Jesse asked, "Dad, why don't you ever go to mass with mom?"

"Oh, I don't know, guess it's just that your mother likes to have an up-close personal relationship with God, taking the sacraments is important to her. Your mother and I, we respect each other's differences," Nick said smiling at his daughter. "Me, I'm content with a long-distance relationship with ritual and worship, but I'm still a Catholic. The pope, I'm sure would disagree, but I have my way to God, and he has his."

Nick, chopping the candied lemon and ginger, continued, "Your mom has a kindred soul in Father Frank, they discuss faith, worship and spirituality with a passionate interest that confounds me. You know Jess, we can't be all things to our partners," he observed scraping the sticky peel from the mezzaluna. "I'm glad they get along so well. I think it's good, especially for Frank."

"I guess so, dad. I know she loved working with him on his cookbook; it gave her creative freedom that her work doesn't. She was excited and had tons of great ideas about the food styling. But why do I get the feeling that despite saying a lot about mom, you've actually told me very little about you?" Jesse said, folding the limoncello and ginger into the mascarpone and milk.

"That's because you are astute and, in that regard, not my daughter for nothing."

"Speaking of daughters and impending sons dad, how is mom coping? She's been quite, I dunno'…remote lately. We go to lunch, I hope to have a frank talk about how the pregnancy's going, her plans for mat-leave, but all she wants to talk about is how to redecorate my old apartment and shouldn't Josh and I consider an open-concept kitchen. I just can't get near her, if you know what I mean."

"Oh, I do know what you mean. Don't push her Jess, she's doing alright. I keep a close eye on that. But at the end of the day, no pregnancy is without anxiety of some kind. She knows we love and support her, that's good enough for now." Nick concluded, putting the gelato into the freezer.

"If you say so," Jesse said with a sigh.

"And, she has her faith. Which reminds me, we

were thinking of prospective god parents and thought about you and Kate," Nick said, smiling.

"Kate and me? Is that allowed?

"Sure, it is."

"Okay, but why not me and Josh?"

"Because unlike Kate, Josh wasn't baptized in the Catholic church. In short, you must be a Catholic to sponsor a child into the Catholic religion, right?"

"Right, makes sense. Yikes, I should know that if I'm gonna' be a godparent."

Nick laughed at his daughter's ignorance. "Before we move on to the semi-freddo, let's open that pinot noir and talk a little religion."

ALDO WAS ATTACHING his financial details and documents to the email he was forwarding to Piraeus Bank, when the tantalizing aroma of lamb souvlaki and the sound of his daughter's voice told him it was time for dinner. *And..Send! Done. No fuss, no muss. I love the digital age.* He smiled to himself in satisfaction, then feeling hungry, eager to share his plans with the family, made for the kitchen.

"Ooh, is this from The Bouzouki? They do the

best souvlaki on 'The Danny', moist chicken, tender lamb, I think they're the only ones left grilling over charcoal. You can't beat that," he exclaimed, giving his daughter, and granddaughter a peck on each cheek.

Lidia, putting the food on platters, the dips in bowls, added, "You know they make their own tzatziki, really thick and garlicky, their own taramosalata too. I just can't seem to get enough of it lately. I should cut back though, too much salt, makes my ankles swell."

"You'd put it on your granola, if I let you," Nick said, passing the wine.

"Oh, gross dad, salty fish-egg paste on cereal? Anyway, I can't stand taramosalata," Jesse said, making a face.

"Good, then more for me," Lidia said, spreading a generous amount on a triangle of warm pita, devouring it in two quick bites.

Nick turned to Aldo, "Had a good nap then? Jesse knocked on your door a few times, but you didn't answer. Must've been out like a light," he said, passing the feta salad to his father-in-law.

"Nap? I wasn't napping, d'ya think I'm some crotchety old geezer who needs his warm milk and nap? I was busy, that's why I didn't answer," Aldo replied, plucking an olive from the salad, popping it into his mouth.

Nick responded, "Oh, it's just that you seemed tired, so I assumed you were napping. Anyway, what had you so occupied that you couldn't answer your door?"

"Researching, wheeling, dealing. You know, the things you need to do to begin an adventure," Aldo exclaimed, enjoying intriguing his family. Lidia looked quizzically at Nick, sensing this had something to do with what transpired earlier that day.

Nick, picking-up his cue, inquired, "Sounds interesting Aldo, what adventure is this?"

"Yeah, c'mon nonno. We're hanging on tenterhooks here," Jesse said, somewhat condescending, expecting something fairly mundane.

"Next month, I'm going to Greece!" Aldo beamed, proud of his news.

"What? Dad, you said you hated cruises, don't like being confined in a ship. Remember the last and only cruise you ever took was with mom? When you were grumpy the whole time," Lidia warned, shaking her head.

"Who said anything about a cruise? I've booked a direct flight to Corfu, so I can finalize the paperwork on my recent acquisition. To say nothing of looking it over and meeting the staff."

Before Nick and Lidia could jump-in with their

questions, Jesse, helping herself to more souvlaki interjected, "I think that's great nonno, you should spoil yourself. Anyway, like they say, a change is as good as a rest."

"You're not listening to me. I'm not going for a rest, I'm going for an adventure," Aldo asserted, taking a resolute bite of spanakopita.

"Dad, what is this? What have you acquired in Corfu and why does it have staff?" Lidia insisted, her palms beginning to sweat.

"I bought a little seaside taverna in Corfu in an online auction, The Asteri, it means 'star'. I think, it and I, are destined for each other," Aldo said dreamily.

"Destiny? Stars? You sound like a kook, dad. You've been hanging around Voula too long. I'm glad she's gone, she was a bad influence," Lidia said, raising her voice. "As for this on-line auction, assuming it's not a scam, well I just pray we can get your money back," she said, banging her fork down on her plate.

Lidia glared sideways at Nick, expecting him to take-up her cause. He preferred not to notice and instead directed his attention to slathering just the right amount of luscious tzatziki on his lamb, reasoning that the flight had already been booked and Aldo was astute enough to heed destiny when it beckoned.

Jesse quietly watched the drama unfold from the sidelines, knowing it was best to keep out of it when Lidia and Aldo went head-to-head. Aldo, unperturbed by his daughter's expected disapproval, calmly explained the scheme:

"I've bought an interest in a taverna /bed and breakfast with Costas and another investor in Corfu, Costas' hometown."

"What? We just had dinner last week with Costas and Elena, they said nothing about this," Lidia said indignantly.

"That's because I asked them not to until our bid was accepted, which it was late this afternoon," Aldo responded, continuing, "I'll be running the taverna, Elena and Costas will do the bookings through their travel agency and the other partner will manage the B&B. But I'm their 'boots on the ground' in Corfu. I can't wait to get there." Aldo sat back, grinning broadly.

"Oh really, and where did you get the money for this venture?" Lidia asked, archly.

"Not that it's your business, but I've a tidy investment accrued from Filly's life insurance and the sale of our house. And *she'd* approve of my new venture," Aldo said, confidently.

"How do you propose to run a business without even speaking the local language?" Lidia said, becoming agitated.

"The same way I proposed, to make a new life in Canada, fortunately before you were around to tell me not to," Aldo bellowed, jabbing a blunt finger at his daughter.

As Lidia opened her mouth to make another protest, he shouted over her, "Furthermore, all the staff speaks English, as all the tourists do. Prince Philip was born there! And they even have a cricket team, it's practically 'Little Britain', except for that stupid Brexit. And me and the investors are going to make it a new destination spot for Canadians. So there." Aldo folded his arms across his chest and smirked.

Lidia rose, saying, "I've had enough, I'm going to lie down. Make sure you clean-up." She fixed her father with an icy stare.

The rest of the table went quiet, Jesse and Nick looked towards Aldo, who looked down, busy cutting-up his dolmades and said, "Give her a day or two, she'll come around. You know what she's like, breathing fire and fury at first, then when she's calm, you can reason with her. Now, let's finish our dinner in peace. After, I'll show you the property online, okay?" He smiled and raised his glass to Nick and Jesse.

Jesse got up, saying, "I think I'd better check on mom."

"Suit yourself," Aldo said shaking his head, topping-up Nick's glass of wine.

"MOM?" JESSE GENTLY opened the bedroom door; her mother lay quietly on the edge of the bed. She sat down beside her and took her hand. "You okay? You crying?" Jesse asked, caressing her face.

Lidia opened her eyes and looked up at her daughter, "Why do I always have to be the bad cop, eh? Your dad gets to be 'Mr. Nice Guy, Good Cop'. If something's broken, I want it fixed, NOW. I can't just leave things to Nick, the great procrastinator."

"I know mom, Dad's approach to life's DIY is to do nothing until eventually it sorts itself out."

"All of you laugh at me, 'the laser', homing in on all the potential disasters. But if a closet is opened, I close it, a drawer in disarray, I tidy it. I can't stand things out of order; my family's lives included."

"We don't laugh at you mom. Well, hardly ever, and anyway the 'good cop, bad cop' thing worked for me as a kid, you're a team, on the same side, just doing it differently," Jesse said smiling.

"Someone has to be the voice of reason, especially with Aldo. He gets carried away; it's the gambler in him. And don't believe that bull about my mom being okay with what he's doing. Mom hated his gambling.

"When I was little, he would often lose his wages and finally their mortgage payment, in a poker game. So, mom took me and left. To get us back he had to agree to a strict allowance and that was that. We were mostly fine from then on, with some lapses. But he seems to be going back to his old ways, getting into trouble. I just want him to be safe. I just want us all to be safe," Lidia exclaimed.

Jesse leaned over her. "He's okay mom. Costas wouldn't get him into anything dodgy, you know that. It actually sounds like a good opportunity." She put a hand on her shoulder. "This isn't really about nonno, is it? It's really about you and the baby. You can tell me if you're scared."

Lidia sat up a little and wiped her eyes, "Yes, I guess so. I get anxious, have sleepless nights. If the baby stops kicking, I worry until he starts again. I thought I was okay after the tests came back negative. I was elated, it was going to be fine. Then that old devil fear clutched at me and won't let me go." She stared wide-eyed, at Jesse.

Jesse embraced her saying, "Ssh now, the baby's okay, you're okay. I know it and he will be bright and strong and what and who he's meant to be. I'm here for you mom, and I can't wait to meet my little brother, even though he'll be a spoiled brat." Jesse laughed; Lidia couldn't help but laugh too.

"Hey, have you thought of names yet, mom?"

"Yes, we're calling him Antonio Fabio, after both of Nick's dads."

"What? I thought for sure dad would go for like, uh 'Barolo' or 'Coriandolo'," Jesse joked.

"Don't even think about mentioning those to Nick, he'll likely change his mind and actually name our son 'Barolo'."

"Don't worry mom, like billions of Italian boys before him, in the end, he'll just be called, Tony."

TREATS AND TRICKS

PULLING THE SHEET pan from the oven, Javi put the finishing touches to his specialty movie snack, Frangelico caramel corn, folding-in just enough toasted hazelnuts to give extra crunch. The coup-de-grace: a generous sprinkling of pink Himalayan sea salt and a light flurry of roasted fenugreek seeds, imparting an intriguing hint of smoky, maple syrup.

He pinched-up a small cluster of the caramel corn and crunched on it thoughtfully, *mmm…damn, I'm good,* he smiled to himself, satisfied that all the flavors were perfectly balanced before portioning the treat into the two small glass bowls standing by.

The vodka is chilling, glasses are frosting, now if only I could get my daughter to stop dumping her stuff all over the entranceway, he mumbled, picking-up several batik scarves, tidying her numerous boots and shoes, always carelessly kicked-off upon entry.

Grabbing her overflowing school bag, out tumbled an array of travel-size beauty products, half a pack of Camel's, a deck of tarot cards, one crystal crucifix earring, several textbooks, a sloppy binder, full of loose assignments. Just as Javi went to yell for Lucinda, he spied a bright green foil wrapper.

Stooping to pick it up, looking at it in disbelief, he saw it was a condom, and not just any condom – a 'Trojan Twisted', *My god,* Javi turned it over in his hands in disbelief. The entrance monitor blinked red, *She's here!* he shoved the condom into his pocket, everything else back into Lucinda's school bag, then flung it into the hall closet. Composing himself, he smoothed back his hair, tucked in the tail of his shirt, and stepped out into the foyer to greet his guest.

As the elevator doors opened and Becky emerged, Lucinda rushed past her. Stopping the elevator, she shouted over her shoulder, "Hi Becky! Dad, I'm staying over at Charlotte's tonight. Leave you two love birds alone. Arrivederci!" she laughed throwing a few air kisses. Before Javi could protest, the elevator doors closed, and she was gone.

"You look like you just missed the last bus," Becky said, looking concerned at Javi who stood silent, staring at the elevator.

"I've just had a shocking revelation. Let's go in and I'll tell you about it. I think I'm going to need a big martini and a little advice," Javi replied, opening the door.

Settling on the couch with their martinis and popcorn treats, Javi held up his discovery, "I just found this in Lucinda's school bag."

"What? "Becky grabbed it from him and read the label, "Trojan Twisted… well, at least she's having safe and fun sex. Kudos to her. Seems like a chip off the 'ol block," Becky chuckled, giving Javi a little punch on the shoulder.

"I'm glad you're amused, 'cause I'm certainly not. My daughter's only fifteen."

"Sorry, I forgot. It's just that she looks older, more like nineteen," Becky replied. "Have any idea who the stud is?"

"She never mentions any boys at her new school. So far, she's made some friends on the girls' soccer team. Mostly though, she hangs around with her best friend, Charlotte. The only male I know she sees on a regular basis is her tutor, Christopher," Javi said, shrugging.

Becky cut-in with, "Bingo! Then it's the tutor, betcha' anything," she smiled in satisfaction, popping a cluster of caramel corn in her mouth.

"What? No, he's probably twenty-two at least, in first year law. What would he have in common with a fifteen-year-old high school kid?"

Becky raised her eyebrows knowingly at Javi.

"Oh c'mon…when would they, you know, 'do it'? He's actually tutoring her, if the improved grades are anything to go by. Anyway, they always meet at the agency's office," Javi said, skeptically.

"And afterwards?" Becky asked.

"Afterwards she goes out with Charlotte."

"You sure about that?" Becky smirked.

"Um, no, now that you point it out. I just take her word for it. I never phone Charlotte's mom to check," Javi said, putting an olive-laden skewer in his mouth, then pulling it out slowly, deduced, "So, it appears I'm paying this smart-ass kid to tutor my daughter in more ways than one."

Javi's eyes narrowed, folding his arms, he leaned back against the cushions.

Becky, wary that she'd instigated a fight advised, "Look, that's just the first conclusion I jumped to. There's no real evidence that it's the tutor, it may just be a guy at school, that's why she never mentions a boy, keeping him on the down-low, Charlotte being the decoy."

"Oh, Charlotte's the decoy alright. But I think you hit it right with Christopher being the perp… I'll get that little pedo," Javi said with conviction.

"First, you better make sure of your facts. You can't fire-off, half-cocked at someone who may be entirely innocent. Even if Christopher is your man, he may not be aware of Lucinda's age. She could've easily lied to him. You should do some investigating first," Becky said.

"Yeah, beginning with following her to the tutorial – and beyond."

"Just be careful. If you're wrong, she'll have a hard time forgiving you, but if you're right, well, I'll certainly back you in stopping it. I think for all Lucinda's worldly posture, she's quite naive. I mean she's only ever attended all-girl schools, right?"

"Yes, by her mother's dictum, and now look what happens. She falls prey to a lecherous tutor," Javi surmised, grabbing a handful of caramel corn.

"Oh, don't be so dramatic, they're hardly Heloise and Abelard."

"They will be if he's seduced my daughter – then his nuts are mine!"

"Relax Javi, after all we don't even know if she's

actually used these," Becky said, picking-up the offending article, "Um, have *you* ever used these, twisted things?"

"What? No, have you?"

"Uh-Uh… d'ya want to?" Becky smiled precociously at Javi.

"Well, I'd certainly like to investigate further, but this is evidence," he said, snatching it from her hand.

SLEUTHING

JAVI HUNCHED DOWN behind the driver's seat in Becky's Mazda, as she sat at the steering wheel in a baseball cap and sunglasses, surveying the street. They parked across the road, a few doors down from Scholastic Tutorial, waiting for Lucinda to emerge from her session.

"Aha! There she is…and yes, there's our man. Christopher, is it?"

"Yep," Javi peeked over to affirm, "They're getting into his car."

"I know, I see them. Well, Starsky, what d'ya want me to do?"

"Duh! Follow the car, Hutch," Javi said impatiently.

Becky did as she was asked, pulling-out into rush hour traffic, which fortunately was flowing in the opposite direction, as it seemed they were headed downtown. Nevertheless, it was difficult to keep Christopher's car in view as there were traffic cones for a few kilometres merging two lanes into one.

Becky had some tricky manoeuvring to get close enough to keep up with the lights and remain unnoticed, getting the horn and the finger from a van driver she cut-off.

At one point, it seemed they had lost them and Javi got angry, "Why don't you get a decent car."

"There's nothing wrong with this car, it's only two years old," Becky retorted.

"There's everything wrong with this car, it's not an automatic for a start."

"Oh, sorry Javi, it doesn't fly either," Becky shouted back at him.

"Look! There they are, turning into the campus. They're headed for; let's see…hey, that's my old fraternity!" Javi said indignantly, as he watched Christopher's car turn into the driveway of the Kappa Epsilon Gamma fraternity house, parking in the back lot.

Becky pulled up one building before the entrance.

"Now what?" Becky asked, feeling a little peeved.

"I'll wait for a few minutes, then I'm going in and sorting this out," Javi said.

"I'll come with you," Becky offered.

"No, you stay here and keep an eye out. I'll be back, hopefully with Lucinda."

"I'd rather go with you, but if that's what you want…just promise you won't go ape-shit on them."

"I promise," Javi said as he got out of the car and headed towards the familiar frat house.

Once in the foyer, he looked through several open doors, until he heard Lucinda's voice and the clack of billiard balls. Standing in the doorway of the games' room he spied her, laughing, a beer bottle in one hand and a pool cue in the other, taunting Christopher as he leaned over, preparing to take a shot, "C'mon Chris, call it! Call it!" she shouted.

"Okay girl, watch and learn. Red ball in the side pocket." He jabbed the cue decisively at his target, but missed the shot, sending the ball bouncing off the rail, hitting a green ball out instead.

Lucinda whooped and started a victory dance, holding her beer and cue in the air, when suddenly she saw her father. Christopher looked toward the door, "Oh. Hi Mr. Ortiz…uh what're you doing here?… Lucinda?" he looked from father to daughter.

Lucinda was silent as Javi stepped forward. "I'm

here for my daughter, who is *not* supposed to be drinking." He snatched the beer from her hand. "But *is supposed* to be with her girlfriend, Charlotte. Isn't that right Lucinda?" Javi said tensely.

She looked down; her face flushed with anger.

"Hey, what's going on?" Christopher asked, nonplussed, putting his arm around Lucinda's shoulders.

"Don't touch her." Javi pulled Lucinda away. "You know she's only fifteen?"

"What? No. She said she was nineteen and doing upgrading to prequalify. Honestly, Mr. Ortiz, I had no idea." Christopher held-up a hand in disbelief.

Lucinda shook free from her father's grasp. "God! How can you embarrass me like this? I'm going back to Argentina; living with you is like living in Jurassic Park. You're so…. antediluvian!" Crying, she bolted from the room, out of the building.

Before Javi could run after her, he needed to make his point with Christopher.

"You're a law student, correct?"

"Yeah. So?"

"So, look-up statutory rape, cause that's the charge you'll be facing if you see my daughter again, understand?"

"Understood. No worries, I never want to see either of you again. As for your nasty accusation, we're just friends, I did not have sex with her."

Christopher threw his cue on the table and folded his arms in disgust.

"Good."

Javi left, jogging down the stairs to the street, looking around, he couldn't see Lucinda, hoping Becky caught hold of her on her way out.

"Did you see her?" he asked leaning into the driver's window.

"Yeah, but she was too fast for me, she headed to the subway."

"Shit. Well, we might as well go back to my place. She probably needs to cool down before coming home to face the music," Javi said getting into the passenger seat.

NIGHT MARE

THE SUN HAD long past set on the terrace, the LED lanterns flickered, Javi went in to fetch a sweater for Becky and poach the Camels in Lucinda's school bag. Returning, draping his sweater around Becky's shoulders, he took a seat beside her and lit up a cigarette.

"Hey, what're you doing?" Becky said, waving the smoke away. "I've never seen you smoke before," she said, indignant.

"Gave it up in my teens. But tonight, I just feel like it. Luckily, my juvenile delinquent daughter has been indulging in that illicit activity as well. So, I decided to have one too, on her. Maybe I'll just finish off the whole damn pack," he said insolently, blowing smoke rings.

"You'll regret that in the morning," Becky advised, standing, moving away from the pungent cloud gathering around Javi.

"Ha! Won't be the first time dawn's rosy fingers served me that cold breakfast," he said cynically.

"Oh, boo-hoo! You can be such a baby, Javi. You know this isn't all about you, don't you?" Becky said, raising her voice.

"I do? And why isn't it? I'm the one who's been lied to. I'm the one whose trust has been abused," he replied angrily, butting out his cigarette in a nearby planter.

"And you're *not* the one who's been shunted from pillar to post, sent from country to country, no less. Ignored until you act up.

"No wonder Lucinda acts up. Put your hurt feelings aside and consider hers. She got a crush on Christopher, wanted to impress him, just because he noticed her, for her beauty, her charm, and not because she'd done anything wrong."

"Well, I can see whose side you're on. Look Becky, I'm protecting my daughter, not condemning her. I do actually love her, you know," he said, holding out his hand for hers.

Becky brushed past him, headed for the door.

"I'm not on any one's side. I just want to help you see her side, okay? It's late, I'm going home. Please keep me posted and if she doesn't show-up soon, you should call the police."

He let her find her way out. He needed to think:

Where the hell can she be? We've contacted all the usual suspects, asked them to contact her, she won't answer to any of us. Who else loves her? Who else does she love?... Ah-ha! That's where she is.

JAVI TURNED-OFF HIS headlights, keeping a sharp look-out through the early morning mist as he bumped along the park's uneven gravel path following Wilket Creek leading to the circular driveway in front of the stables. The paddock and track were lit with three spotlights, shedding wide cones of light on the entrance from the stables and the two bends. A lone rider on a bay Appaloosa was cantering from the dark clammy mist into the eerie light of the second bend.

Horse and rider were oblivious of their watcher, he could see the white cord of Lucinda's ear buds as she kept cantering, fixedly, mindlessly on and on around the track, in and out of each shaft of illumination, submersed in darkness, then emerging into light.

Javi was transfixed, he had never regarded his daughter in such a distant, objective way…who was she really? Who was he to her, the rider, bent on her own circular motion, in and out of the light? Seen, known, then hidden, a shadowy figure. He knew that feeling, that way of being. He realized she was his in a way he'd never felt before.

Impulsively, he flashed his high beams to get Lucinda's attention just before she cleared the next bend, going from darkness into the light again. Frida shied, reared, then jumped the rails, galloping towards the path. He caught a look of terror on his daughter's face as she passed the car, yelling, trying to control her runaway horse. He quickly backed the car up, turned it around and followed them, hoping Frida would slow down enough for him to pull up alongside, then cut her off before she got out onto the main road.

As the pathway widened, he saw two sets of headlights coming towards them. The park patrollers on ATV's; one swerved around to block the horse's way, the other headed-up alongside. Javi stopped his car and ran towards his daughter.

Lucinda pulled-up too hard on the reins, Frida reared again, and this time threw her. Lucinda fell sideways onto her shoulder, rolling out into the ditch. Both patrolmen moved quickly, one grabbed hold of Frida's bridle and between them they managed to calm the rampant horse.

A TROJAN HORSE

LUCINDA HAD BEEN home from the hospital for a week, a long, invalided, uncommunicative week. Her mother and Hans sent flowers, Lidia did too, Becky sent a goodie basket full of chocolates and other treats. There were visitors, Charlotte, her new tutor Lauren, a girl named Phoebe who was captain of the soccer team, Jesse, and Kate.

Javi could hear them talking and laughing in her room, but when he poked his head in to offer food and drink, the visitors fell silent and Lucinda just shook her head, so he withdrew. Since her left arm was in a sling against her chest, making it immobile for a few weeks, Javi hired a private home-care worker to attend to her daily needs. Lucinda made it clear to him that she didn't want his help, not even to tuck her in.

Javi was worried, not only about her broken collar bone and imminent final exams, but what he most feared, her broken heart and inevitable anger towards him.

He had respected her wishes, tolerated her insolent silence, and now had had enough; tonight, they would talk, come hell or high water. He was resolute as he peeled the onions, cutting them and the chorizo into large chunks, then crumbling the queso and warming the tortillas in the oven. Alternately threading onion, then sausage onto the wet skewers, he realized how he would approach the issue.

Turning the sizzling food over on the built-in grill, he decided to take a Trojan horse approach. Lucinda had only a fruit smoothie for lunch, her goodie basket was empty, so he decided to hold-off dinner until he knew she'd be good and hungry, starving even, if he knew his daughter, who had a very healthy appetite. He assembled the super choripan; grilled sausage, onions, queso and chimichurri sauce, wrapped it in the warm tortilla and again in tinfoil, placed it on a tray then knocked on her door.

Hearing her whisper, "Okay, come in," he plunked the tray down on her desk and left, leaving the door slightly ajar. He heard her get up from the bed, then struggle, trying to unwrap the foil, a moment's pause, then an exasperated shout:

"And just how am I s'posed to eat this thing?"

Pausing a moment, he came to her rescue.

"Just sit down and I'll bring it to you," Javi said, unwrapping the choripan. "Voila," he offered her the warm tortilla oozing with sauce and melted cheese.

She balked, turning her head away, "I know what you're trying to do, and I don't want it. I've lost my appetite."

"Oh really? Well, I'm hungry and me and this super chori are going nowhere, so bon appétit! Hope you enjoy eating air." Javi took a big bite off one end, the sauce dribbled down a corner of his mouth. He wiped it away, enthusing, "Oh man, this is great. Mmm, mmm, I'd forgotten how good this was. But really, mine is better than your abue's, I have to say," he mumbled smugly, going in for another big bite.

Lucinda grabbed the choripan from him, devouring the rest in two famished bites.

"Whoa, I'd hate to see you eat when you do have an appetite," Javi laughed, pulling a little string of cheese from her chin.

"This is good dad, but not better than my abue's, nothing touches hers," she said, her eyes tearing up.

"I know, you miss her. And I know it hasn't been

easy for you, sent away from home. But you're home now, with me. It's just you and me kid, and remember we'll always have Argentina," he said playing for a laugh, putting-on his best 'Bogie' imitation.

Lucinda rolled her eyes and giggled, "Oh dad, that is the worst!"

While her guard was down, Javi stood-up and decided to broach the burning issue, "Here, I think these are yours," he said quietly, handing her the Trojan Twisted and half-pack of Camel's.

Lucinda was embarrassed for a moment, then indignant, "I can't believe you went through my things!" she yelled.

"I didn't, these fell out of your school bag when I was tidying-up last Friday night. It's what made me suspicious of you and Christopher," he said calmly.

"Oh… Dad, Charlotte put that stupid thing in my birthday card, as a joke about my seeing Chris. But, I swear…"

"I know, he also said things hadn't gone that far. I believe you," Javi said, as he gathered the napkins and foil on the tray.

"Okay," Lucinda said, tearing open the condom packet and throwing it in the waste basket. Look, you can take these away, too" she handed him the cigarettes, "I'm finished with them. Phoebe'd kill me if she knew her MVP smoked."

Javi put them on the tray, stopping at the door, he asked, "Tomorrow, would you like to go see Frida?"

"Yeah, I really would. I'm so worried about her. All the way in the ambulance, I kept hoping she wasn't hurt, and that they wouldn't put her away wet."

"No. Don't worry, I made sure she's okay. I've been to the stables and she hasn't even been off her oats, much like her mistress."

"Um, is there any more chori out there, dad?"

"Of course, I have some more warming in the oven, if you wanna' come out."

"Okay. Hey, it's almost time for 'Raised by Wolves'," Lucinda said, indicating her favorite British sitcom, "Can we eat…"

"In front of the tv? Sure, I'll set it up," Javi agreed, heading for the kitchen. They hadn't talked in the way he planned, but they had a new and better understanding, nonetheless.

A FOND FAREWELL

"WELL, THAT'S THE last of it," Aldo said, putting a sweater in the now full bag destined for the charity bin, the rest of his belongings to be stored at Cheech's.

"Okay, let's take these and the boxes out to the car, then come back for the luggage," Cheech said, grabbing several garment bags.

"Right, we may need to take it in three trips though," Aldo added, loading the boxes on the dolly, following his friend to the car.

When all of Aldo's things had been cleared, he took one last look around his old room, then at Cheech. "Feel like a beer before we go?"

"Sure, why not?"

Cheech sat at the island, as Aldo poured their beer.

"How's Nick gonna manage getting your furniture down into the basement apartment?" Cheech asked.

"Josh and his buddies said they'd help. I think Lidia wants to paint first, freshen things up."

"Oh, that's good… Listen Aldo, I'm sorry things didn't work out between you and Voula, you made a nice couple," Cheech said, taking a sip of his beer.

"That's water under the bridge. I'm actually glad she turned me down. I didn't really want to get married, just wanted to hold on to her, keep everything the same. But life is change, and I'm looking forward to my next adventure in Corfu.

"Don't get me wrong, I love Voula, and I love Canada, it's a great country, been very good to me, but the winters get me down and I'll just be in the way here."

"So, how's the family dealing with your next 'adventure'?" Cheech asked, a little warily.

"Nick and Jesse understand, Jesse's even got dibs on the first room available after our 'B and B' reno, on family discount, of course. Lidia, well, she's being stoic, doesn't like it, but accepts it."

"Anyway, I guess when little Antonio comes, they'll be glad of your room for an office and that ground floor bathroom," Cheech said.

"Yep, and Jesse's apartment can be rented to help when Nick goes part-time," Aldo explained.

"Ya' know Aldo, Corfu sounds nice to visit, but I couldn't just pull-up stakes and move there, like you. I can't say it isn't handy me having a friend there though, I'd love to get away in the winters too."

"The winter climate is cool, more like fall, not hot like Florida, but still nice, and no snow! There'll always be a room for you, buddy. And thanks for putting me up in the meantime," Aldo said.

"'Me casa e tu casa', as they say," Cheech responded.

Aldo looked wistful, "You know Cheech, I can taste the sea, in my dreams, like when I was a kid in

Pescara. My favorite dish was pesce in acqua pazza, our trattoria's specialty. At dawn, mom and I would go down to the port, we bought what the boats had just brought in. The smells, the shouting, the haggling, such an exciting place. I enjoyed working in the trattoria, I left school at fourteen to go full-time. My poor mother needed me, I was her wing man. She taught me all I know about food, and love."

Aldo and Cheech drained their glasses. Aldo put them in the dishwasher, then turning to his friend declared, "Let's get going, I'm hungry. We can pick-up some calamari on the way home."

SEA OF DREAMS

SIX WEEKS LATER, home seemed a long way away for Aldo, not only in real space, but in emotional time, as he walked along the sunset shore, barefoot, trouser legs rolled-up. This was his favorite time by the sea, to linger in the waning day, sinking into the sun-soaked sand, feeling the mellow ebb and flow of life; gulls bobbing aimlessly, people stretching out to receive the blessing of the dying sun, a languid moment in the twilight of lucid dreaming.

Shielding his eyes from the sun's rays, Aldo stood

and looked towards shore and his new home, Asteri, its brilliant, white-washed facade glowing in the twilight, like a star. He recalled with a wry smile a fragment of, *Sea Fever*, the one English poem he learned decades ago as a 'greenhorn' from his first and only Canadian girlfriend…

> I must go down to the sea again,
> To the lonely sea and the sky,
> And all I ask is a tall ship,
> And a star to steer her by.

Aah, sweet Deborah, five years older, E.S.L. teacher… no, Diana! I used to sing to her in bed, 'Oh, please stay by me, Diana,'…Paul Anka; never liked him, but she did, not enough to stay by me though, Aldo laughed, his reverie interrupted by the animated figure of Nikos, shouting, jumping, and waving a white napkin to flag his attention:

"Boss! Boss! There's a gues' here, needs shek-in!"

Aldo waved back, "Okay, I'm coming!" *sheesh, you'd think the damn place was on fire just 'cause a guest appears. Oh well, at least he's eager,* Aldo grumbled as he slogged his way to the shore pushed along by the incoming tide. *Hmm, maybe too eager,* he rolled down his trousers, *have to keep an eye on Nikos.*

Nikos was five foot four, wiry and high-wired, always on the move, darting here and there. A maître'd, interpreter, cultural envoy, and Aldo's indispensable factotum, self-appointed. He could be anywhere between twenty to thirty on account of his chubby face, schoolboy shock of curly black hair, always mussed-up, standing on end, and wide-eyed, open-mouthed air of breathless anticipation.

He was married with four noisy, excitable children and one tall, stolid, Albanian wife whose hefty, rolling-pin arms were always crossed against her ample bosom, in discontent. Aldo suspected that the long hours at work offered Nikos a refuge from his 'domestic bliss'.

"Welcome to the Asteri, Ms?…"

"Dupré, Lola Dupré, but you can call me 'Lo'," she said, with a beguiling smile.

"Aldo Campanile, proprietor." Aldo extended his hand.

Lola took his hand in both of hers. "Mm now, let's see…there's a good strong lifeline, virile too," she laughed holding his palm open, "oh, but my, my, money goes out quickly, comes in easy though. You're a gambler, aren't you, honey?" Lola grinned.

"I like a flutter now and then. Nikos, put the lady in our best suite," he said, turning to his confederate, with a wink.

"Oh? Oh! Yes boss, right away," he nodded, taking the first of their glamorous guest's trunks to the room adjacent Aldo's.

Aldo turned to Lola, "Ah, before you go up Lo, join me at the bar for a sundowner?"

"Love to, just so long as it's long, icy and bourbon."

He ushered her in, and watched her walk ahead, slim hips swaying; taught, shapely calves crossing, perched on stylish stilettos; a proud, naughty round bum beckoning him to follow.

She slid effortlessly onto the bar stool, then searched in her purse for her Marlborough's, "May I?" she asked, holding a cigarette between two long, brown fingers capped in fantastically bejewelled nails.

"Why not? I'll turn the fan up," Aldo said, putting an ashtray on the bar. Reaching over to light her cigarette, he asked "So, bourbon on the rocks good for you?"

"Sure, but what I'm really craving is a Morrison Mule. Do you know it?"

"No, but if you tell me, I'll try."

"It's a few ounces of ginger ale, splash of Campari, squeeze of lime, twist of orange and two fingers of bourbon on crushed ice."

"One Morrison Mule coming-up," Aldo said,

getting-out the jigger, pouring-in the bourbon, he asked, "why 'Morrison Mule'?"

"Oh, it's named after Jim Morrison, you know, bad boy singer of the Doors? He used to stay at the Pontchartrain Hotel in New Orleans, and sure loved his bourbon. So, Benton Bourgeois at the Hot Tin Bar did a twist on the Moscow Mule, named it after him," Lola explained, blowing out a lazy stream of smoke.

Aldo placed a Collins glass onto a coaster, "How's this?"

Lola took an appreciative sip and smiled, "Perfect, just like *N'awlins*," she drawled ironically, laughing.

Aldo poured himself a Heineken, and they settled-in for a cozy chat when there was a loud bang from reception; Nikos struggling with the rest of Lola's luggage, shouting, swearing "Theé mou! …oh, sorry, boss," he peeked his head around the corner, smiling sheepishly. Aldo chuckled.

"Oh my, d'ya think he needs some help?" Lola asked.

"Nah, he's fine, just a little clumsy. I hope you don't mind me saying though, that's a heck of a lot of luggage for three weeks."

"I need it all for my act, I'm a tribute performer. The trunks are my professional wardrobe and props.

This tour I'm doing Diana Ross, Tina Turner, Donna Summer and Beyoncé, just to keep it fresh. I'm booked-in to the Club Disco here; I mostly do the resort circuit and cruises."

"So, you're a singer, eh? I thought you might be in show business, or modelling."

"Well, I'm not near tall enough, or pretty enough for modelling," Lola demurred.

"You look pretty enough to me," Aldo said, giving her an appreciative smile.

"Guess I walked into that one. My, but you're a flirt!" Lola laughed, stubbing-out her cigarette.

"Can't help it, I'm Italian," Aldo said, shrugging his shoulders.

"Oh, yes?" Lola said, tilting her head, looking him up and down.

Aldo suddenly wished he were smartly dressed. He cleared his throat, and said, "You must be tired, I won't keep you. If you'd like to go to your room, everything's ready. We're not open to the public for dinner on Sundays, but if you'd like to dine here, we can do you something, or take a stroll, there's nice little spots nearby."

"Well thank-you, I think I'll do that later. I've been to Corfu several times, so I know my way around," Lola said, as she rose to leave, straightening her skirt, heading for the door.

Aldo looked after her, intrigued.

"No, Nikos! There'll be no more of that greasy crap here," Aldo shouted, glowering down at the defiant figure.

"But boss, you no understand, the Brits, they all want their *fiss and sheeps*!" Nikos yelled back, rising on his toes.

"I don't care, we'll clean-out all the frozen order, put it on a lunch special, just get rid of it, then basta, no re-order of frozen '*fiss and sheeps*'. Ever. Got it?"

"Got it, boss," Nikos conceded, unconvinced, shaking his head.

Aldo, feeling conciliatory, explained, "Look Nikos, we're trying to pimp-up this place, make it sophisticated, appeal to a more upscale crowd, better tips for everyone, right?"

"Only if they come, boss." Nikos grimaced.

"They'll come. Especially the Canadians, they love Mediterranean food, eat it all the time; in Toronto, half the restaurants are either Italian or Greek. So, we change the menu to feature the fresh seafood here; fritto misto, but mostly grilled, maybe a cioppino. We'll do updated mezes, big flavourful salads, some with legumes and cous-cous, a ceviche.

"Then a coupl'a simple pizzas and pastas, a few Greek lamb classics. Desserts focussed on fruit with local honey, or the kumquat liqueur and we're set. Simple, fresh, tasty, beautifully presented, 'cause you eat with your eyes first, right?"

"If you say so, boss." Nikos shrugged continuing to set tables.

"And no more flowers on the tables, distracts from the food, only tea lights in the evening. We can get some big amphoras for reception, the bar, and those niches along the walls, that's where we'll have flowers. And nix the bouzouki music, everybody does that, from now on, only pop and jazz like, Bublé, Bocelli, Sinatra, and Nat King Cole."

"Yes boss," Nikos said listlessly, as he banged down a dinner plate.

"Whoa, 'Opla', spare the new china, eh?" Aldo said, extending a cautionary hand as he walked away.

Aldo headed upstairs to check on housekeeping, when he met Lola on her way out. She was dressed casually, but beautifully, in aqua silk Capri's, sleeveless white linen cropped, tent-top, a row of coy bows, loosely tying-up the opened back. Clusters of sparkling bangles jangled on her long shapely arms, her colorful pedicure peeked-out from embroidered kitten-heel mules.

"Good morning, Lo! Did you sleep well?"

"Like the proverbial baby. I see you've got new mattresses and linens, very nice." She nodded approvingly.

"Joining us for breakfast?"

"Oh no, my morning regime is lots of warm water with honey and lemon, a little light yoga, and a jog or brisk walk to the club for rehearsals. I'm performing tonight, I'd love it if you could come, if you can get away for a bit," Lola said, placing a hand on his arm.

"I'll see what I can do; we're not that busy yet, so yeah, I'd love to see your act."

"Good then, see you tonight," she said, fluttering a few bejewelled fingers in farewell, as she continued downstairs.

LOLA DID TWO shows, a young British comedian opened for her, he and a local DJ kept the punters amused in between. Aldo caught the second show when the crowd was effusive and a little drunk. It went well; she had a strong, clear soprano, great range, and well-choreographed moves, her costumes, glamorous and flamboyant. He was impressed; she really was a knock-out, a talent worthy of Broadway.

After her show, they walked along the seashore, talking wistfully about their hometowns, hers in Louisiana, but now New York, his in Italy, then Canada. They talked of their families and the lives they'd lived there, agreeing that people really weren't much different the world over.

They talked about their dreams, Aldo's was fulfilled in making his success and family in Canada, and now in Corfu, being useful, productive, and in charge once again.

Lo's dreams were distant, far ahead of where she was now, to be a renowned song writer, jazz vocalist, then buy a little mountain retreat in Corfu, she loved the mountains, so cool and quiet. There she could go to renew her spirit, write, retreat with like-minded friends, and ultimately, retire with a beautiful garden, a faithful King Charles Cavalier spaniel, a few chickens, and some beehives. She loved honey, swore it was the secret of perpetual youth and believed bees were sacred. She might even get a little donkey cart, paint it up like the Sicilians do, install velvet cushions, and ride it into town.

When they got back to the Asteri, Aldo insisted on making them a spaghettata di mezzanotte, midnight spaghetti, an Italian tradition, to be shared with friends, at home, at midnight, after a good night out. They shared it under the stars, from a big deep bowl, slurping-up the long oily strands, washing them down with a smooth, amicable Chianti. Chatting, giggling, they climbed the weary stairs to dreamland and parted with a kiss at her door.

OH, LA LOLA

ALDO TURNED-OFF HIS electric shaver then slapped on some Acqua di Gio. He regarded himself in the mirror, turning his head to the left, then the right, checking the sag on his jaw line, the slight droop on his once chiselled cheekbones.

The neck was good though, he reckoned, lifting his cleft chin, running a hand down the still firm flesh. His salt and pepper mane was full. And as for wrinkles, only a few deep creases at the corners of his eyes, clear and blue as the Adriatic, a few etched across the high noble forehead;

Shows I'm a man of thought, gravitas, not some airhead, numb skull who doesn't know enough to be worried about the evils of globalization or the state of the damn rainforest.

Satisfied, he put on his freshly pressed, glazed-cotton shirt, tucked it into his still respectable waistband and headed downstairs to prepare for the staff meeting. Walking through his kitchen, above the cacophony of chopping knives and sizzling saucepans, rose the dissonant chant of, "Oh, Lola, Oh, la-Looola," the guys shouted, turning towards him, grabbing their crotches, laughing.

Annoyed and baffled, Aldo collared Nikos in the dining room, "Hey, what the hell's their problem, what's going on?" Aldo jutted-out his jaw, belligerently.

"Ah, it's Lola, they laugh because she is your girlfriend," Nikos said, looking down, pretending to be engrossed in folding napkins.

"Girlfriend? Lola? No, we're just, you know, friends. Anyway, what business is it of theirs, and why the snickering?" Aldo demanded.

"Uh, well boss, uh, your girlfriend, who is not girlfriend…well, she is tranig," Nikos said looking up, swallowing hard.

"Training? Training, for what?"

"No, no boss!" Nikos wrapped a napkin like a kerchief around his head, fluttering his eye lashes, looked-up at Aldo and said in a falsetto, "Tranig, Lola is Tranig!"

"What? You mean *tranny*? *Transvestite*?"

"Yeah boss, that's right, transvesty! You got it!" Nikos exclaimed.

Aldo went pale, speechless, as if he had just wandered into a 'B-movie' about his life.

WHERE'S ALDO

LOLA, IN JOGGING gear, hoodie and wrap-around sunglasses, finished her post power-walk stretch and headed across the causeway to the Asteri, determined to find out what was up with Aldo. Striding to the front desk, she pounded on the service bell until a frantic Nikos came running, "Yes miss, can I do for you?" he said out of breath.

"Where's Aldo?"

"Ah, he's out right now, leave a message?"

"I've been leaving messages for three days, you do pass them on, don't you?"

"Oh, yes miss, always, but boss, he is too busy I think for answer."

"Bull shit! I know when I'm being swerved. What's wrong? He's nowhere to be seen, I knock on his door, I can see a light from beneath it and hear the TV, so I know he's in, but just won't answer!"

"Oh well, it's mystery. Like I say miss, he too busy to answer," Nikos shrugged, smiling unconvincingly.

Lola, who hated taking 'no' for an answer, turned on her heels, *Huh, there's more than one way to skin this cat,* she bounded up the stairs, taking them two by two. Once in her room she half-filled the ice bucket from the tap, twisted yesterday's news into a long, tight spiral, grabbed her lighter and stood in front of Aldo's door. Then on tippy toes, beneath the smoke detector, Lola lit her paper torch, holding it as close to the detector as possible, *I sure hope this place don't have sprinklers!* It didn't, but an almighty siren, loud enough to wake Zeus, blasted, and Aldo finally opened his door. Lola moved swiftly, jamming a high-top in to block Aldo's door from closing.

"What the hell are you doing!" Aldo yelled.

"My imitation of the damn Statue of Liberty," Lola yelled back, dousing the burning paper in the ice bucket as Nikos came rushing down the hall.

"Boss! Boss! Why you set fire to restaurant?"

"It's not on fire Nikos, just calm down and go back to work, okay?" Lola said calmly.

Nikos retreated, exasperated, but glad not to know.

"Well, you might as well let me in, cause I'm not leaving." Lola challenged.

Aldo just shrugged, turned his back on her and took a seat on one of the two chairs in the room.

Lola shut the door and took the seat facing her elusive friend, "Well, don't you look a sight. Greasy hair, scruffy stubble, a tee shirt that looks like last week's menu. Not exactly an Italian stallion." She smirked.

"Shut-up Lola. The state of me is my business, I don't need you to come in here and gloat. Think you're pretty slick, don't you? Sick is more like it, playing stupid 'tranny' games with people's affections, setting me up to be a laughingstock to my staff," Aldo glared at her through fierce blood-shot eyes.

"Oh really, and you're so innocent, didn't even notice my Adam's apple?" Lola pulled down the neck of her hoodie.

"To be honest, I wasn't looking that far up," Aldo said surprised.

"Well, who can blame you," she said cupping her fine firm breasts, "they're spectacular, bespoke and all mine, cause I just made the last payment on them."

Aldo joked, despite his vengeful mood, "Go big or go home, eh Lo?"

That's right, sugar, they're the finest prosthetics you can buy," Lola said as they broke-up laughing.

Lola pulled-down her hoodie, tore off her sun-glasses and exposed her un-wigged, clean visage to Aldo, who saw the lovely, heart-shaped face of a vulnerable, effeminate young man.

He relaxed, sat back in his chair, and said, "Alright Lo, tell me your story."

"I'm not a transvestite or gay, I was born the wrong sex is all. I am a woman, and I'm in the process of gender reassignment, but really more like, gender confirmation.

"But it's hard, especially where I come from and who I come from. My little hometown in Louisiana wasn't happy about boys who want to be girls. School was hell, for years I was bullied and beat-up. Then at eighteen, I left home, and found a different abuse working the clubs in New Orleans.

"And my daddy, the 'right most holy on high', Reverend Reginald Dupré, of the first Baptist Church, didn't like me neither. There 'weren't no room in his heaven' for the likes of me. When he died, I thought I could finally come out and start becoming the woman I was meant to be. But my mom, she loves me, just couldn't face the neighbors and her church.

"So, whenever I go home, I am Darnell Dupré, web designer. But as my re-assignment progresses, I won't be able to go home anymore. And right now, I'm working my tail-off to get enough money to finish the process. Until then I'm stuck in an in-between world."

Aldo, sitting forward, clasping his hands together, said thoughtfully, "Us Catholics, we have a name for that place, limbo… but I may have a way to help you get to heaven."

Lola raised her voice in surprise, "Oh yeah, Zorba? I'd sure like to hear that. 'Cause when I finally get to 'heaven', I'll dump all this tribute stuff and go legit as a singer-song writer. Jazz, I love jazz, that's my voice, my heart, my idiom.

"Don't get me wrong, I put everything into my act and it's good, but I can't deny the cloud of freak show that surrounds it. It's fake, I don't want to be fake anymore, I want for the rest of my life to be real. When I'm fully transgendered, I'm finally gonna own it."

EARLY THE NEXT morning, the Asteri's kitchen staff was surprised to see their proprietor, shaven, dressed and wielding a cleaver over a side of lamb. Some looked down, and mumbled greetings as they shuffled by. "Hey boss, hello boss, morning boss." Others just took-up their stations and began prepping for lunch.

Aldo put down his cleaver, blasted-up the disc player to Tom Jones' *She's a Lady*, picking-up his cleaver, hacking-into the haunch, he bellowed in his baritone, "She's a Lady, whoa, whoa, whoa, she's a lady," then turning to his staff, holding-up his cleaver, he shouted, "C'mon you pricks, you like singing, so sing!"

They joined-in, getting the message, loud and clear.

Chapter Three

SUMMER

EXPRESS DELIVERY

IT WAS SEVEN p.m. on a wet, July Thursday, half the fluorescent lights in the newspaper's office were dimmed, the cleaner's trolley was parked in the hall as Samira vigorously vacuumed the carpet, in danger of balding what nap it had left.

Lidia, weary, in search of a stimulant, rummaged through the leftovers in the lunchroom tea basket, *Licorice-nettle, lavender-hibiscus, yuck.* Then picking-up the perpetually hot coffee flask, a tarry, acrid liquid dribbled into her cup. "Oh, for goodness' sake, why do people keep leaving the dregs to distill. This looks positively poisonous."

"I'm sure it is, and that's why you should back away slowly, this very instant," Shelton said, chuckling.

"I didn't hear you come in, guess you heard me grumbling?" Lidia sat down wearily on a nearby chair.

"How could I not, even above the roar of that blast vacuum, which makes it impossible to do any work. Miss Mew, I am here to rescue you, both of us actually. I see you're as tired and hungry as I, so I'm whisking us both off to my favorite little boîte, Persimmon, where the waiters are pleasant, the wine decent and the menu honest."

Shelton held out his hand to Lidia, who rose listlessly, holding her now heavy belly, following him to gather their jackets and umbrellas from the cloakroom, then off to a cab and dinner.

The restaurant's decor lived-up to its name, the upholstery, drapes, and tiles were themed on the warm persimmon colors punctuated with accents of black, gold and turquoise creating an exotic, stimulating effect. Shelton helped Lidia onto the banquette, her protruding belly now a burden, as she angled sideways to slide onto the seat.

He sat opposite his companion and waved-off the dinner menu, ordering from memory, "Let's see," he squinted his eyes and recited, "We'll start with the eggplant zaalouk, then a tagine for two of your wonderful agadir, some pomegranate and mint couscous, a carafe of ouled thaleb syrah for me, mineral water for my companion, and to finish, m'hanncha with one ginger tea, one Turkish coffee."

"Of course, sir, right away," the waiter said, happy to serve a decisive and appreciative regular.

"What are Agadir and m'hannacha, Shelton?" asked Lidia, unfolding her napkin.

"Agadir is whitefish baked with olives, artichokes, preserved lemons and tomato with a touch of harissa, you'll love it. The m'hanncha, I warn you, is positively addictive; flaky layers of phyllo with almond filling, baked in date syrup, very luscious."

"Mmm, sounds like it. Gosh, I'm tired. Thanks, for taking charge of my feeding and watering tonight," Lidia said, scooping-up a glob of smoky eggplant.

"My pleasure, your Mewship. Tell me, how does planning for the 'interregnum' progress?" Shelton asked, sampling the wine, finding it satisfactory.

"Alright, I guess. Siobhan is really gung-ho. She's more internet savvy than me and certainly enjoys the limelight," Lidia sighed. "But I reviewed her 'Killer Cook' Christmas podcasts and I can't help noticing she's gone all 'Jamie Oliver' on us," she observed with a wince.

"What do you mean, 'gone all Jamie Oliver'?

"You know, she's picked-up his annoying verbal ticks like, 'I'm *literally* massaging this marinade into every nook and cranny of the pork shoulder', as if she could do it, what, figuratively? Nonsensical," Lidia said, tearing off a piece of pita.

"I see what you mean." Shelton barely got his response out before Lidia went on.

"And another thing, why is it that she has to warn the audience, 'Now, I'm *going-in* with a fistful of chopped basil,' Really? She's not invading Afghanistan, just adding more stuff to an already over-spiced dish!"

"Shocking, you must have a word with the producer," he advised.

"Oh, I couldn't do that Shelton; James would just take it as sour grapes."

"You know Miss Mew, I think Brunhilde's actually done you a favor," Shelton said, finishing-off the zaalouk.

"Oh really?"

"Yes," Shelton said, serving them fish from the tagine. "If left to choose your own replacement, you'd have a very unpopular decision to make between two of your good friends. This way, you get to stay 'Ms. Nice Guy'. You see, Brunhilde knows you're just not ruthless enough for that job."

"Or ambitious enough? Like Siobhan?" Lidia said, swallowing a morsel of fish.

"Well, let's just see how she progresses. Meanwhile, concentrate on your new family project, these intrigues will unravel as they may." Shelton smiled, patting her hand. "Mm, the fish is exceptionally good tonight. How do you find it?… Lidia?" Shelton inquired, looking up, concerned at the suddenly uncomfortable look on Lidia's face.

"Ow! Oh, dear god that hurt… I feel a little queasy," Lidia said, her eyes watering, hands on her belly.

"What's wrong? Is the baby kicking, is that it?… Lidia!" Shelton went over to her.

"No, ow! They're contractions. Oh god, I think my waters broke. Help me up Shelton!" Lidia cried.

"No, no. You stay there, the cab stand's just outside," Shelton said, hailing a waiter. "It'll be here shortly. Just hang-on!"

The other guests looked-on in alarm as Lidia, holding her belly, lamented, "Oh please! I'm not due for five weeks."

Shelton pulled her up, saying, "The cab's here, I've got your things. Can you make it to the door with me?"

"Yes, yes, I can make it."

"Dad!" a tearful Jesse rushed from the waiting room towards her father as he hurried in from the pelting rain.

Grasping her tightly, Nick, breathing heavily, asked, "How is she? Has the baby come?"

Shelton, coming back with coffees, answered, "Yes, he came quickly; I barely got her here on time."

Jesse broke in, "They're both okay, dad. I've been in to see mom, she's just really tired. We're waiting for the doctor; they said he'd be here shortly."

Shelton handed Nick a coffee, Jesse helped him off with his coat.

When Nick had barely brought the cup to his lips, a figure in a white coat appeared, "Mr. Ponti?" he inquired.

Nick stood immediately, "Yes, I'm Nick Ponti."

"I'm Dr. Walker, Mr. Ponti. I delivered your son, both he and Mrs. Ponti are doing well. Would you come with me please?"

Nick followed the doctor down a long corridor to a glassed-fronted viewing room, "There he is, number four," Dr. Walker indicated the fourth incubator in the first row.

"Oh, he's so tiny…and so bald, poor little guy." He waved in the direction of his blue-eyed, red-faced son, whose spindly, splotchy little legs twitched-out from his diaper.

A breathing tube was taped to his nostrils, a feeding tube to his mouth, several monitors were taped to his chest and his perfect little hands were anxiously clenched.

Nick began to pine, "I need to hold him, talk to

him, he's all by himself." Desperate, he pressed his hands against the window. "Please, let me touch him. Can't I just go in and touch him?"

Dr. Walker put a hand on his shoulder. "Not just yet. He's fine, the nurses are watching him closely. Wouldn't you like to see Lidia now?"

When they entered her room, Lidia was dozing, but woke as soon as Nick sat on the bed and took her hand. "Oh Nick, he's alright, isn't he?" They both cried and hugged each other.

Dr. Walker stood by, waiting for calm before speaking:

"Mr. and Mrs. Ponti, your son is stable and all indications at this stage are that he'll progress well. However, being five weeks premature raises issues about lung function." The doctor explained, "boys' lungs fully develop during the last five weeks of gestation, so he'll need to be on the ventilator for a while yet, we also have to make sure that the lungs drain properly and no fluid builds-up. We're administering surfactant, which will help his lungs inflate properly."

"And later development? I've read that premature birth can affect brain structure," Nick said warily.

The doctor took a thoughtful pause, uneasy with projecting. "Studies show that some premature children develop learning disabilities, such as short-term memory deficit, spatial cognition and slower cognitive processing. But with specialist education support their outcomes are good. I must stress that it is not a foregone conclusion that your son will have learning difficulties."

"We understand. I'm just so glad he's doing alright. I'm very tired now, but later, can we see him?" Lidia asked, lying back on her pillows.

"Of course, and you will be able to touch him in the incubator, but not hold him just yet. Okay?" Dr. Walker said, rising, "Get some rest, Mrs. Ponti; you've had quite a stressful experience. If you need something, use the buzzer. In the meantime, I'll check back in a couple of hours."

Nick headed for the waiting room, to update Jesse and Shelton.

"A MILLION THANKS for your help tonight, Shelton," Nick said giving him a hug, "I'm so glad you got her here in time, otherwise…"

"Otherwise, your baby would've been born in a restaurant. It was a good restaurant.

Nevertheless, they don't do delivery and the only thing I'm good at in a medical emergency is fainting," Shelton said laughing.

"Look guys, you should go home," Nick said looking from the weary Shelton to Jesse, "I'll keep you posted; Doctor Walker says everything's going to be fine."

"Well dad, if you're sure. I'll be back in the morning, then you can go home to rest and freshen-up, okay?" Jesse said, giving her father a kiss on the cheek.

"Sounds good, and thanks again you two," Nick said as he headed for the nursery, to watch over his newborn son and sleeping wife.

THE NEXT DAY, Father Frank paced around the rectory's twilit garden, puffing intently on his fifth cigarette. He had visited Lidia and the child earlier; she was still drained by her trauma, but determined that Antonio would pull through. They prayed silently together, afterward she said little, staring through him from dark-rimmed, worried eyes to the future. He had wanted to hold her then, but couldn't, just left his useless arms by his sides, then took his useless self away.

He'd let her down when she most needed him, denying her the absolution she had wanted, withholding it, a cowardly act, leaving it all on her shoulders. He wanted now the confessional, the anonymous intimacy of its dark revelations and the blessed light of absolution, but he didn't dare; now, the shadows were where he felt he belonged.

Frank sat on the stone garden bench and lit his next cigarette from the last, inhaling deeply, he decided; I'll *have to perform the baptism, but first speak to the Bishop…apply for the Rome sabbatical… I need time for reflection, study, and most of all, prayer; the best theology done on the knees. Then I'll either emerge a better priest or perhaps no priest at all.*

He rose, crushed his last cigarette beneath his heel and went in to make the call.

EXPECTING THE UNEXPECTED

FOUR WEEKS LATER, with one day left until Antonio was discharged and finally home, Lidia leaned against the nursery's doorway, arms folded across her chest, contemplating the pastel, floral paper, Josh had just hung behind the crib. The opposite wall would be hung with the same mural paper, the rest of the room was painted in a pale butter shade. The crib, rocking chair and dresser were a pale Wedge-wood blue.

"You don't think it's overwhelming, do you?"

Josh got down from the ladder and joined Lidia by the door.

"No, the flowers are big, but they're not a strong color, so I don't think they'll keep him up at night," Josh said, smiling.

"Or distress him, like poor old Oscar Wilde, 'This wallpaper is killing me. One of us has to go,'" Lidia mugged, laughing.

Josh laughed too, thinking how good it was to see Lidia elated, back to herself again. Then hearing a booming voice from downstairs, they both looked to each other.

"Hey! Anybody home?"

"It's dad! Leave this for now, come down and see Aldo," Lidia said rushing toward the stairs, Josh following.

"Bella!" Aldo took his daughter up in his arms, giving her a big kiss on both cheeks before letting her down, remarking, "You're so skinny sweetheart, didn't they feed you in that hospital?"

"Thanks dad, but I think I look just fine," Lidia retorted.

"Oh no, no, I didn't mean…you look great bella, just a little, you know, slimmer. C'mon, gimme a break, I haven't seen you since you gave birth."

"I know dad, just rattling your cage. Where's your luggage? Josh will help you in with it."

"Uh…no need, here comes help now," Aldo said holding the door open for Lola, hurrying-in, bearing two suitcases.

Panting, putting them down, she declared, "Oh my, but it's hot in this town. I thought Canada was a cold country." Lola fanned her face with her hand.

Aldo introduced Lola, "Josh, Lidia, this is my new friend, Lola, from Corfu. Well, really from Louisiana but…"

"Oh shush, Aldo," Lola stepped forward, reached-out and shook Lidia's hand, "Pleased to meet you, I'm Lola Dupré, but y'all just call me Lo. Aldo and I met in Corfu where I was performing, I'm a singer."

"Oh, a singer, how nice," Lidia said smiling wanly, feeling a little disconcerted.

"Josh Patel, Lo. I'm Aldo's grandaughter's partner," Josh said shaking her hand enthusiastically.

"So Lo, I guess this is your first visit to Toronto. Where are you planning to stay?" Lidia inquired looking down at the unfamiliar luggage.

"Oh, um I'm not visiting exactly. I want to rent a place and stay awhile, for professional reasons," Lola said, smiling.

"I meant to email you Lidia, about Lo maybe renting Jesse's apartment, being that it's all spruced-up and furnished, right?" Aldo reasoned, looking from one woman to the other for a nod of approval.

"And just where are *you* going to stay, dad?" Lidia asked testily.

"With Cheech, all my gear's there," Aldo said.

"Well, we were thinking of advertising to rent the suite out," Lidia said, relaxing, pondering the possibility.

"Oh dear, I'm sorry, I don't mean to impose. I thought Aldo had already asked you. But I understand if it's not in your plan, having a brand-new baby coming home and all. It's a busy time for you," Lola said, shooting Aldo an annoyed look.

"There's one thing you need to know about my dad, he acts first, asks later. But you know Lo, we may be able to work something out. Come through, and you can have a look at the place," Lidia offered, being relieved that her worst fear, her father and Lo shacking-up in the basement, was unfounded.

"HAVE ANOTHER BREAST, Lo? There's a half here going begging," Nick said, offering the platter of chicken to Lola.

"Oh no, but thanks Nick, you're a wonderful cook. I've got to watch my weight, auditions next week," Lola said, taking a sip of her water.

"What's the show?" Lidia asked.

"Kinky Boots, so it's singing and dancing. I have a friend in production which might help a little, there'll be stiff competition though, so I've got to work hard on my 'party piece'," Lola said, knitting her brow.

"I'm sure you'll knock'em dead, Lo. You certainly have the legs for it, and I'll bet your voice is beautiful too," Nick said, admiringly.

"Oh yeah, you should see her act, she does a fantastic Tina Turner, younger version of course," said Aldo.

"A tribute act, is it? A kind of burlesque, right?" Lidia said cattily.

"Lidia!" admonished Nick.

"It's okay, there's some truth to that. Tribute acts are kind of in that tradition, that's why I want to take my career in another direction. But a girl's gotta' pay her rent, right landlady?" Lola observed, an unspoken touché hanging in the air between them.

LATER THAT EVENING, Lidia sat up in bed waiting for

Nick to finish clean-up. He entered the bedroom door yawning, pulling his shirt over his head, tossing it on the divan, he unbuckled his trousers, then caught Lidia's frown, "What? Okay, I'll put the shirt in the laundry hamper."

"It's not the shirt Nick, although it'd be nice if you'd pick-up after yourself. No, it's the fool you made of yourself at dinner over that 'Lola'," Lidia said sarcastically.

"What? I was just being a good host to our guest and new tenant, who is a friend of *your* father's," Nick retorted, tired and annoyed, kicking-off his trousers, heading for the bathroom.

"Oooh! Your legs are so beautiful Lo, bet your voice is too, and have another breast Lo. *Puhleeze*, that's above and beyond being a good host. And I notice you managed to hide your disdain of musical theatre pretty well!" Lidia shouted after him, crossing her arms.

When Nick got into bed, he turned to his grumpy wife and gave her a loud smooch on the cheek, something which usually disarmed, if slightly annoyed her.

"Look cara, I think we're both overtired and anxious about tomorrow. Let's not argue, do you want our beautiful baby boy to come home to a fractious family? Eh? Well, do you?" Nick smiled at Lidia and put his arm across her waist.

She stroked his arm, "It's just that I've had way too many surprises this year, I really didn't need one more. But count on dad, he's always the wild card," Lidia sighed.

"I think this is a blessing in disguise, with a new baby, we need the extra income. And Lo seems a sensible sort. I'll bet we'll barely know she's here."

"You're right, Nick. She does seem nice; I do like her. Sorry I was a bit sharp, hope she doesn't think I'm a bitch," Lidia said chewing her lip.

"You, a bitch? Never. I think you two will be 'bff's' in no time." Nick gave his wife a reassuring hug, then turned-out the lights.

GINGER AND LEMONS

"HEY! HERE'S MY little champ," Aldo beamed at his new grandson, as Nick laid Antonio in his carrying seat on the kitchen table.

Lidia said, "You can pick him up dad, just–"

"I know the drill, just support his head. You never forget." Aldo cradled his new grandson in his arms.

"Ciao, Antonio," he said stroking him under his

chin. "Oh, what beautiful blue eyes, just like your mom's. And what's this all over your little nose and cheeks? Freckles!" Aldo said, smiling at his grandson who smiled and gurgled back.

"Yeah, where'd he get all the freckles from? His hair's kind'a ginger too," Lola said, peeking over his blanket, "hm, maybe more strawberry blond."

"Oh, the freckles must be from the light treatments they gave him for jaundice. I guess it just brought out some pigmentation," Lidia surmised.

"They look like they're keepers to me," Josh added, admiring his potential, baby brother-in-law.

"You know, I had a second, or was it third cousin, in Pescara who had lots of freckles. Her mom would scrub her face with lemon then make her sit in the sun, poor Serafina. She hated that," Aldo recounted, handing the baby to Jesse.

"Why'd she do that, nonno?" Jesse asked.

"To bleach them, I guess. Foolish notion. She thought Serafina would be passed over by the desirable local boys. Ha! She ended-up running-off with a novitiate from the monastery, I guess he didn't mind about the freckles," Aldo said, laughing.

"See, freckles are in his genes, after all. Anyway, I think they're really cute," said Nick, preparing Antonio's bottle.

"I'll say. He has a lovely little smile too. May I?"

Lola extended her arms, to receive the child.

"Sure Lo, be my guest. Josh and I have to get going anyway," Jesse said, handing him over, then picking-up her purse.

What's the rush? I thought we were going to have some lunch…order pizza, 'wet the baby's head'?" Nick said disappointed.

"I need to get more gesso today and Curry's closes in half an hour," Jesse responded, annoyed.

"Jess, I haven't even had a chance to hold the baby, can't you prime your canvases tomorrow?" Josh asked.

"No. I want to do it tonight. Don't worry Josh, Antonio's not going anywhere for at least eighteen years, but *we* do need to get going! Bye dad, bye mom," Jesse said, giving each a peck on the cheek.

"Yeah, bye guys. See you later," Josh said, perplexed, heading for the door. He rushed to catch-up with Jesse. "Hey," he put a hand on her shoulder. "What's going on? You didn't tell me about getting gesso today, I would've remembered."

Jesse turned to Josh. "I do need the gesso, but I just thought having a full house may be a little too much for mom."

"She seemed okay to me. Anyway, it's only family," Josh said, opening the car door.

"Nevertheless, she's still weak and needs to rest,

especially now that the baby's home." Jesse was resolute, buckling her seat belt. Josh suppressed an objection, judging it best to just let the matter drop.

LATER THAT EVENING, when the Ponti house was quiet and the excitement of finally having their baby home was calmed, Lidia found Nick in the nursery, in the rocking chair, reading a book to a snoozing Antonio.

"Oh, here you are. What's that you're reading?" Lidia whispered, tilting her head sideways, trying to read the title.

"*Freddy Goes to the North Pole*," said Nick, closing the book.

"Who's Freddy?"

Who's Freddy? Freddy is the most famous pig in all literature, a bon vivant, a diplomat, explorer, poet, and philosopher. The most excellent pig, he's the 'Pooh' of pigs, but much smarter than that silly bear," Nick said, indignantly.

"Really, well I've never heard of him."

"I know, that's because you had a deprived childhood."

"Well, since you never read them to our daughter, I guess she's had a deprived childhood too then?"

Lidia countered.

"No, not at all, I just knew she was more of a *Charlotte's Web* child, than a *Freddy the Detective* sort, which by the way, is my personal favorite of the series," Nick said, gently placing his sleeping boy on his back in the crib.

"Speaking of your daughter, don't you think there's something up with her? I mean she almost yanked Josh out of here, when clearly, he wanted to stay. She could've got her gesso tomorrow," Lidia said quietly, leaning over the crib rail, looking down at Antonio.

"I know. She was certainly in a huff. Do you think she's jealous?" Nick asked.

"What, of me? And maybe Athina? I guess it seems that everyone's having babies, maybe she's feeling the 'maternal urge' and a little left out?"

"No, that isn't what I meant. I thought that she's jealous of all the attention Antonio's getting, you know, sibling rivalry," Nick speculated, heading downstairs.

"Nah, she's too old to be jealous of a baby, must be something else." Lidia pondered, following Nick.

LOLA LEANED AGAINST the wall, hands on thighs, rib cage heaving, catching her breath. She had high-kicked, pirouetted like a dervish and even hand-sprung into the splits, which judging by the throbbing pain in her thighs was a rusty move. She opened-up her clear, vibrant, contra-tenor and poured forth all the right notes, in tune and on time, with bravura and even a little tenderness. Now it was up to them, the producers, and directors; will she be an Angel, or in Ensemble, or just out of work?

After guzzling some water, Lola got her stuff, and headed to the change room, when a runner caught-up with her, handing her a note from one of the producers, 'Love your energy. You're more than just Ensemble talent, so let's talk, meet me at seven tomorrow night in the Four Seasons DBar Lounge, no wig, no make-up, just shirt and jeans.'

"Tell him I'll be there and thanks!" Lola instructed the runner.

Well, I'll be, maybe I've got the right name and the right moves to be the lead, Lola, after all.

AFTER A RESTLESS sleep and an 'antsy' day of going through her wardrobe, hating everything, then going shopping for just the right jacket and shirt, Lola started to get ready for her rendezvous with the producer.

Hope I don't run into the family on my way out...huh, maybe they'll just think Lo's got a gentleman caller? If I get this part, they'll find out anyway, she thought, putting on her new tobacco colored linen jacket, straightening the collar of her new ink-blue silk shirt. She donned her black newsboy cloth cap and put on her Dolce & Gabbana aviator sunglasses. She laced-up her new tan Oxford brogues, straightened the legs on her black jeans and turned to regard herself in the mirror, *hmm, maybe the red paisley silk puff in the pocket, to match the red socks, then I'm good to go.* Lola gathered-up her keys, tucked her portfolio under her arm, looking out for 'a clear coast', she hustled off across the back alley to the subway.

At the DBar Lounge, Lola found a seat facing the entrance, ordered a Perrier with lime, and anxiously awaited the producer. Thirty minutes and two Perrier's later, when he failed to materialize; Lola decided to leave, calling for the bill, when a very tall, thin blonde, wearing a black tee-shirt, sporting the Kinky Boots logo in red sequins, approached.

"Darnell Dupré? Chris's running late and sends his apologies, but Nigel, the associate producer has a window now, if you'd follow me to his suite," she said, and without waiting for his answer, turned and walked to the door, stopping at the bar to charge his tab to the company.

After an awkward, silent journey, she led him into the suite's lounge, where she left him to wait for Nigel. He appeared shortly, looking rumpled and fatigued, his mass of yellowed salt and pepper hair standing on end, his greasy, horn-rimmed glasses perched at the end of his bulbous, pock-marked nose, "Darnell?" Nigel greeted him. "Come." Nigel ushered him into his office, his desk was littered with empty coffee cups and a full ashtray, which stank up the chaotic space.

The associate producer sat on the edge of his desk, extended his hand towards the portfolio Lola carried. Nigel lit a cigarette and leafed perfunctorily through Lola's resume. "Hmm 'Cats – understudy, 'Grease' – acting part, some off-off Broadway, summer rep-Shakespeare in the Park-Twelfth Night," flipping quickly through the rest to, cabaret-tribute? Good money?" his blood-shot eyes focused over his specs at Lola.

"Pretty good, puts butter on my bagel," Lola responded feeling a little uneasy.

Nigel quickly riffled through Lola's photos, then tossed the portfolio aside.

"Here," he handed Lola a curled-up music sheet. "Look-over the first stanza while I set-up the camera. We need a British accent, or at least the inflection."

Lola did as she was told, quickly taking-in the solo in question, mouthing/singing silently, starting to panic on how she should deliver it, a quiet voice within her counselled, *c'mon Lo, this ain't Verdi, just Cyndi Lauper.*

"Here, put on the mike and stand there in front of the screen while I take a reading," Nigel said, adjusting the lamps and soft boxes. "When I say 'ready', you go. But first, just give me something for sound, ok?"

"Ok," Lola cleared her throat, and sang the first line of the solo, "What a woman wants…"

Nigel passed his hand across his throat. Lola stopped singing, she cleared her throat again, still studying the music, pacing, humming to herself, focussed on the lyrics, Nigel motioned her to get back on her mark in front of the screen. Lola dropped the score, looked into the camera as Nigel cued her in. She delivered the stanza in perfect pitch.

"And cut." Nigel stepped out from behind the camera, standing very close, face to face with Lola, he unclipped the mike, slipping a few nicotine-stained fingers beneath the placket of his shirt. "That was nice, very nice, now take off your shirt," he commanded.

Lola felt intimidated. "Why?" she asked, folding her arms across her chest.

"For the Polaroids, this isn't just a drag queen part, we need a lead that's also butch. So, bitch, can you give me some butch?" Nigel smiled wryly.

Lola considered for a moment, then met his gaze, "Yeah, I can do butch," she said, unbuttoning her shirt, tying it around her waist.

"Okay now, put your arms up. No! Not like that, it's not a mugging for fuck's sake, here let me show you," he leaned in, roughly pushing Lola's elbows up and back. "That's it, hands behind your head."

Grasping Lola's jaw, he firmly pushed her head to a left profile. Running his hand along her jaw line and bicep he said, "Good, stay like that." He got a few shots in then, "Look down, at your shoulder. Deep breath, expand the chest. Now flex, flex your biceps.

"Okay, put your shirt on, we're done. We'll let you know," Nigel said, handing Lola her portfolio. She finished buttoning her shirt, grabbed the rest of her things and quickly left the suite, feeling shaken, but not quite sure why.

THE NEXT DAY, Aldo visited his daughter and new grandson, then went downstairs to check-in with Lola, who was still in an agitated state.

"Well? How'd it go? Did ya' blow their socks off, Lo?" Aldo said, hoping for a positive response.

Lola paced nervously, barefoot, in jeans and a tee-shirt, sans make-up, wig and prosthetics, "I honestly have no clue. All I know is that Nigel, the associate producer, is one scary MF. I mean, he was rough; he kind'a came-on to me but bullying too. I don't know what his game is," Lola said, chewing her thumbnail.

"Maybe he's just a power-tripper. Probably has a small dick and is pissed-off that he's just 'associate producer'. He's a miserable misogynist," Aldo speculated with a laugh.

"You mean he's someone who hates girls and hates boys who are girls?" Lola said, sarcastically.

"Something like that," Aldo replied.

The gasman rang the doorbell upstairs, Lidia put Antonio in his cot and led him downstairs to Lola's apartment where the metre was. "I guess we should look into having it installed outside," Lidia said, as she descended the stairs.

"Well, that'll cost you around six hundred bucks," the gasman responded, following.

Lola's phone bleeped as Aldo was about to expound on his misogyny thesis.

"Really? Well yes, yes, sure I'll be there. Tomorrow at two, great! Thanks." Lola began jumping. "I got a call back! I got a call back!"

"Great!" Aldo said, beaming.

"Yeah, and it's with the producers this time, not Mr. Creepy!" Lola grabbed Aldo's face with both hands, and gave him a big, loud kiss.

"Six hundred –, Lidia was half-way down the basement stairs, when she stopped abruptly, the gasman nearly stumbling over her. "Wha –, her astonished utterance hung in the air, as she took in the situation before her.

The gasman looked over her shoulder with a smirk, "Bad timing folks?"

"No…no, c'mon bella, let the man through," Aldo said, as he took Lidia by the elbow, leading her down the rest of the stairs to a seat on the couch.

"Are you okay, sugar?" Lola said, concerned, bending down, peering into her eyes. "Aldo, get her some water." Lola sat down beside Lidia and took her pulse.

"Hot milky tea with lots'o sugar is what she needs," offered the gasman, hooking his thumbs in his belt.

"Thanks Dr. Oz, when you're done, you can leave by the garden entrance," Aldo said indicating the back door.

"Sheesh." Aldo shook his head, then heard the baby crying upstairs, "I'll go." He bounded up the stairs, relieved, *thank-you Saint Antonio!*

Lola, satisfied that Lidia's pulse wasn't racing, handed her the water. She took it, and looking up, bewildered at what now seemed a stranger, asked, "Just who are you, and why are you really here?"

Lola recounted her story and why Aldo brought her to Canada, to professional opportunities and the Ontario Hospital's, affordable, gender re-assignment program. Lola gave her the truth, but a judiciously edited truth.

Satisfied, Lidia went upstairs to tend to her son and confront her father, who was in the nursery, the picture of grandfatherly love, rocking and singing to a squalling Antonio.

Lidia interrupted this familial idyll, planting her indignant self in front of Aldo, demanding, "How dare you assume I'm a narrow-minded bigot."

Aldo looked-up at her innocently. "What do you mean, bella? What's Lo said to you?"

"That you told her she should hide her trans-gendering from me, as I'm not able to 'handle it'! Me, who has always voted Liberal, sometimes even New Democrat and on one occasion for the Green Party! Two of my best friends are gay and second cousin, Rosario, 'resolute bachelor', wore mascara and painted his nails, even the family pretended not to notice!"

"Lo's not gay. And I meant you might not handle her situation well. You just had a premature delivery. I didn't want to give you more stress. It was just easier that way." Aldo shrugged, handing Antonio to his mother.

"Oh yeah, easier, easier for you dad. Whatever's *easier* for you, eh?" Lidia said, taking her fussing child, heading downstairs to feed him.

WHAT'S LOVE GOTTA' DO WITH IT

"SO, THE WHOLE thing went up in smoke," Cheech affirmed, shuffling the cards as Aldo set down their beer. The club was quiet for a Friday night as most people were out of town at their cottages or travelling.

"Yep, best thing in the long run. Though I

would've followed through and married her, despite the legal implications," Aldo said, taking a sip of cold beer.

"It was a crazy scheme anyway. Marrying Lo just so she could have the treatment on the government…that's even criminal, isn't it?"

"Criminal? What crime's been committed…who's to say why two people marry? You gonna tell me there aren't regular marriages where one of the parties is in it for more than just love? As Ms. Turner says, 'What's love gotta do with it?' Lo does that fantastic, by the way."

"Hey, Aldo, remember we used to go to The Colonial to see Jackie Shane?"

"Do I ever, what a great 'R and B' singer. Filly loved her hit song…what was it called now?"

"*Another Way*," said Cheech.

"No!… *Any Other Way*."

"That's it! Great song. But she wasn't, you know, a real girl, was she?" asked Cheech.

"A 'real girl'…she was a transvestite, dummy! Maybe even transgender…and that was in the sixties."

"Yeah, she wasn't a drag queen though, just dressed and sang like a normal woman. Nobody made a fuss about it. Guess in some ways she was a pioneer."

"Yep, and a real talent. Wonder what happened to her?" Aldo said.

"Dunno, just disappeared from the scene. Probably went back to the States."

Dealing the cards out, Cheech, returning to the topic of Aldo's nuptials, said with a sigh, "Ya know Aldo, I feel a little let down. I was looking forward to the wedding party. All I go to nowadays are wakes, the food's crap, but the booze is generous."

"I know, but there wouldn't have been a party as I'd need to keep my marriage on the down-low from the family. Anyway, I'm really glad she got the lead in Kinky Boots, she's over the moon. Now she can afford the procedure here herself. But it wasn't a really crazy scheme, it could've worked out fine," Aldo said, taking-up his cards, regarding his hand.

"Uh-huh, just like your other crazy scheme, 'The Wheel of Misfortune'?" Cheech smirked.

"What? That was your idea! Anyway, there was nothing wrong with it, who knew our first winner would just drop like that," Aldo said, grimacing.

"Yeah, that was a damn shame, we had to buy two wreaths and it chilled the rest of our players," Cheech said, laying down a card, then drawing one from the pile.

"Damn shame," repeated Aldo, arranging the cards in his hand.

BABY, BATTERED AND FRIED

ATHINA RANG THE buzzer to Jesse's flat, burdened with a diaper bag, two chilled splits of codorniu, a small bucket of extra crispy chicken wings and a baby stroller containing her bleating, fussing newborn daughter.

"Hi ya! C'mon up!" Jesse buzzed her in.

Athina rang the buzzer again, "Can you come down? I need a hand."

Jesse obliged, lifting baby and seat from the stroller, while Athina followed, toting the rest.

"Aah that's good." Athina settled into the couch, giving the baby her bottle while Jesse put out the food and opened the bubbly.

"I never thought I'd be so grateful for the invention of the kneeling bus. When they first came out, I thought, 'Oh, how nice for moms and the old folks. Honestly, I don't know how our moms managed to take us all over town on those old streetcars and busses."

"The drivers helped and people, well, they just helped each other, I guess," Jesse said, shrugging, putting a glass down for Athina.

"Yep, those were the days. God, I sound like an old curmudgeon," she said, putting the baby over her shoulder to burp. "Oh, that's a good one, good girl!" Athina smiled at her satisfied daughter, then giving her a soother, nestled her in the baby seat. Athina reached for her glass when Jesse proposed a toast:

"To Dimitra, Gesuela,"

"To Dimitra, Gesuela, Clytie!" added Athina.

"Clytie?" Jesse said raising an eyebrow.

"Oh yes, *Clytie*. Not my choice Jess, it's Ainsworth's tribe, they pressured us to name the baby after his fearsome great auntie Clytie, 'she who will be obeyed'. The best I could do was bury it as a third name. I hope she forgives me," Athina said, grinning at her daughter.

"Well, third name…so what, she doesn't even have to know, does she?" Jess said, taking a sip of her bubbly.

"Hope not, cause if she finds out, there'll be payback."

"To Clytie then, may you be as fearsome and great as your great, great auntie!" Jesse said, laughing.

"To Clytie!" Athina affirmed, drinking to her daughter's namesake.

Athina and Jesse dug into the crispy wings.

"Oh my, how I've missed you, you lovely, greasy,

over-spiced, crunchy little things," Jesse said, holding-up a drumette, "it must be at least three years since I had these."

"I wish I could say the same," Athina said, licking her fingers. "All through my pregnancy these little demons were all I could think of, when would the next fix be, where could I get them, how to hide my shame from Ainsworth who found my craving gross. He even thought our baby might be born battered and fried," Athina said, giggling.

"And reeking of eleven different herbs and spices," Jesse added. They both laughed, tearing into more wings.

"So, how's Lidia and Antonio doing? I haven't seen them since he left the hospital."

"Doing well, Antonio is a little freckled fatso. He doesn't cry much, mostly eats lots, poops lots, laughs and gurgles," said Jesse, wiping her greasy hands, pulling out her phone, to show Athina the latest pictures of her little brother.

"Well hasn't he made up for lost time, lots of freckles, big blue eyes, and strawberry blonde hair, not like Lidia's, she's more honey blonde. Has your dad's broad shoulders though," Athina said, handing back the phone.

"Yep, made for football," Jesse agreed.

"So, the baptism is all set for next month? You

and Kate are going to be comares? No compare, is that right?" Athina asked.

"That's right. Apparently, it's 'kosher' to have two godmothers and no godfather, so long as they're both confirmed in the Roman Catholic faith."

"Greek Orthodox is different, the parents don't need to be married, but the koumbaro and koumbara have to be married in the Greek Church. So, freshly united cousin Alex and wife, Dora, are the lucky couple, or so my parents tell me. I just go along with it, it's easier that way.

"Mom's busy organizing the 'big fat Greek christening party' as we speak. She's determined that I'll cash-in on all the money and gifts she's given her friends' kids in the countless christening parties she's attended. 'Now,' she says, 'it's your turn,' like I care. But she does, and that's the point. The more focussed she is on her project, the less focus on getting me and Ainsworth married."

"Don't you want to get married?" Jesse asked.

"It's not exactly my priority at the moment, what with Ainsworth working all hours on filming his scripted series for Netflix. He's doing so well, but isn't around much, work being pretty demanding. That's okay though, I really don't mind his becoming a TV mogul," Athina laughed.

"No, I guess not. So, you'll be living in Montreal

for the foreseeable?" Jesse said.

"Yeah, we're looking to buy a condo in the old town, I love that area. So many beautiful loft conversions," Athina said, pouring herself another glass of bubbly.

"Sounds great, you're lucky property's more affordable there. If it wasn't for my getting this teaching contract, I might be interested in relocating," Jesse said, thoughtfully.

"You mean you and Josh, right?"

"Of course, he's from Montreal, don't forget. But it's not doable now. Anyway, he's happy here, growing 'The Dep' as a community hub of sorts. So, no plans for now."

"Not even for a family?" Athina asked.

"What? NO! I want to start focussing on my art practice. I'd like to go to Europe next summer and visit some of the artists in my Face Book group who have open studios."

"I get that, Jess…You don't have to be defensive about it," Athina said, holding-up the last wing, offering it to Jesse, who declined.

"I'm not defensive, after all what happened to *your* professional aspirations? Have you given-up on being a sommelier?" Jesse challenged.

"No, I'm registered for the online courses this September, I figure between feedings and naps, I can squeeze in the time," Athina said, picking-up her baby daughter, cuddling her close. "And you're not giving-up your naps for a long time, right princess?"

"I don't want to just 'squeeze in' time for my work, it really matters to me. Teaching is very demanding, I need something that's purely 'me', not dictated by a curriculum or eked-out of stolen family time." Jesse got up to clear away the mess.

"Jess, don't you want kids at all?" Athina asked, with a sudden realization. Holding Dimitra, following Jesse into the kitchen, she waited for her response.

Jesse stacked the dirty dishes and glassware by the sink, squirted-out a generous amount of detergent and turned-on the tap. As the basin filled, she glanced over her shoulder at Athina and said, "No, I don't think I do."

"Really? Does Josh know?" Athina asked, rocking her baby.

"We haven't discussed it."

"Don't you think you should? I mean he seems quite paternal. Don't you think he wants kids?"

"Probably, lately he keeps going on about how great it is that I'm a teacher and get summers off, asking me about maternity leave and – Jesse's voice rose, as she dropped a plate on a glass in the sink, cutting her finger.

"Oh god, Jess. Squeeze and hold it up," Athina said, seeing the red gush from the side of Jesse's index finger. "Where's the bandages?"

"In the cutlery drawer," Jesse said annoyed, tying a paper towel beneath the cut to staunch the bleeding. "Get a couple of large ones."

Athina got the bandages and set Dimitra down on the counter beside her. "Gimme your finger; I guess it should be clean enough." Then bandaging the wound tightly, she said, "There, you should take it off in a bit and give it some tea tree oil. But that'll do for now."

"Thanks," Jesse said, sitting down at the kitchen table.

Athina picked-up Dimitra and joined Jesse, concerned, and wanting to get to the bottom of her friend's distress.

"Sorry, if I snapped at you, it's just lately I feel so pressured. It seems everywhere I turn someone's shoving a baby at me, and if I don't make the right comments or seem all gooey-eyed and winsome, then there's something wrong with me."

"There's nothing wrong with you, Jess. Not everyone wants to have kids, so what? More babysitters for the rest of us." Athina smiled, putting her free arm around Jesse's shoulder.

"Josh might not see it that way. I'm afraid that if I

tell him, I'll lose him," Jesse said, picking at her bandage, tearing-up.

"You don't need to decide anything right now, it's early days. You'll work it out between you when you've been together longer. Anyway, I should go, mom's expecting us for dinner, and I need to get this little monster changed," Athina said, giving her daughter a finger to grasp.

Just then, Jesse heard a key turn in the lock. "Josh's here, he wanted to see Dimitra, he'll drive you home," Jesse said, wiping her eyes.

Josh walked into the kitchen, smiling, opening his arms. "Well, hello ladies! Here I am. And who's this little angel, eh?" Josh bent down tickling Dimitra under her chin. "May I have the pleasure?" Josh took the baby, cradling her in his arms and began to coo and make funny faces.

Jesse got up, went to the sink, put on some rubber gloves, then drained the water, to clear-up the broken glass. Josh waltzed over with the baby, showing her to Jesse, enthusing.

"Isn't she a beauty, Jess. Just look at those long lashes."

Jesse glanced over at her. "Yeah, gorgeous. Josh, Athina needs to get going, would you give her a lift?"

"Absolutely."

"I'll just get my things Josh, then meet you and her ladyship downstairs," Athina said, wanting a moment alone with Jesse before she left. "Don't worry Jess, he loves you. That's obvious. It'll work out. If you need to talk, anytime, I'm here." She gave her friend a kiss and a hug.

Hearing the car pull away, Jesse pulled-off her gloves, opened a bottle of Chianti, poured herself a glass and stared anxiously out the kitchen window, at the dark, storm-threatening sky.

TWILIGHT TIME; SECRETS AND SHADOWS

LIDIA WATCHED THE hummingbirds buzzing in and out of the nasturtiums, monarch butterflies drinking the late summer nectar from her buddleia, lazily flapping their wings in drunken content. The burnished sun, sunk low on the horizon, lit-up the alleyway where dozens of tiny insects hovered and hummed, busily winding-up the dusky day.

She picked the last fig from Nick's tree, the one his godfather gave him twenty-two years ago to plant in their new home. She'd had her plans for the garden then, to create an abundantly floral court-yard, no tomato stakes and bean poles, but a romantic, fragrant oasis. The garden was hers, the kitchen, his.

Nevertheless, she grudgingly gave up a little spot, a sun trap in the south corner against a brick wall, and it flourished. She didn't expect much fruit, but year after year, it bore enough for several delectable frangipane crostate, and now, placed before her, the one last beautiful, ripe, purple fig, her special treat.

Lidia looked down at her son, kicking and fussing, refusing his bottle, sleepy, grumpy, but determined not to let the light die without him; his little fists flailing against imaginary bonds, his high-pitched, scratchy voice, bleating and straining to be understood. His mother cradled him, staring away, not really listening, resigned that one of them would soon wear the other out. It was only a matter of who and when.

Hearing footsteps behind her she looked to the basement stairs.

"Oh, sorry Lidia, I didn't know you were out here," Lola said, turning back, holding her cigarettes and ashtray in one hand, the other clutching her silk kimono.

"Don't be silly Lo, come and join us. You might even be able to give this one a lesson on how to squawk in key," she said, barely mustering the strength to laugh.

"Mercy me, don't he have a lot on his mind. Looks like he just can't wait to start talkin' and walkin'," Lola said, tickling one of Antonio's busy feet. "Here, let me take him, you look done-in sugar," Lola said rocking the noisy, squirming bundle.

"Thanks, I need a break," Lidia said, stretching and yawning.

"No problem, it'll keep my hands off those cigarettes. I quit three months ago, but I've lapsed, it's the hormone treatments, I have night sweats, and get edgy; smoking calms me down."

"Ever tried massage? I know a spa that offers great therapies, their practitioners are really good. I'm due for a 'me day', you could come with me," she said, biting into the warm juicy fig.

"I'd love that, good massage might help," Lola agreed. Then getting-up with the baby, she strolled around the garden, singing soft and low to him, until eventually Antonio quieted down and nodded off to sleep, blissfully unaware of the consternation he caused his weary mother.

Sitting back down, handing the baby to Lidia, Lola said, "That's better, I think he's down for the count."

"You have a gift, Lo. What was that lovely song?"

"Oh, that's an old Creole lullaby, a douce berceuse, that one was 'Dodo, Ti-Pitit Manman'. My Haitian granmè used to sing it."

Lidia looked thoughtful, then said, "You know Lo, I'm glad you're here. I guess I was a bit, well, less than welcoming to you, being wary about what Aldo was up to next."

"I understand. I'm glad I came here too; it's changed my luck, moved my life forward, I've even applied for citizenship."

"Good for you," Lidia said.

"Thanks, but I know your dad kind'a sprung me on you. He's such a live wire, nothin' seems to get him down for long, there's always a plan. He's a survivor, not surprising, considering how he was raised," Lola said, curbing the urge to reach for a cigarette.

"What do you mean, 'considering how he was raised'?"

"I mean what his dad was like, you know, fond of the belt and the bottle?"

"Not really, but go on," Lidia urged, suddenly feeling alert.

"Oh now, I don't think I should… Just forget I said anything, it's not really my place."

"You might as well tell me now. I want to know, Lo, *please*," Lidia insisted.

"Well, okay. This is what he told me when we first met and were talking about our childhoods. He said his dad would get drunk, then come home and belt his wife and son, until the son got big enough to belt him back.

"One night he saw his dad, very drunk, leaving the tavern, heading for home. Aldo, fed-up with it, decided not to go home, to stay out all night with friends.

"He returned in the morning, saw his mom's face badly bruised, his dad claimed she slipped on a grease slick on the kitchen floor, said Aldo didn't mop-up properly. Aldo said he'd done his job right; the floor was clean and dry when he left. His mom said nothing, but by noon she was dead, cerebral hemorrhage."

"Oh my god, I knew nothing of this story," Lidia whispered.

"Wait – it gets worse. When the cops and the doctor come, dad repeats the story, blaming his son. Aldo accuses his dad, but since he wasn't a witness to the beating, fled the scene, no one listens, believing the father instead. The town turn their backs on Aldo, so he grabs as much cash as he can, takes off, and eventually emigrates."

"I'm flabbergasted. Why did he never tell me this?" Lidia said.

Lola put a hand on Lidia's arm, "Maybe he was protecting both of you, himself from the guilt of his mom taking the beating he didn't protect her from, and you from a bad family history.

"Likely, he told me because we weren't close, we'd just met, were practically strangers, it was safe for him to unburden."

"I guess you're right. I'm glad you told me. It's better to know, but did Aldo say what ever happened to his dad?"

"Well, that's the strangest thing. Without Aldo's help, the father and the trattoria went downhill fast. Apparently, one night, drunk, he tried to cook himself something, slipped-on some spilled oil, was found dead on the kitchen floor the next day."

"So, 'the whirligig of time brings in its revenges'," Lidia quoted.

"Yep, 'what goes around, comes around', he tripped on his own lie," Lola echoed the sentiment.

"I guess," said Lidia, pensively.

The sun had finally set, covering them in shade, Lola shivered.

"We'd all better go in to bed."

She rose and helped Lidia out of her chair.

"Now mind how you go on those steps, sugar. Nighty-night." Lola called, over her shoulder.

Thanks, Lo, nighty-night to you too," Lidia responded, carefully mounting the stairs.

Chapter Four

FALL RECKONING

THE FIRST WEEK of autumn found the weather in Toronto still warm; the roses and sweet peas were in their last brave blooming, the mums, zinnias, and dahlias, growing brilliant in their season. The once bad-tempered wasps filled the hanging honey traps.

Nick and Jesse were back at their respective teaching posts. Aldo returned to Corfu after Antonio's christening and Lola was almost finished the Kinky Boots' run, eager to proceed with gender reassignment. Father Frank was off to Rome on his sullen sabbatical.

Even though Lidia was kept busy with the growing needs of Antonio, when everyone returned to work, she felt a little blue, and lonely, left out, with only a baby to talk to. She called Shelton, who had no time for catching her up on office gossip.

Then she tried Siobhan, who was all about business, alerting Lidia that she had some suggestions for her next column, a piece of Lidia's professional life she guarded jealously and fought to keep during her leave.

Later, Brooke, Siobhan's P.A., emailed with an invitation to 'a little brunch party' at the office, to show-off her new baby.

Ha! a P.A.? Who does that Siobhan think she is? I never had a P.A.... Okay, so Brooke's a barely paid, 'not quite bright' daughter of an influential friend, but still! I'll bet this brunch is her idea of smoothing things over. Perhaps Antonio and I should put in an appearance, if only to do a little reconnaissance, Lidia thought, as she emailed back her acceptance.

The visit yielded more than she expected. In the lunchroom, where the brunch was held, she spied several changes. The old Mr. Coffee with it's chipped and permanently stained carafe, yielding whatever bulk brand 'Joe' was on sale, had been retired for a gleaming new espresso-latte maker, whose diet was restricted to Fair Trade shade-grown grind. Gone too were the assorted vile flavoured tea packets, replaced with a fancy, embossed tin of loose-leaf, organic rooibos.

The fridge was stocked with coconut water, organic juices, and almond milk, instead of the usual coffee cream, assorted soft drinks and a jug of Smirnoff's discreetly stashed away in the back, ready for late meeting 'de-briefings'. Lidia was in awe, *huh thought we were tightening our belts, how'd she get this from Brunhilde?* Then the penny dropped, *Of course, Siobhan gets it wholesale from her connections, probably threw a few perks the boss' way too, like free dinner at her celebrity chef friend's new restaurant.*

When the brunch, with its ooh's, aah's and coochy-coos, was mercifully over, Siobhan led Lidia out to her former desk.

"Oh, this is nice," Lidia said, running her hand along the back of Siobhan's new desk chair.

"Yes," she said sinking into its soft, grey leather. "Had to get rid of that shabby cloth one, this one's ergonomically correct. My chiropractor recommended it; since the twins, I've been a martyr to my back. You're lucky, yours is so nice and sturdy," she said, handing Lidia a manila envelope of column topics. "Oh Lidia! Don't look at me like that, the chair was on sale. Anyway, we all deserve a little perk, don't we?" Siobhan said smiling, swivelling in her new chair.

"Yes, we do, when we've earned it. Thanks for the brunch. I'll look this over, and when I have time, get back to you," Lidia said through tight lips, hoisting her baby's carrier, straightening her back, walking out with what she hoped was dignity.

When Lidia got home, and settled Antonio down for his nap, she poured herself a glass of iced tea and sat down at the kitchen table with Siobhan's envelope of 'suggested' topics to be covered in her, *Manners Matter* column. As she pulled the sheet from the envelope, the first suggestion caught her eye: Ghosting; a recent phenomenon where one accepts a job, then just, inexplicably, never shows-up; *huh, guess I'm well-qualified to address this issue, being a bit of a ghost myself.*

THE NEXT WEEK, a farmers' market set-up in the adjacent park, and Lidia decided to take Antonio to see the sights, sounds and colors. She met other 'stay at home' moms and dads, but mostly moms, and made a few new acquaintances in the neighbour-hood.

It was one mom, Mandy, who made her own baby food and suggested Lidia should too, especially since there was such fresh, organic produce, practically in their backyards. She gave her a list of a few helpful food blogs, which Lidia visited with interest.

So, armed with a little knowledge and determination, she commenced learning the art of making baby food. Since the task consisted mostly of cleaning and chopping vegetables and fruits, steaming, then pureeing them, she figured she could master it without too much frustration, making Lidia approach this learning curve with confidence, sure that her worst critic, Antonio, would be lenient.

After one particularly inspiring market day, she bought, among other vegetables, several delicate bunches of baby beets. They looked so promisingly tender and sweet, not like the woody, earthy mature ones. Lidia loved beets, especially Nick's beet risotto, so if Antonio balked at them, she'd just hand them over to Nick. No problem.

She followed the instructions on one blog which recommended baking them unpeeled, wrapped in foil, to preserve nutrients and facilitate peeling afterwards. It went well, peeling was a bit messy and tricky as the beets were small and still warm, but nothing Lidia couldn't handle with some latex gloves and a few paper towels.

She then dropped the tiny whole beets into the blender, filling the carafe. But before adding spring water as per the recipe, she looked around the counter, her eyes resting on a little bottle of powdered coriander. *Yes, why not? It'd add a bit of sweetness, I want my baby to like beets, and not just get hooked-on carrots, like those carrot-junkie babies Siobhan told me about, with their orange skin, 'OD'ing' on beta-carotene. Huh, probably just an urban legend though, Siobhan loves to exaggerate. Anyway, here goes,* Lidia opened the jar, inhaled its fragrance, *Ok Mr. Ponti, now who's a chef, eh?* she thought, taking a pinch of the ground spice and with a flick of her wrist, ejected it into the blender.

Then she measured a few ounces of spring water and poured it in.

One step she neglected was chopping the beets first, but Lidia figured that they were so small and soft, the blender could handle them whole.

"Okay, now replace lid, then rock and roll!" she turned the dial to high, and immediately the lid blew off, the beets clunked erratically around the carafe, then chunks of red beet and mush shot out every-where.

"Aah!" Lidia jumped back, splattered by flying beet. Antonio cried and Pickles ran in circles barking, until Lidia finally had the presence of mind to turn the contraption off. After she picked-up Antonio and wiped a little beet mush off his cheek, offering it to him from her finger, he made a face, then smacked his lips in approval. She laughed.

"Well Antonio, I guess I've learned my first important culinary lesson, never leave out a step." Then surveying the mess, she added, "and we don't have to tell Nick, right Pickles?" She looked to where the dog had been, only to see a trail of red paw prints leading to the hall. "Oh shit! Pickles!"

ON THE WEEKENDS, Nick took Antonio to the Y's water-baby swim program, the park and even to ComPanis to meet with the guys and make plans for Thanksgiving. It was decided that the Ponti's would host this year's feast, it being Antonio's first Thanksgiving.

Javi couldn't come, as he was taking Lucinda to a lodge in Muskoka where they'd canoe down winding rivers, hike through blazing fall forests, build roaring bonfires, roast marshmallows, watch the mystic Northern lights, do all the things she was eager to experience as a new Canadian.

That left Lola, Becky, Paul, and Kate, whose two sisters had plans with boyfriends: Lidia, Nick, Jesse, and Josh as celebrants. Paul invited Ramona, who declined, not yet feeling ready to meet the ex, especially during a family celebration with their mutual friends.

THANKSGIVING DAY, THE air was crisp, the day bright. Inside, the seasonally adorned mantle and hall table were welcoming, where a tall spiral of wheat sheaves, tied with sisal, sat on a round, colonial pewter tray, surrounded by an arrangement of miniature pumpkins and gourds.

Everyone felt in good spirits. Lola was in the apartment kitchen putting the finishing touches on her contribution of Southern fare, corn bread dressing and sweet potato casserole. "And y'all are done," she declared, shaping the tin foil round the top of each dish, before putting them in the oven. She set her phone alarm, put on some lipstick, grabbed her small-batch bourbon, a baggie of sliced oranges and limes, bottle of ginger ale, then headed for the stairs.

"Well, what have we here?" Lola declared loudly, sashaying into the kitchen. "Three sober cooks, and on Thanksgiving. That just won't do, now let's get this party started. Nick honey, show me your highballs. We're gonna kick back on some Morrison Mules."

They laughed at her wit, as Lola shook-up the cocktails and cranked-up the jazz. Handing a frosty glass to each, seating herself opposite them at the island, she proposed a toast, "To good friends and family, wherever you may find them."

"Here, here!" the men joined in.

"Mm, that soup smells good Nick, what's in it?" Lola asked resting her glass.

"Here, have a taste, tell me what you think," Nick said, offering her a spoonful, which she took carefully, blowing to cool it off.

"Tastes a little earthy, like chestnuts and mushrooms…then shallots and sherry, but there's a sweet undertone, what's that spice?"

"Coriander, my absolute favorite go-to spice. So subtle, yet it has just the right note to bring the flavors together," Nick replied, taking a spoonful himself.

"Well, I'll be. I don't really associate coriander with Italian cuisine, more Asian, in my experience," Lola said, taking another sip of her Morrison Mule.

"Coriander's native to Southern Europe, too. Its name derives from the Greek word, koris, meaning 'bed bug', on account of the appearance of the seeds. But I think the biblical reference is more poetic–" Nick was just about to quote his favorite passage, when Lola, cut in with:

"Manna, the House of Israel called thy name; and it was like coriander seed, white; and the taste of it was like wafers made with honey: Exodus 16:31.”

“Hey, that’s right,” Nick said smiling, “how’d you know that?”

“My daddy was a preacher. I may not know my coriander from a bedbug, but I do know my bible,” Lola said winking, taking another sip of her drink.

UPSTAIRS, ANTONIO SNOOZED while Lidia and Jesse went through the ornately carved *cassone*, an antique cedar chest from Lidia’s family. She was sorting out the heirloom linens, beautifully, painstakingly, embellished with handmade lace.

“Just look at these Jess,” Lidia said spreading out a pair of pillowcases on the bed.

“They’re gorgeous; who did these, mom?” Jesse asked, fingering the lace borders.

“I’m not sure, all I know is that the technique is called ‘punta in aria’, literally stitches made in air, and for the women in my mom’s family, it was a cottage industry. Theirs was a long line of artisans in lace. They made it for the wealthy, for their tables, weddings, baptisms and for the church. In fact, my mom’s great, great aunt Renata, was so renowned as a designer and artisan that some of her work is in the Vatican.”

"No kidding?"

"That's what your nonna told me. I even have some of her designs, but the parchment's pretty fragile. Anyway, I have four sets of bed linens, two counterpanes, four tablecloths, a set of cuffs and a jabot. These are nonna's entire trousseau. Oh, and I almost forgot, Antonio's christening gown and bonnet," Lidia said, holding-up the garments.

"That gown is so elaborate; he looked like 'Little Lord Fauntleroy'."

"I know, but you must admit it's beautiful work. I like to think that with every stitch, a blessing. We'll never meet them, our talented forebears, but I like to think that, through this we have their blessings. And it'll be yours now," Lidia said, turning the bonnet in her hand, admiring the lacework.

"Mine? Why?"

"Because you're next in line to use it, trust me, this is my last rodeo."

"I don't want it mom. Just keep it for Antonio, for when he has kids, okay?"

Lidia, preoccupied with wrapping the outfit in tissue, went on, "And you can pass it back to him, when the time comes, since you were both christened in it."

Jesse became agitated. "You're not listening to me mom. I said, 'I don't want it!'"

Lidia looked-up, startled at her daughter's emphatic declaration. "Oh. Well…um…well then, I guess I'd better just hold it here, for safe-keeping?"

"Yeah, I guess you'd better. Now let's pick out one of these tablecloths for tonight, okay?" Jesse said, reaching out for the stack of cloths. "This one is really pretty, mom. Simple lace insets with little rose buds embroidered throughout, as if someone just tossed them there. I love this one." Jesse held-up her favorite for Lidia's approval.

Lidia nodded. "Yes, that one'll do. Now go along downstairs and make a start with the table, while I straighten-up here."

"Certainly, Mrs. Dalloway, and will you do the flowers yourself?" Jesse responded in her 'Downton Abbey' accent.

"Oh always, 'my de-ah', always," Lidia responded, haughtily.

They both chuckled at their insider joke.

After Jesse disappeared down the stairs, Lidia sat quictly on the edge of the bed, passing her fingers up and down the lace border of the baby's bonnet, wondering about her daughter's mood.

THE THANKSGIVING FEAST was well underway,

everyone was into their second course, Antonio was thoughtfully mushing some sweet potato around his tongue, unsure if he liked it, Pickles skulked beneath the dining table, waiting patiently for Nick to sneak him a treat.

"These Cornish hens are really tender, Nick. Did you get them from the market?" Kate asked.

"Yes, they're free range. But it's Josh's baste, the maple butter, whiskey, and cumin, that makes them really special," Nick responded, pulling a leg off his bird.

"Thanks, Nick," Josh said, smiling, pouring more wine for he and Kate.

Becky turned to Lola, "I love your cornbread dressing, the butter and pecans are a nice touch for the topping. My family used to make cornbread, I guess what you'd call Johnny cakes, but they weren't as light and tasty as this and they were sweet," Becky said, lifting a forkful to her mouth.

"It's all in the quality of cornmeal you use. My momma always favored a medium-fine white meal, plenty of sweet butter, and eggs; I separate mine: beat the whites then fold in the yolks. Then use good quality chicken stock, turkey if you got it, lots of poultry seasoning and no sugar, ever. That's for Yankees. Grits, corn bread, it's really all in the same family as polenta."

"Ha! Except in Sicily where they only feed it to the pigs," laughed Nick.

Paul observed, "Well, having travelled through the southern U.S., I have to say Lo, I just don't like grits, but I do love this dressing. One thing you guys do really well there is barbeque. I just couldn't get enough of it."

"I know. What y'all do here is grilling, but call it barbeque. Real barbeque is usually ribs or a bone-in pork butt, cooked low and slow over hardwood charcoal. Basted for eternity with a sweet-savory sop 'til it falls from the bone. Can't beat it, but not exactly heart or waist friendly," Lola advised.

Turning to Antonio, Lola said, "And how're you doing my little man? Managed to get lots of that sweet potato on your new designer shirt?"

Lola wiped the orange drool from his chin. Then Lidia, seeing that he was starting to fuss, gave him a small bottle, and remarked, "Who knew Givenchy made kids' clothes, Lo? That shirt does look really cute on him."

Josh added, "It seems everyone's getting into the kids' market these days. There's some neat products out there, like Athina's stroller. The car seat is part of the stroller, then you can just lift it and the baby out, voila! Real simple, makes having a kid a breeze."

"Uh, a convertible stroller seat makes having a

child a breeze?" Jesse challenged. "What, are you nuts, or just stupid?"

Everyone looked down at their plates, pretending they hadn't heard the crude remark.

Josh put his fork down, his eyes wide in disbelief, he responded quietly, "Well no Jess, I don't mean *literally*. It was just a casual observation."

"Oh, I know that Josh. I was just kidding, okay?" Jesse tried to recover the situation.

After that potential storm was avoided, Kate took up the thread, observing that, "I know what you mean Jess, about parenthood being no joke, what with day care and housing prices going through the roof. It's insane."

Josh added, "The 'North American Dream' of single-family home ownership is so over, not sustainable. Europeans and New Yorkers have been raising families in low and medium-density housing for generations.

"They don't seem to have suffered for lack of the perfect, poisonous, suburban lawn, and the long, fossil-fuelled commute into the city."

"I know, we just have to be creative with the space we've got," Kate said.

"Exactly," Josh affirmed. "Jess and I have no intention of being enslaved to a million-dollar mortgage, making banks and real estate agents rich.

Our space is more than adequate, and when the time comes to expand, Jesse's studio will make a great nursery. Right, Jess?" Josh smiled across the table at her.

"I don't believe this! How dare you assume that I don't need a space to practice my art. It's not a 'bored housewife's hobby', Josh. It's what I really care about. You are such an idiot!" She banged her fork down on her plate and ran upstairs to the bathroom, locking the door.

Josh excused himself quietly and went upstairs to talk to Jesse, leaving everyone momentarily silent and not sure what to do.

"Jess, please open the door," Josh said, jiggling the knob. "C'mon, we need to talk, you don't want everyone to hear us, do you?"

The door opened; Jesse sat down on the edge of the tub.

"Well?" She looked-up at him through teary eyes.

He sat down beside her, putting his arm around her shoulders, "Is this about work, Jess? I know you've had a hard time lately, but you don't seem to want to talk to me anymore, just withdraw to your studio, or bury yourself in lesson plans."

"It's about all of it Josh. All the expectations everyone else seems to have about my life," she said, pulling off a piece of toilet paper to wipe her eyes.

Then shrugging his arm off her shoulders, she turned to him and asked, "Why do you assume I want kids? Is that why you're with me? A nice Italian girl who'll have your babies, keep your house and sweep all of her aspirations under that big oriental carpet of yours?"

Astounded, Josh opened his mouth to speak, when Jesse jumped-in ahead of him, "Well, guess what! I'm not that girl. Don't stereotype me."

Josh, his color rising, raised his voice, "Oh don't play the race card Jess…not with me. I love you, that's why I'm with you, and that's why I want to have a family with you."

"Yeah, without even consulting me first. How can you love me Josh when you don't even know me?" Jesse said, staring hard into his eyes.

"You're right, guess I don't…so, what's next?" Josh shrugged.

"I'm going to leave, by myself. You can stay and enjoy the party and all the baby talk, fill your boots with it, okay? Just don't follow me," Jesse said rising, pushing past him.

Josh waited until he heard the back door slam, then rose to join the family.

"ARE YOU OKAY?" Lidia put her hand on Josh's arm.

"Yeah, guess so. Um, Jesse left, doesn't feel too well, but wanted me to stay. If that's okay," Josh said quietly, feeling awkward, looking to his hosts for affirmation.

"Of course, Josh. Here you need a top-up," Nick said, passing the decanter to Paul sat at mid-table.

"There you go," Paul said, pouring more wine. "D'ya want more potatoes? There's warm ones in the oven, I'll get them."

"No, no. I'm fine thanks. I'll just finish this," Josh said, picking at the rest of his meal.

When dinner was cleared, and dessert served, a choice of apple pie and/or pumpkin cheesecake, Josh begged-off, having had enough of the farce, wanting to head home.

"Thanks Nick," Josh said listlessly, taking his doggie bag of desserts, I'm sure Jess'll appreciate the cheesecake."

Nick patted him on the back as he turned to leave; Josh, his nearly son-in-law, and despite his concern for his daughter, the young man seemed to him a pitiable, sympathetic figure.

WITH MID-NOVEMBER'S EARLY frost, the trees shed their brazen mantles, but now on St. Martin's Day, with Mercury's sudden rise, there came the 'second summer', a brief respite before the onslaught of winter. It was so warm that Javi suggested he and Nick enjoy their beer on the terrace.

"Oh, this is nice," Nick declared, closing his eyes, turning his face towards the sun. "Hard to believe we're only a few weeks away from a frozen hell."

"I know, the weather was perfect for our Muskoka trip, Lucinda loved it. It was great to see her in awe of the whole 'northern experience', I felt like I was experiencing it for the first time too," Javi said.

"So, it's all good between you two?"

"Oh yeah, after the boyfriend drama and the fractured shoulder we've been getting along just fine, except she's a slob and I like everything neat and, in its place," Javi chuckled.

"I guess you're the odd couple, then. Well, I wish that's all that was wrong with Jess," Nick sighed, sipping his beer.

"I know, Becky filled me in. So, it was quite an 'interesting' Thanksgiving then?"

"Yep, full of surprises. Jesse has always been one to bottle-up her feelings, then explode. But this is more than just a temper tantrum; I'm afraid it's a life-changer."

"Oh, how so?" Javi asked, waiting for the over-flow of head to settle before pouring them out more beer.

"After the 'explosion', I invited her to meet for a drink after work. She opened-up, was quite blunt; said teaching wasn't for her and that I shouldn't have pushed her into it. That was a shock; I didn't think I was that kind of parent."

"You mean the kind you moan about all the time, the helicopter parent, the pushy micro manager?" Javi said wryly.

"I really thought she'd love teaching and promot-ed the idea –heavily. Apparently, I was wrong."

"So, what's her 'plan b'?" Javi asked.

"Not sure, I do know she put Josh on notice that she doesn't want children, he does, so they have to work that one out. I'm worried that she'll burn all her bridges, Javi."

"That's exactly what she seems determined to do. If she were twenty years older, I'd say she's having a mid-life crisis." Javi laughed.

"And Lidia is taking it all with uncharacteristic optimism. She said, 'Well, Jess knows for sure what she doesn't want, now all she needs to discover is what she does. So, we'll leave her to it'," Nick said, his voice raised in disbelief.

"What? Has Lidia been body-snatched? Wow, I guess having a second child really changed her perspective," Javi observed.

"Whatever, just don't do as I did, do as I say Javi, or you'll be in for it too," Nick said, shaking his head.

"What? Me influence Lucinda's life choices? I can't even get her to hang-up her clothes or make her bed," Javi chortled. "Oh, speak of the devil…I didn't hear you come in," he addressed his daughter, who appeared at the terrace door. "Come out and say hi to Nick."

"Hi Nick," she said giving him a little wave. "How's Jess? I haven't heard from her for a while."

"Busy, but give her a call, she'd love to hear from you."

Just then, Lucinda's phone 'pinged' with a text message, "Miss U already! p.s. left your earrings here… fratboy@netmail.com." Lucinda read it, smiling slyly.

Javi said, "Who's that, Charlotte? You just saw her five minutes ago."

"Yeah, I know dad, but I left something at her place." With that, she turned away, heading for her bedroom.

"Can't hold her attention for more than a nano second unless I open the fridge door or jingle the change in my pocket."

"Welcome to my world. Now, how are you and Becky?" asked Nick.

"Fine, she still won't move in, or get engaged, so I'm backing-off, taking it slow. She's the one for me, just needs time to realize she feels the same," Javi said, taking a sip of his beer.

"Good move, now that Paul's hooked-up, I guess there's no worry he and Becky'll get back together," Nick speculated.

"Have you met Ramona?"

"Briefly, when I stopped by the showroom. She's very attractive, dark, looks to be mid-thirties," Nick replied.

"So, younger lady, eh? Sly dog." Javi grinned.

"He's got that boyish charm, women of all ages fall for it," Nick recalled.

"Charm? Immaturity more like," Javi countered.

"Whoa, who's pointing fingers now?" Nick laughed.

"What? I'm a responsible family man," Javi said looking innocent.

"Let's just leave it at 'family man' shall we?" Nick smirked. Just then his phone rang, "Sorry, I need to take this."

"No problem, more beer?" Javi offered, rising for replenishments and the bowl of spiced nuts he'd forgotten on the counter.

Nick nodded… "Okay, anything else? Yes, yes, I'll be home by four."

"Lidia?" Javi put the nuts on the table and poured them more beer.

"Yes, have to pick-up diapers. I'm amazed at how one tiny body that intakes more liquid than solid, can generate so much waste. I think babies are environmentally unfriendly," Nick chuckled, popping a few cashews into his mouth. "I mean, they just don't seem to care, pooping wherever, whenever, despoiling the planet for the rest of us."

Javi laughed. "And speaking of the rest of us, how's Frank doing in Rome, polishing his Holiness' papals, hoping to become a Monsignor?"

"He's been very quiet, but we did get one rather long letter from him, and a gold St. Anthony medallion blessed by the pope for Antonio."

"What'd the letter say?"

"Something about his needing more prayer and guidance to make a decision, which is more about calling than about faith, or faith in calling…I can't remember exactly, rambling on about St. Paul and the Corinthians, The Acts of Paul and Thecla…he can be so obscure at times. Anyway, the gist is that he's applied to extend his sabbatical until Christmas."

"Really? I'm sorry we didn't get a chance to talk before he left. I just assumed he had parish fatigue, or something. He doesn't really give much away, does he?" Javi said, taking a deep draught of beer.

"How do you mean?" Nick asked.

"Well, for someone who hears so much of his fellow man's woes, he never talks about his own issues, at least not to me."

"To me neither, though I think he does to Lidia."

"They're close aren't they, Nick?"

"Yes, they seem to have a spiritual bond. She trusts him, he's her confessor and I think, in some ways, she's his."

"I'm glad he has someone to confide in. Remember how shy he was in school? Wouldn't say 'boo' to a ghost, but always a good listener," Javi recalled.

"You know, the only way he seemed to be able to open up, really express himself was in English class, he was a really good poet," Nick said.

"Remember Nick, in Grade Twelve, Sister Monica sent some of his work to a literary journal and they published it. He was so embarrassed, but it gave him the confidence to enter some contests, he even won a few, I think."

"That's right, but his mom put a stop to that ambition. The widow Kelley was a real ball-buster. Even though he and I were only children, and my guardians were really strict, they didn't dictate my future, not like Frank's mom," Nick sighed.

He put his empty glass on the tray and pushed his chair out, "Well, I'd better be off. Diapers to buy etcetera…thanks for the beer, you sit and finish yours, I know my way out."

"Ciao Nick, talk again soon, eh?" Javi replied, leaning back in his chair, wondering about their absent, enigmatic friend. He took out his phone, considered dropping him an email, then thought better of it, deciding instead, to leave Frank to his self-imposed solitude.

JUST AS LIDIA was putting a casserole of chicken legs with lemons and green olives in the oven, there was a tapping on the kitchen window. She waved with her free hand, shouting, "Be right there!" as she shut the oven door and went to admit her visitor.

"Well, hello stranger! Haven't seen you for awhile," she said, giving Josh a kiss on the cheek.

"Sorry, looks like you're busy. I won't stay, just wanted to drop-off this duck rillette and cranberry compote for you to try."

"No, c'mon in, we'll try it together," Lidia said, leading him into the kitchen, where he slung his coat on the back of a chair and sat down.

"It seems I'm very popular today; you just missed Lucinda; she dropped-by after school for a hot chocolate, then took Pickles and Antonio to the park, so I decided to grab the opportunity of making dinner early," she said over her shoulder, preparing a tray with two tumblers, plates, some crostini, and pâté knives.

"Oh, then I am intruding. Guess I should've called first," Josh said, frowning.

"Don't be silly, I just bunged the chicken in the oven and the mac n' cheese will take no time. I use some evaporated milk and mascarpone instead of making a béchamel. Nick pretends not to notice, and gobbles it up anyway," Lidia laughed.

Lidia put the tray on the kitchen table, then grabbed a bottle of red wine, "Ah, we're in luck, I think I can squeeze at least two glasses from last night's pinot.

"Thanks Lidia," Josh said, as she poured them each a glass.

Josh reached for the rillette, snapping open the lid, he said, "This is an artisan product I'm stocking for the festive season. It's made by a small game and poultry producer outside of Guelph. They raise all their fowl free-range and organically. I visited their operation last weekend, and asked Jess to come too, pack a picnic and make a day of it, but she was busy with marking. It was such a beautiful day; I love the countryside in the fall."

"Oh well, perhaps another weekend? It's nearing end of term after all," Lidia said, turning the rillette crock around, surveying the stencilled label. "Love the Baskerville font; the container reminds me of the English marmalade jars my mom used to save."

Josh spooned-out the deep-garnet cranberry compote on top of each savory rillette-laden crostini, noting, "The compote is mine, I made a ton of it in a big pressure cooker I got at restaurant supply, fresh cranberries, knob of fresh ginger, a few cloves, some crab apples, green grapes, coriander seeds, brandy and maple sugar."

Lidia picked-up hers and bit-in. "Mm, lovely! So luscious, the cranberry is nice, sweet, and tangy, a hint of the ginger's heat coming through. I could definitely eat more of these," she said, swallowing the last bite, reaching for a second crostini.

"Thanks Lidia, I'm glad you like it," Josh said, not touching his sample, preferring to sip the wine instead. "Jesse wouldn't try it, says she's on a diet, doesn't want any rich food until Christmas."

"I guess she's just trying to eat healthy before the

gluttonous season, and I expect her colleagues will have celebrations that she'll attend as well."

"Colleagues? Huh, what colleagues, Lidia? She rarely talks about them and when she does it's with derision. I doubt if she's popular at the school."

"That's a bit harsh, Jesse's sometimes reserved socially, but she was never unpopular," Lidia retorted.

"Sorry, forgot I was talking to her mother. It's just that lately she either gives me the cold shoulder or swings from impatience to anger at a moment's notice. It's exhausting, it makes me feel like she's brewing something and not telling me about it. Has she said anything about me, or us, to you?" Josh asked, his voice tight with anxiety.

"Well, she did talk to me after Thanksgiving, more of a rant really. Remember, she's only twenty-one Josh, and you're what, twenty-eight? So, for you, settling down and having a family fits with approaching thirty, but Jess is barely out of her teens.

"She doesn't need the pressure right now, especially since she's struggling at this school. I think, in some ways she feels a failure, and is angrier with herself than with anyone else," Lidia reasoned.

Josh, listening intently, responded, "I didn't quite see it that way, the age difference I mean. She seems so mature and serious and yes, I know she can be very self-critical. But I have my needs and life-plans too, and I want to know where I stand."

"I'm sorry, I can't tell you that. That's between you and Jess," Lidia said, firmly.

"Fair enough, but there's several years' gap between you and Nick, right? And didn't you 'settle down' and start your family around her age?"

"I did, yes. I guess that's why I can relate to her point of view," Lidia responded thoughtfully. "Just don't push her right now Josh, relax and take time with each other over Christmas, after her teaching duties are over and she's relaxed, okay?"

"Okay, I'll grin and bear it until Christmas," Josh agreed, as he rose to leave.

Lidia followed him to the door. "Oh, you cut your hair, it looks nice," she said, smiling.

"Yeah." He passed a hand over the back of his head. "I did it for Jess, she was always bugging me to ditch my man-bun."

"Well, thanks for the delicious treat, and you can talk to me anytime, especially if you bring more treats." Lidia chuckled.

"Will do," he said walking out the door, then turning back remarked, "And please Lidia, there's no need to share our conversation with Jess."

THE LINDEN CLUB was Lidia's oasis, where for two hours, once a week, she used to escape for a mani-pedi, facial and deep muscle massage. Pampering time she hadn't managed since Mothers' day, so this Sunday, she and Lola were indulging themselves in all the treats the spa had to offer, including complimentary chocolate truffles and champagne.

While Lola was getting her Dead Sea mud body-wrap and steam bed detox, Lidia was having a hot stone treatment and massage with Magda.

As the therapist laid the hot stones along her spine, Lidia pondered a niggling issue.

"You're married, aren't you, Magda?"

"Yes, for now," Magda laughed.

"Do you keep secrets from your husband?"

"Ha! How do you think I'm still married?"

"So, you don't think that honesty is always the best policy?"

"Oh please, Lidia! The truth is so overrated. I mean, do you really want to know that those jeans make your ass look fat? Or would you rather just wear them and be happy?"

"Actually, I think I'd rather know. But I mean keeping secrets that are, well, deeper than that, more important, especially if they got out," Lidia pursued, wanting Magda's sincere opinion.

"Oh, deep secrets, eh?" Magda removed the stones and rubbed Lidia with warm oil, then started in with her Kansa wands. "That's another matter, even more reason to be silent. You know it's selfish to start spreading the truth all over the place; it only ruins the marriage for both; you just end-up with a clear conscience and an empty bed."

"Ow! That hurt!" Lidia scowled.

"Sorry, your tendons are so tight," Magda said, easing-off on the pressure.

"And what about keeping other people's secrets?" Lidia asked.

"Well, all I can recommend is, if you want a secret kept, tell it to a Scorpio, they're good at 'omerta'. They make the best spies, and—

"Yikes! That's enough on the tendons, Magda!" Lidia shouted.

"–assassins, they know how to kill efficiently. I'm Scorpio," Magda said, "My husband though, he's Gemini. A blabbermouth, both awake and asleep, poor man gets away with nothing," she said, smugly.

Then dimming the lights, covering her client in warm towels, Magda advised quietly, "Lidia, secrets are secrets for a reason. Trust me when I say, to tell your secrets or another's, is to open-up Pandora's box, all the troubles just rush out."

Lidia turned over on her back, laying silently, eyes closed, breathing in the lotus flower aroma wafting from the diffuser. Her mind wandered to Italy, imagining her father as a frightened young man, with secrets, deep secrets perhaps. *Do I really want to open them or leave them alone? And the truth of me, and Frank?...Let God and time take it...because now, I just can't.* Lidia sighed heavily, as she rose and began to dress, resigned to time, and resolved to silence.

THREE'S A CROWD

ALDO WAS GRUMBLING loudly, digging into one of the large packing boxes, flinging bubble wrap and newspaper everywhere.

"Ha, gotcha! Just had to be in the bottom of the god-damn box, didn't you?" Aldo cursed, hoisting-up his heavy, copper-bottomed stock pot.

He hadn't yet finished settling into his rental across the bay from The Asteri. Its chief attractions were three small bedrooms for visiting family and friends, a large second floor terrace facing the sea, and its own dock, where he could tie-up the ancient motor launch he bought from Nikos' uncle.

Today, Aldo was creating a new cioppino recipe for the restaurant, more like a bisque, lighter on the tomatoes and cod, heavier on the saffron cream, nixing the capers and chili. He began by sautéing finely minced fennel bulb, shallots, garlic, and spices, dropping-in a tablespoon of passata, ladled in the fish stock fumet, then a final glug of pernod.

His assistant was busy scrubbing and sorting the clams, scallops, and mussels while Aldo deftly detached the tails and claws from the live lobsters, slipping them into the simmering fumet, then plunging the bodies into a pot of boiling water for reserve stock.

After two minutes, he scooped-out the tails and claws, cracked them and pulled-out the meat. His helper tipped the shellfish into the bubbling fumet as Aldo chopped the cod and lobster meat into large chunks.

"The shells are half-opened Aldo, it's ready for the rest."

"Okay, here we go." He pushed the succulent flesh from the cutting board into the pot, "now just another little stir, off with the heat and in with the saffron cream."

Aldo stirred the contents gently, not wanting to break-up the fish. Then added salt and white pepper, a handful of chopped cilantro, replaced the lid and let it simmer for a few minutes while he checked his emails.

"Oh, great timing, kid!" he exclaimed upon reading the first one.

"Who's it from, Aldo?" his helper asked, peering over his shoulder.

"Jesse, she wants to come in December, says she wants work in the taverna or housekeeping."

"Why?"

"Dunno."

"She's coming alone?"

"Looks like it."

"But that's the off-season, no need for extra help."

"Even if it wasn't, I couldn't hire her, not with so many young locals out of work, wouldn't look right."

"Anyway, I thought you promised me –

"I said, we'd talk about it… I'll get back to her later." He closed his iPad. "Now let's see how this cioppino is doing," Aldo said, lifting the lid, inhaling the warm, enticing steam. He dipped-in a spoon and took a thoughtful sip, "hm…"

"So, are she and Josh finished, Aldo?"

"No idea Voula, but pass me that, will'ya? This cioppino needs a pinch more coriander."

NICK HURRIED IN from the cold, dropped his case on the bench, hung his coat on the peg and headed towards the kitchen, from where he heard his wife shouting, "Oh! Son-of-a –

"Hey, what's wrong?" he asked.

"Oh…you're home early," Lidia said, looking flustered and furtive, snapping-down the cover on her Notebook, yanking the camera cable from its port.

"Yeah, and what've you been up to?" he asked, standing over her, reaching to open the device, "Watching porn again?" he chuckled.

"No and it's none of your business," she said, pushing his hand away.

"Oh dear, worse than I thought then, you've been blowing the mortgage money on eBay, haven't you?"

"It's just a little project I'm working on."

"For the column?"

"Nope. Something of my own."

"Oh, c'mon Lidia, you know I hate secrets. I'll find out eventually," he persisted, quickly snatching the Notebook as she reached for it.

"Huh, this is a blog, 'Kitchen Klutz'… and are those your hands? They are!" he said, looking at two hands with several bandaged fingers, one grasping a very long, sharp knife, the other, a honing steel. The caption read, 'Steel yourself, this could get dangerous!'

"And what's our baby doing in that picture with beet mush all over him, and my Pickles, trailing red paw-prints everywhere – Lidia, what the hell's been going-on here?"

She sighed impatiently, "Don't get so worked-up. I just had the idea of turning my culinary challenges, small triumphs, and big disasters into a blog, so that other people who are 'kitchen klutzes' could learn from my mistakes and have a good laugh too. I think the pretentious, competitive, culinary aspirations of the 'foodies', just make it very intimidating for the rest of us and takes the fun out of trying to learn." Lidia looked at her husband, levelling her accusations in his direction.

"Oh great! The blind leading the blind. Yes, let's celebrate incompetence, that's just what the world needs more of." He shut the cover and leaned back, crossing his arms.

"How dare you put me down, that's just the sort of attitude I'm fighting against. I think you're jealous. You always blather on about doing a blog, but true to you, only procrastinate, while I actually do something. And yes, the world does need this, at least my three-hundred subscribers think so. So there!" she folded her arms, then stuck her tongue out at him.

"Really? four-hundred?" he leaned forward with interest.

"Give or take," then pulling the Notebook towards her, she opened the screen, "and see my dashboard, it shows how many, and from where I'm getting views. Aside from Canada and the States, I get a lot from Britain, Australia and for some reason, Japan is pretty interested too, though I think they just love pictures of chubby red-head babies and cute dogs," she said, showing him the screen.

"How long have you been doing this?"

"About three months."

"How'd you get so many subscribers in so short a time?"

"Siobhan. I guilted her into promoting the blog to her connections, they post my link on their blogs and vice-versa, but you have to post new content regularly, that's key. And I joined a food bloggers association, they have loads of practical advice. That's where I got the idea for giveaways.

"I sent out ten-dollar Amazon gift cards for the best 'kitchen klutz' anecdotes. The subscribers loved that. When I get sponsored content, I plan to do Kitchen Klutz merchandise, aprons, and mugs. So eventually, I hope to monetize this," Lidia said confidently.

"Good for you, cara. Sorry, I was being a shit about it, maybe I am a teensy bit jealous, but I'm more than proud of you," he said, sending her an air kiss.

"Thanks. You know, leaving work was really hard for me, and Siobhan, taking over like she did, just turned the knife. I need this to feel connected, and I guess, empowered," Lidia responded. "But I'd feel more empowered if I could upload this damn video Lucinda helped me with. Maybe it needs to be re-sized."

"Lidia, I'd help if I could, but I struggle with downloading scanned docs. Can never find the damn things afterwards. They just disappear into obscure folders!" Nick paused thoughtfully, then said, "Promise me one thing?"

"What's that Nick?"

"Stay away from the crème brûlée torch."

As they laughed at the image of Lidia wielding such a fiercely incendiary device, Lola tapped on the kitchen door.

"Avanti," Nick shouted.

"Hi y'all," she said, emerging into the kitchen

bearing an empty cookie tin. "I just wanted to return this and thank Lidia for her addictive Malteser, Rice Crispy squares, and to tell you that I'll be out of town until after Christmas."

"Oh? Getting some r-and-r in the sun? I guess you're tired after the extended run," Lidia said.

Nick got up and pulled-out a chair, "Have a seat Lo, want to join us in a little glass of Barolo?"

Well, seeing as it's Barolo, I certainly will," she said smiling, then turning to Lidia. "No, it's not a vacation, I got a gig in a satirical drag review in New Orleans for a few weeks, 'Tina Re-Turner and the Stylettos, at least I get to do Tina. And the club's decent, attracts a lot of good fans, stage-door Johnnies too, which I'm long done with. Then I plan to go see my mom, and maybe stay over Christmas."

"You don't let the grass grow, eh? Kinky Boots has barely ended, don't you need more of a break than a week over Christmas?" Lidia asked.

"Yeah, I plan to take time off in June. Aldo's invited me to Corfu for two weeks, I can do some song-writing and arranging, then back here, to focus on the reassignment process, and making more money."

"I thought you've applied for citizenship. You'll be in the province's health insurance plan, it covers these procedures, doesn't it?" Nick said, handing her a glass of wine.

"Yes, it does, but not until I'm a citizen, which I won't be until at least next November. In the meantime, I'm on the hormone treatments and going for counselling, all of which I'm paying for myself," she said, taking a sip of wine.

"Reassignment surgery? Wow, that's a big step, Lo. I'm glad you've got counselling," Lidia said.

Nick nodded his head in silent agreement, trying to quell the queasiness of the images such invasive procedures evoked.

Lidia asked, "Aren't you afraid?"

"Afraid? Of the surgery?" Lola said.

"Well, yes."

Nick cut in, asking, "But not only that, aren't you afraid of the hostility you might face?"

Lola started to laugh, Lidia and Nick look nonplussed, feeling they had said something wrong.

"Let me tell you about growing-up black in America. My hometown of god-fearing, law-abiding, homophobic folk was pretty peaceful, if you towed the line to fit in, otherwise you were bullied and ostracized, sometimes exiled, sometimes end-up dead, *accidentally*.

"In America, 'armed and dangerous' for black people, mean the cops, who could and would stop you anytime for the crime of driving a nice car 'while black', walking in a white neighborhood, 'while black' or just for 'being black'. I learned to comply, and just pray that the officer wasn't having a bad day, or out for a trophy."

Nick shook his head in disbelief.

Lola continued, "Let me ask you, the police cars here say, 'To Serve and Protect', right? So, do they deliver on that promise to you?

Nick and Lidia looked sideways at one another.

Nick responded, "Mostly, I guess…yes."

"See, I don't know how that feels, because it's the talk we're given, but not the walk we're forced to take. So, to answer your original question, am I afraid? Hell, yes. But I'm more afraid of not living this life God gave me, authentically. And if some folks are uncomfortable with that, then that's their problem. I'm done accommodating the haters."

Nick said, "Well my friend, you've got guts. I don't know that I'd be that brave about any of it."

"Honestly, right now, the thing I fear most is telling my mother," Lola confided. "My support group urged me to go home. Spend time with my mom, help her understand what I'll be going through. I just pray she accepts my decision," Lola said, looking down at her glass.

Lidia asked, "Have you discussed re-assignment with her before?"

"No, never. I don't think she even realizes what it

would mean for me. As far as she knows, her son likes to dress-up as a woman and make a show of himself. But gender reassignment?

"She'll struggle with that, not only because of her religious beliefs, but because the long-awaited infant she gave birth to twenty-six years ago, her sweet baby boy, will be gone forever. It's like a death to her, but a rebirth for me, which is why I think of it more as gender confirmation. I'm dreading this visit, but I couldn't do it without her knowing, even if it's the last time I ever see her again," Lola said, her eyes glistening.

Lidia put her arm around Lola's shoulder, "Give her a chance Lo, she's your mom, she'll come around. You'll have a good Christmas; this'll bring you two closer together."

"Lidia's right, Lo. Even though she may feel she's losing a son, she's actually gaining a wonderful daughter," Nick said, trying to lighten the mood.

Lola, wishing she felt as optimistic, smiled apprehensively, as Nick poured them more wine.

A WHITE WEDDING

BECKY, KATE, DANIELLE, and Monique, armed with

Paul's Amex gold card, were plowing through the racks of formal wear at one of Toronto's high-end retailers, their capricious requests abandoned by an exasperated sales staff.

"Maybe we should just go to Prada," Danielle blurted-out, after the voluptuous Monique pushed open the dressing-room doors, presenting herself triumphantly in a very low-cut, figure-hugging, floor-length plum charmeuse gown, with Swarovski-crystal bodice trim and matching opera-length gloves. As she twirled around, admiring herself in the bank of full-length mirrors, the department's manager emerged to check on the progress and chaos this group might be making.

"That's striking on you dear, with your stature, you can certainly carry it off... much too much for a smaller woman," she said through a taught smile, her eyes running up and down the bodacious spectacle before her.

Nasty cow, that's just code for you've way too much figure for that. Maybe, I'll just let my daughter buy that dress, then she can tell everyone where she got it! thought Becky, who let her ire pass, unexpressed.

"Um, excuse me, but have you anything like – this," Danielle asked the manager, holding-up a very short, embossed black-velvet number. "But with, like a pleather metal-stud corset and black faux suede lace-up breeches? I'm a vegetarian, so no leather, right? See, I was a Goth, but now I'm into Steam Punk and I think that an outfit like this, accessorized right, would be a good transition-look for me."

The manager smiled benignly saying, "I'll see what I can do, dear."

As she headed toward the staff lounge and a bottle of Tylenol, Kate intercepted her, grasping her elbow, steering her aside, she whispered, "Look, don't let that we're here for wedding gear fool you. It's for my dad's second, ill-considered marriage to a much younger woman, so my sisters and I don't care too much about the solemnity of the nuptials, if you get my drift.

"And the red head over there, the one with my dad's gold card in her cold grasp, is his first wife, so, like she cares how much we spend, right?" Kate said nodding, looking for assent.

"Oh, right dear, hear you loud and clear. I'll see what I can do about that pleather corset then," she said, feeling strained.

"Good, and while you're at it, I'd like to see something in, black satin, with a flocked, net veil. And well, maybe just a bit of bling on the headband, okay?"

"Right away, dear!"

Now, who said working for commission's a bad thing? Kate thought, as she joined her mom on the divan in front of the dressing rooms.

AFTER MUCH WRANGLING amongst each other and arguing with their mother, the girls stopped fooling around, and chose appropriate dresses, giving Paul's Amex card a chance to chill. Weary and hungry, Becky decided to treat them to lunch at a nearby sushi bar. As the waiter distributed their menus, Becky ordered sake, tout-de-suite, leaned back on the banquette, loosening her cashmere scarf.

"Isn't it a *leetle* early ma?" Monique said disapproving, using the annoying moniker she and her sisters picked-up from their maternal grandma.

"Huh, too late you mean. I should've had a shot for breakfast, 'Dutch courage' for the gruelling experience of shopping with you three. I'd forgotten that joy, it was happily suppressed in my subconscious along with the horrific childhood and disappointing marriage," Becky said, taking a sip of the warm, potent liquor.

"Oh boo-hoo! Ma's having a bad life, girls." Danielle sighed.

"Yeah, I know, with her handsome, rich boyfriend, and new travel business. Oh ma, how do you cope?" Monique mocked, sticking-out her lower lip and stroking her mother's hand.

Becky laughed, pulling her hand away, "You really are the worst children!"

"You think we're challenging, just wait 'til you meet your grandchildren," Danielle said, chuckling.

"Okay, enough torturing ma, let's get some eats in, I'm starving!" Kate said, scanning the menu for the dishes she wanted.

While they waited for their orders to arrive, Becky decided to inquire about her daughters' view of their father's fiancé, "So, how do you all get along with this Ramona?"

"She's okay, ma. Her little boy is cute, well-behaved, good manners and kills at Lego Creator," Monique said.

"Yeah, Brendan's a cool kid. Ramona's not around that much though, she's busy with real estate, and she and pa go out a lot, so he has a nanny. Me and Monique babysit him sometimes. We've actually seen more of Brendan than we have his mom," Danielle added, pouring herself some sake.

"Is that right. Well, I guess since Paul's moved in with them, you see him less too, outside of work, I mean," Becky observed, taking a sip of her miso soup.

"Yes," Danielle sighed, "but the upside is, we'll be able to rent our own place and have some money in the bank for a change."

"Yes, and what we're giving you three from the sale of the house is going straight into secure, long-term investments, right? No using it to swan-off to Caribbean all-inclusives on a whim," Becky said, levelling a serious look at her daughters.

"Understood, ma. But, since there's already been quite a few showings, we'd better start looking for a rental, right guys?" Kate said, chop-sticking some barbequed eel.

"Right, but we don't need to sign for anything until ma and pa have accepted an offer. You know, I think it's really nice of Ramona to waive her commission on it," Monique said, dipping her tempura into the ponzu sauce.

"Enough with the 'ma and pa' girls, that hillbilly thing's giving me a headache!" Becky interjected, massaging her temples.

Kate, mindful of her mother's annoyance, picked-up the thread, pointing-out, "Don't be too impressed by that, Monique, you know dad will be paying his way, so 'quid pro quo'."

"Oh Kate, you're so cynical, can't you just give Ramona a break?" Monique retorted, grabbing the last California roll.

"I will when I find out just what kind of a break

dad's giving her, I mean I'll bet he hasn't even arranged a pre-nup," Kate said, pushing her empty plate away, opening her purse to check her hair and refresh her lip-stain.

"God, I'd never even considered that Kate; I think we should've sent you to law school," Becky said pointedly, taking-out her phone to text Paul.

THE NEXT DAY, as requested, Paul showed-up at Becky's door, wondering what her urgent summons was about.

"Hi, thanks for coming. Here, gimme your umbrella, you can hang your coat over there," Becky said, indicating the coat stand.

"So, where's the fire?" Paul asked, as he took a seat on the sofa.

"No fire exactly, just a matter we need to reach an agreement on – soon. Oh, but before we do, here's your card back."

"Thanks, Beck. I know the Hecates can be a nightmare to organize. Even though this wedding's a low-key affair, registry office, champagne reception, I didn't want it to turn into the Rocky Horror Picture Show, especially given our resident Goth," Paul laughed.

"Steam Punk," Becky said.

"What?"

"Danielle's into 'Steam Punk' now."

"Oh, right. And the difference is?"

"I think Steam Punk has more breeches, grommets and aviator goggles," advised Becky.

"Well, thank god none of that paraphernalia was in evidence when they showed me their outfits. They all look very nice, thanks."

"I do think they look lovely, even though they're not really thrilled. After all, this event isn't all about them, just somewhat about them, right?" Becky said, leading into her real purpose.

"What do you mean 'somewhat' about them? I think it's about them that our family is changing, expanding. Why? Have they been grumbling behind my back?" Paul demanded, sitting upright, looking concerned.

"Oh no, no. They like Ramona and Brendan; it's just that, well Kate raised a valid concern, which needs addressing," Becky said taking a seat opposite Paul.

"And that is?"

"The issue of our business' security and our children's' inheritance, considering your new legal obligation,"

"New legal obligation? What the hell are you

talking about? I haven't mortgaged the business or anything," Paul said, agitated and confused.

"No, no. You miss the point, Paul! I mean your marriage, that's a legal obligation, one that needs to be defined for all our sakes. You need a pre-nup Paul," Becky said, emphatically.

"Oh, so you think Ramona's a gold-digger. Well, I just think you're jealous and using the kids against me, why else would you drag them into this?" Paul challenged.

"Why? Paul, because they are in this. Their futures and livelihoods are in this, you need to make sure the business is secure from any possible future claims against it."

"I see. So, you think Ramona and I won't last, eh?"

"Well, it's been known to happen," Becky said, wryly.

"Yeah, and whose fault's that?" Paul sneered.

"You can be as bitter as you like, but you know I have a point, especially as Ramona's got a child, a potential beneficiary and dependent, who isn't even our girls' blood relation," Becky shouted, standing, hands on hips.

Paul jumped-up to stare her down, "Unlike their new step-brother, who'll definitely be a blood relative!"

"What?"

"That's right, Ramona's pregnant," Paul said smirking, grabbing his coat from the rack and heading for the door.

"Why didn't you tell me?" Becky shouted after him.

"Cause it's none of your business," Paul shouted back, over his shoulder.

"And the girls?"

"They'll get over it," Paul said pushing the elevator button.

Becky, fuming, seized his umbrella and pitched it at him, "Here idiot, you'll need this, and a good lawyer!"

LAWYERS, GUNS, AND MONEY

JAVI REACHED OVER, getting the snifter from the nightstand, "Oops, watch it, Beck. You're dribbling that twenty-year old brandy all over my new Frette sheets," he said laughing, holding the crystal glass up to her lips.

"Oh sorry, your highness," Becky sputtered, a little inebriated.

"All better, now?" he smiled at her, leaning over for a kiss.

"Yep, all better now," she said, kissing him back.

"So, are you and the girls really gonna 'lawyer-up?" Javi asked, snuggling up to her.

"Looks like there's no alternative. I just can't reason with him, never could, he's so emotional. And now that there's a baby in the picture, he's even worse," Becky sighed.

"Who'da thunk it, eh? Two of my oldest friends, daddies at this age. Well, I guess he and Nick can compare baby food recipes, chiropractors and sleep deprivation tips," Javi laughed.

"You know, I think you men should do the child-rearing and leave running the universe to us," Becky said wistfully.

"Seriously though, Becky. Sometimes going legal can just ratchet-up the money and the enmity. I'm sure you don't want that," Javi advised.

"Oh, don't I? Paul's so selfish; he didn't even tell the girls about the pregnancy. Guess he thought he'd just spring it on them whenever it suited him. Huh, I'm not so sure that wasn't Ramona's idea. Seal the deal before anyone can have second thoughts," she said cynically, taking another sip of brandy.

"Why do you care?" Javi asked, looking at her sideways.

"Why? Because of the girls, obviously,"

"Are you sure that's the only reason?"

"Of course, it is. What're you implying?" Becky said, sitting-up, shrugging-off his embrace.

"Well, it just seems to me a little incredulous that you didn't think of this before, like two months ago, when the announcement came out and not three weeks before the nuptials," Javi said, his arms across his chest.

"Oh really? Well, the timing just gives me more leverage. Anyway, whose side are you on?"

"Yours, always. You know that," he said, taking her hand. "It's just that this legal embranglement might chill the marriage, especially given the timing."

"Tough, I'm sticking to my guns, to protect my investment, but most of all, for the girls' sake," Becky affirmed.

"Okay, as long as that's all there is to it," Javi said, getting-up, pulling-on his boxer shorts and tee shirt.

HAVING THE CAKE, EATING IT TOO

RAMONA WAS AT the island in her expansive, slate, and bronze kitchen, putting the finishing touches on the salad, when Paul came up behind her for a hug, brushing her long dark ponytail aside, he planted several light kisses on her neck.

"Mm, is it my birthday or something?" Ramona said, smiling with satisfaction.

"Every day should be a celebration of you, my love," Paul said, hugging her tight.

"Okay, and just how many glasses of wine have you had?"

"Oh pshaw! I'm drunk on love!" he laughed.

"Well, just make sure you're giving those filets lots of it, 'cause I don't want them burned, there's nothing else in the house to eat."

"It's under control, they're resting as we speak," he responded, taking her hand. "Speaking of which, shouldn't you take a rest, get off your feet for a minute? Come and sit down with me," he said, leading her to the distressed-hide banquette.

"Oh, that's better." Ramona stretched-out her legs, kicking-off her shoes to flex her toes.

"Are you excited about the wedding, sweetheart?" Paul asked.

"Sure I am…is there a problem?"

"Um, a minor one. It's not me, it's Becky, we've just had some pretty heated words over business," Paul said, hoping Ramona would help him out.

"You mean your family's business?"

"Yes. All of a sudden she's got it into her head that we need a pre-nup, in order to protect her and the girls' financial interests."

"Oh, does she now…what a bitch!" Ramona said, sitting-up.

"I know, this just came out of the blue at me, she's even hired a lawyer, just got his letter today, summoning me to a preliminary mediation at his office next week."

"And what did you say?"

"I said 'no' to the pre-nup, and I'm not interested in making her lawyer richer than he already is," Paul said firmly.

"So, what next? Do you have a plan?"

"How would you like to be married tomorrow, at the registry office?"

"Why? Just to accommodate your ex's paranoia, we're supposed to rush our plans and have no celebration with friends?" Ramona asked, with growing anger.

"No, we can have the celebration as planned. I just want to get us married before 'Cruella' turns this whole thing into a Greek tragedy and my kids against me."

"Forgive me if I seem a little slow, but what difference does when we get married make?"

"Like 'Cruella' pointed-out, it's a legal commitment and I want to show her and my girls that we are committed, have a united front. And as for the pre-nup, I think I can make you, the 'very-soon-to-be' Mrs. Deauville, an offer you won't refuse. Sweetheart, we're gonna have our wedding cake and eat it too," Paul said, grinning slyly.

"Okay then. I'm in," Ramona confirmed, reaching over for a kiss.

TURNING THE TABLES

KATE DROVE THE company's Land Rover into the wooded enclave of Wychwood Park, as her mother, sitting next to her, mumbled a running complaint about the character of her ex-husband, his relations and their twenty-three-year marriage.

God! What a load of grief. I'll never, ever marry, Kate pledged to herself.

"We're here Mom, you can quit the grumbling now," she said, unbuckling her seatbelt, looking over at her mother, still engrossed in her grievances while scrolling through emails.

"What? Oh! This is it?" Becky stared at the large, Tudor-style home with its casement, leaded-pane windows, stacked chimneys, and steep copper-roof that dominated the cul-de-sac. In the grounds, all the tea roses were wrapped neatly in burlap for the winter, the yew hedges adorned with discreet white lights, the rhododendrons, variegated holly, red and yellow dogwoods grouped artfully in the middle of the circular cobbled drive, glowed vividly, lit from beneath.

"Why didn't you tell me she lived in Wychwood Park?" Becky said peevishly, banging-on the antique lion's-head doorknocker.

"Because you didn't ask, okay? Calm down, it's only an address," Kate retorted, already regretting attending this meeting with her mother.

Paul answered the door smiling, he greeted his daughter with a kiss, Becky with a "Thanks, for coming." He hung their coats and showed them into the study, where Ramona was waiting, sat at the head of an oval Duncan-Phyfe mahogany table.

She rose to shake hands with Becky, greet Kate warmly, and offer them a drink from the wet bar. As she poured them each a glass of white wine and Paul a scotch, she remarked, "I'm sorry we didn't meet earlier Becky, in a purely social context, but Paul tells me that you and Kate have some concerns about our marrying," she handed them each their drinks and continued, "so, we thought it was best to just sit down and 'clear the air'." Ramona, looked to Paul.

"That's right, we don't need lawyers, do we Kate? You know, it never occurred to me that you were upset, I just wish you had spoken-up earlier," Paul said turning to his daughter, who now felt more than a little anxious and ashamed.

"Sorry, dad. It just built-up, I guess," she said shrugging. "All the changes in the family, I just wanted to make sure that we didn't get lost in the shuffle."

"Yes, especially since there's going to be a new stepbrother in the mix, Paul. You chastise Kate for not being forthcoming, while withholding quite a lot yourself," Becky scoffed, taking a sip of her wine.

"Ah, that's my fault, I'm afraid. You see, I had several miscarriages trying to have just one child, and was so thrilled, well, we both were," Paul reached over for her hand, "when we found I was pregnant. But given my history and on the advice of my doctor, we thought it best to keep it to ourselves until the fifth month."

"I'm sorry Ramona, and I truly hope everything will go well this time. But it still doesn't alter the fact that my daughters and I need reassurance about the company's future," Becky responded matter-of-factly.

"Good! Which is why Ramona and I have made a legal agreement, well, trade is more accurate, that'll not only secure her good faith in our enterprise, but even expand its reach, and of course its worth," Paul chimed-in, enthusiastically.

"C'mon Paul, enough! I feel like we're playing Clue– was it Colonel Mustard in the library with the wrench? Where's the body and whodunit, if you please," Becky said, crossing her legs, pulling her cardigan tight around her.

Opening a legal file with copies of their agreement, Ramona answered, "We decided to trade interests in our assets," she said handing-out the agreement, "I've traded half my interest in this home, which is unencumbered, for half Paul's share in the company."

"And exactly what is that supposed to achieve," Becky asked archly, turning-over the pages of the document.

"Yeah, dad. What does this mean? You're out of the company?" Kate said, worried, leaving her copy untouched.

"No, Kate. It means that I still have an interest and a vote in the company and half-interest in an asset that is more secure than a commercial enterprise, real estate values being on a steady climb. I remain President of Operations at Coach House Flooring. And Ramona, through her connections, will expand our market reach, benefitting us all."

"Connections? What 'connections? I appreciate that you own a real estate brokerage Ramona, but really, it's only domestic projects that'll be 'hit or miss' in terms of contracts for us," Becky scoffed.

"Who said anything about small domestic contracts?" Ramona retorted.

"Becky, Ramona is a DeMarco," Paul said.

"A DeMarco? Oh, a DeMarco, you mean the – Becky said, astounded.

"Yes Becky! Those DeMarco's, who are the largest condo developers in Ontario," Paul said.

"And the fifth largest in Canada," Ramona added, proudly.

"Oh my god," Becky took a deep gulp of wine, steadying herself she said, "And this contract makes you what? My partner?"

"Yes, it does," Ramona said, smiling, extending her hand.

"Mom," Kate nudged her mother under the table. "Well, this is good news guys. Sounds like a plan. Thanks dad! And, of course, you too, Ramona." Kate grinned widely at her stepmother, raising her wine glass.

But Becky kept her hands in her lap, while she took-in the news. Finally, she spoke, "Well-played Ramona, it seems you've not only taken over my business, but my family as well, and you're not even married yet."

Paul countered, "This swap was my idea Becky,

and yes, we're married. Took our vows at City Hall last week."

"If you feel uncomfortable with the business arrangement, I could make you an offer," Ramona said.

"Really? You think you're going to buy me out? No way lady, I'm keeping my hand in this game, if only for my girls' sake. And I've had quite enough of your subterfuge, Paul," Becky said, getting-up to go.

"But mom! Don't you see this is good for all of us. Oh c'mon, let's talk some more," Kate pleaded, rising to follow her mother.

"No, Judas. I'll meet you in the car."

Paul caught Kate at the door, "Don't worry, this'll all be water under the bridge in a few months. Your mom will just have to cope with the situation; she's very good at coping.

"Anyway, she's been a silent partner since we split, it's really me, and your sisters who'll be hands-on running the operation." Then he paused and took her face in his hands. "I love my children, please trust me to take care of your interests."

"I will dad. Love you."

"Love you too, Kate. Drive careful now and put in your ear buds."

Kate paused in the driveway to call Danielle, who urged, "Well c'mon, how'd it go?"

"Mom's really pissed-off, but we sister, we are gonna be rich!"

A MERE TRIFLE

"WELL, HAVEN'T YOU become the little 'Suzy Homemaker'," Becky exclaimed, as Lidia pulled a Black Forest trifle, her recent culinary triumph, from the fridge and set it on the table.

Then handing out the plates and spoons, she retorted, "Better than being 'Suzy Home Wrecker'."

"Ouch! I guess I deserved that. Sorry, Lidia, it's just that I'm still pissed about the way Paul turned the tables on me. And in such a 'win-win' way, for everyone but me; I get stuck with Bridezilla as business partner and my kids treating me like I'm the one who's spoiling their party. ME! The fool who tried to protect their interests from their feckless, moonstruck father," Becky said angrily, plunging her spoon into Lidia's luscious confection.

"Well, it doesn't seem like a feckless plan to me. You're right though, that was a swift move. Didn't think Paul had it in him, to be honest," Lidia observed, digging-in herself.

"Mm, this is yummy… but, no I didn't think he

did either. Ha, must've been Ramona's idea," she scoffed, scooping-up another big spoonful.

"Are you sure you aren't underestimating him?" Lidia asked, picking-up a chocolate curl.

"I dunno, maybe. It's just that I was always the planner, he was the doer. I never thought he was deeper than that, not that he's dumb, just not deep," Becky said, waving her spoon emphatically.

"Is that why you had the affair?"

"I think so, he bored me, so dependable, so predictable," Becky mused, resting her chin on her hand.

"Not so predictable now though, you better keep-up." Lidia laughed.

"You remember last Christmas, when we went skiing with the girls in the Townships?" Becky asked, plucking a cherry from the top of the trifle.

"Yes, you said you felt the old urge, but nothing happened."

"Well, it was not for my lack of trying. Javi was closing-in and I just wanted to see if there still wasn't a spark between Paul and I that needed rekindling. But he begged-off, saying he was too tired, afterwards was distant, so I left it at that."

"It's likely he was falling for Ramona, and just didn't want to get confused," Lidia offered.

"I think you're right, but I didn't know about her

at the time. I thought there might still be a chance for us…now I've blown it, haven't I Lidia?" Becky said, with a little sob.

"No," Lidia admonished, "You said the marriage was stifling, and you really wanted out, don't forget that."

Just then Nick came in, sensing the emotional atmosphere, he asked, "What's this, Becky? Tears in the trifle, c'mon now, Lidia's cooking's not that bad!"

"Just get some trifle Nick, and go away," Lidia said, rolling her eyes.

"Okay, sheesh, I was just trying to – oh never mind," he said serving himself a large portion, before quickly exiting.

"I can't believe how he's moved-on from twenty-three years of us, to a new wife, new baby, new home, all in just two years. No wonder he was so quick to file for divorce after Christmas," Becky said, frowning.

"Did you really expect him to stay on hold for you? Don't you want him to be happy too?" Lidia asked.

"Not that happy, and not this soon!" Becky exclaimed.

"But you weren't happy with him," Lidia countered.

"I was happy lot's of times! Now I'll never be

happy again, probably just die alone with a grumpy cat for company," Becky wailed.

"Nonsense, you're allergic to cats, and anyway, you have Javi," Lidia pointed-out.

"I know, he does love me. I'm just being 'the dog in the manger', I guess." Becky sighed, rubbing her eyes, taking another consoling spoonful of creamy trifle she asked, "Hey, is this Reddi-wip?"

"Yep, it is – Extra Creamy. And I don't care, okay? I tried whipping real cream but ended-up with butter, who knew whipped cream could turn into butter?" Lidia laughed, licking her spoon.

Chapter Five

WINTER

A BRIDGE TOO FAR

ON A COLD, late November evening in Toronto, Nick ambled down the empty hallway of his college, burdened with the last batch of Christmas exam papers bulging from his briefcase. Passing Professor Glen Davies' open door with a nod, before turning the corner into his own office, he saw the door ajar and the desk light on.

"Jess! What're you doing here? It's nearly seven o'clock."

"Since I had the car today, I thought I'd pick you up," she said, getting-up from her father's desk.

He put his briefcase down and slumped into the chair, swivelling around to face his daughter, he asked, "So tell me, how'd it go with the superintendent today?"

"Not bad, fairly good actually," Jesse said, sitting on the couch, hunched over, her hands between her knees. "I expected some old fart who would just give

233

me a rebuke about letting the profession down.

"But she really understood, especially about the brutal timetable, the number of special needs kids crammed into my classes, with no teachers' aid, and the dodgy head of department who constantly short-changed my supply requests."

"And the upshot is?"

"The upshot is that she, Ms. Bancroft, urged me to reconsider quitting altogether, she granted me an unpaid leave for the rest of the year.

"Also offered me a short-term contract, subbing for a mat-leave, at a smaller, more arts-focussed school in September. It'll give me time to decide whether or not I really want to pack teaching in for good."

"Hey, well done, you! And here I worried that you'd burn all your bridges," Nick said, relieved.

"Don't get too thrilled, dad. I still may decide teaching's not for me, I'll maybe just opt for supply teaching to support my art habit." Jesse laughed.

"Anyway, over Christmas holiday, when you and Josh get back from Montreal, we can contemplate that, right? I can help you firm-up your plans," Nick said, brightening.

"Uh, not okay, dad. I'll be having Christmas with nonno in Corfu, so, you'll have to contemplate without me. I emailed him just after Thanksgiving."

"He said, yes?"

"Said he'd think about it. But seeing as I'm his favorite granddaughter, I don't think I need to worry about him saying, no. I really need a break. The change of scene will be good for me."

"And what about Josh, isn't he going too?"

"No."

"Does he know this?"

"I'm telling him tonight."

"Oh. So that bridge is burning?"

"Not sure, depends on him. I know what I want now and what I won't be pushed into. If he can't accept that, then yeah, let it burn." Jesse looked-up at her father, her eyes clear, her manner calm and resolute.

"I like Josh, Jesse, he's a fine person and it's obvious to me that he's very much in love with you, so be kind to him," Nick said, regarding his daughter intently.

She looked back and replied, "I know, he's good and kind, and loving, and I'll try not to hurt him, dad."

"Good. Now let's get outta' here. I'm very tired and very hungry."

IT WAS ELEVEN o'clock by the time Josh locked-up the store, balanced-up the cash and trudged upstairs ready for bed. Jesse was waiting for him, working on her laptop at the dining room table.

"Hey, how'd your meeting go today?" Josh asked a little warily.

"Good, I have an unpaid leave for the rest of the school year, and a short-term contract in September, in a better school," Jesse said, not looking-up from her screen.

"That's great, at least you're not fired," he said, kissing the top of her head, on the way to the fridge. "You hungry?"

"Nope, but there's some salad and pizza there for you."

"Thanks." He popped the pizza in the micro-wave. "Um, can you cover a shift for me tomorrow, one to six?"

"Sure. You going some place?"

"Yes. I gotta' make a trip to see the elves, don't wanna turn-up at mom and dad's empty-handed, now do we?" Josh said, sitting beside her, drawing-out a long string of hot mozzarella from his pizza.

"I guess you don't," Jesse answered.

"Don't you mean, *we* don't? The gifts are from both of us, we're both going to be there," Josh replied, feeling apprehensive.

"Don't count on me, Josh. Nonno just emailed me an invite to Corfu, he's rented a little house, only has one bedroom furnished and a pull-out couch, so I'd like to go and help him fix it up. He's terrible at stuff like that," Jesse said, eyes still fixed on the computer screen.

"I don't believe this! You promised my mom that you'd join us in Montreal for Christmas, she even bought you your ticket!" Josh shouted.

"Oh, don't be so dramatic, I'll pay her back. Anyway, Miriam's Jewish and your Dad's nominally Hindu, Christmas isn't exactly a big deal for them."

"That's not the point and you know it. And look at me when you're speaking!" Josh yelled, banging his fist on the table.

"Don't you yell at me, or boss me around… Okay, I'm looking at you now, satisfied?" she said grimacing.

"No, I want to know why you think it's fine for you to disrespect me and my family. This isn't about religion, it's a four-day break for me, I've already arranged coverage for the shifts.

"This was a way for my family to spend time with us, get to know you better. You should be pleased that they want to know you better," Josh said vehemently.

"I didn't mean to disrespect anyone when I accepted an invitation from my nonno, who is all alone in a foreign country and misses his only grand-daughter.

"I'll be the only one there for him this holiday, your parents have you and each other," Jesse said, indignantly.

"Oh please, I'm not stupid or a push-over. You invited yourself, didn't you? Your 'nonno' can take care of himself, and I doubt if he's alone, Jess. I'm going to bed, you can sleep on the couch, it'll be practice for Corfu,' Josh said, rising, leaving his now cold plate of food on the table.

ROOM AT THE INN

"ABSOLUTELY NOT!" LIDIA was emphatic in turning-down Jesse's request to stay in Lola's apartment while she was gone.

"But mom, she's not here! I'm sure it'd be okay with her," Jesse pleaded, dragging her luggage in from the back porch.

"I'm sure it would, but just because she's a nice person, doesn't mean you can impose on her," Lidia responded.

"Oh, c'mon Lidia if it'll be okay with Lo, why

isn't it okay with you? Our daughter needs a place to stay, woman!" Nick rejoined.

Lidia gave him a dark look. "She shouldn't have assumed that Aldo would say 'yes' to her self-invite, especially when she'd already accepted one from Josh's parents.

"Jesse has a place of her own to stay, and that apartment is Lo's private space. I can't ask her if we can violate her privacy, she wasn't expecting guests, after all, and she's paid the rent to the end of the year."

"I don't, in fact, have a place to stay, mother, otherwise I wouldn't be here begging you. It's not my fault nonno bumped me in favor of Voula's son and granddaughter," Jesse shot back.

Lidia thought for a moment, "Okay baby Jesus, you can have the manger in the den, take it or leave it."

Nick looked at his daughter, grinning weakly, he said, "She'll take it. Right, Jess? It's only for a few weeks. Anyway, I know that couch is pretty comfy."

"Yeah dad, I know you know," Jesse smirked. "Okay, done."

"Uh and you'll babysit for us?" Lidia asked, arching an eyebrow.

"Yes, and I'll muck-out the stables, feed the donkey and polish your little star, okay mom, is that enough humility for you?"

"Yes, I think that'll do," Lidia said, turning away, leaving Nick to help his daughter settle in.

LATER THAT WEEK, Jesse was upstairs in the nursery, sitting on the floor, taking pictures of Antonio, as he laughed and gurgled, jumping vigorously up and down in his 'Jolly Jumper', while Kate tried to assemble the walker they bought him for Christmas.

"Stay still, you little devil," Jesse said, poking him in the belly, "or auntie Athina won't get a clear picture of you."

"Just send a video with the caption, "Jump for Joy, it's Xmas!" That'd be cute. How's Athina doing? Since I'm off Facebook, I've missed her posts. Are they in the new place yet?"

Yep, here, have a look," Jesse handed Kate her phone.

"Ah, Dimitra's so cute, has Athina's eyes and long lashes, lucky girl. Hey, isn't that one of your pieces on the wall behind her?"

"Yeah, I gave it to her for a house-warming gift. Her loft looks nice, eh?"

"Oh yeah, lots of light, great harbour view," Kate said, scrolling through the photos. "And Athina's put on some weight."

"I know, looks good on her, she seems really happy," Jesse said quietly, taking back her phone.

"Well Jess, I guess you and I are the spinsters of the group, which is fine with me," Kate said.

"For me too, for now anyway."

Then, wrestling a plastic figure from Pickles, turning it over, Kate remarked, "What the hell is this supposed to be, a frog, it's green…or no, a dog?"

Taking hold of it, Jesse said, "Um no, I think it's a bear, yeah, definitely an ugly, green plastic bear."

Returning to her task, Kate asked, "You're gonna wrap this, right? When I'm finished? Kid's love wrapping, tearing all your hard work to pieces, it's what they live for."

"That and boxes, so I guess we should save the box and wrap it too. I'll put some discard, textural, colorful stuff in it and he'll have a ball," Jesse said, "Added bonus – the mess will piss-off Lidia."

They rolled on the floor laughing, exciting Antonio, who jumped all the more.

"And, you should put designer logos on each piece," Kate sputtered, trying to contain her giggles. Then calming down, sitting upright, she advised sternly, "Just no bubble-wrap, balloons, sharp or small objects, and nothing with toxic materials, okay?"

"Okay, nanny Poppins. God, I'm not stupid. I'll

wait until he's at least four to choke him with a balloon," Jesse said.

Then, pushing Pickles out of the way, ordering him to lie quiet, searching amongst the packing for the Allen key, Kate asked, "So, Josh didn't take your bailing-on Christmas too well, eh?"

"That's an understatement. 'Specially now that I'm not going to Corfu until after New Year's. So, I'm trying to make it up to him by doing lots of shifts at The Dep, but I think he actually hates me now. Wouldn't blame him if he did," Jesse said, rolling over on her tummy, her head resting in her hands. "I'd hate me, if I were him."

"I know I'd be really pissed if it were me. Why did you lie? Anyway, now you could just go for the four days. Maintain the status quo, keep everyone happy," Kate said, smoothing-out the instructions.

"Because I'm done with keeping everyone else happy. I know what would happen in Montreal; Miriam would drop some 'not so subtle' hints about our future plans, Sudhi would jump in, both feet in his mouth with, why aren't we getting married? My being 'a good Italian girl' means to him that my ovaries are in over-drive and just dying to seed all the clever little Patels he's always dreamed of, his own spawn being a source of everlasting chagrin."

"Well, when you put it that way..." Kate said,

turning the nuts on the frame, "still, parental issues aside, I think Josh is a catch, a really nice guy."

"Yes, St. Joshua is all I hear about now from friends and family, while I'm cast as Mary Magdalene or something," Jesse said, picking Antonio up from the jumper, "Uch, phew, stinky pants."

"Oh god yeah, get it away from me!" Kate screeched, holding her nose with one hand, swatting the air with the other, as Jesse laughed, wafting her baby brother's bulging bottom in the direction of her friend.

THE FIRST WEEK of December visited Toronto with a light snowfall and plunging temperatures. The ice was ready in Nathan Philip's Square for all the enthusiastic skaters, some on their lunch break from stuffy offices and sedentary jobs, some young people on exam break, some unsteady on their blades, not having practised Canada's favorite pastime for a whole year.

The day was heavily overcast, looking more like five o'clock than noon. The fairy lights above the rink twinkled while the speakers broadcast the iconic

Canadian Christmas song, Joni Mitchell's, *River*.

Frank stomped around, trying to keep warm, humming along quietly to the winsome lyrics, he regarded the graceful moves of some of the skaters with envy, wishing he had brought his speed skates, just to glide in and around the crowd, effortlessly swooping along to the music.

Finally, he decided to get a hot chocolate while he waited, when there was a light tap on his shoulder. Turning around, he saw Lidia. "Hi! I started to worry you wouldn't come," he said, smiling, leaning over for a kiss.

"Sorry, I know I'm a bit late," she said, giving him a peck on the cheek. "I had a morning meeting at the magazine, then went for a coffee with Shelton." Looking him over, she remarked, "You look good, Frank. I like the beard, very distinguished with the grey."

"Yeah, silver threads amongst the gold, as my mom used to say," Frank replied, stroking the side of his face.

"But in your case, copper," Lidia observed.

"Yes, in my case, copper. Grab that bench, and I'll get us some hot chocolate?"

"Oh, not for me, thanks, but you go ahead," she said, staking a claim on the seat.

"Ah! That's better, I was freezing," he said raising

the steaming cup for a second sip.

"When will you tell Nick and the guys you're back?" Lidia asked.

"Not sure, maybe later this week. I just wanted to see you… So, how's Antonio?"

"Not much changed since the last picture I sent, chubby, precocious, and a nightmare since teething, his bottom two finally broke through. Now he likes to bite, everything, including me. Come over to see him?"

"Maybe. You know he looks –

"Just like his father's son," Lidia said firmly.

"Right, like his father's son," Frank said with a sigh. "Listen, Lidia, I have some important news. But first, I need to tell you that I'm very sorry," Frank said staring into his cup.

"Sorry? You mean about us?" Lidia turned towards him, needing to see his eyes.

"Yes. I never should've taken it that far," Frank said, shaking his head.

"I had something to do with it too, you know."

"But you trusted me, my motives in asking for your help with the book, which okay, I needed, while knowing I really wanted much more from you than that," Frank said, his voice breaking-up, looking away, "Lidia…I love you."

Then looking back at her, "Please, did you? Do you?"

Lidia exhaled loudly, shrugged, and replied, "Oh Frank, I just needed, *something*...of my own, I, I just..."

He cut-in, coldly reciting his plans, "I've quit the parish and the priesthood, and will serve as a brother at St. Benet's monastery, in Oxford. I'm reading Theology there, get my doctorate, then teach. I leave for England next week," he raised the cup to his lips, drained it quickly, crushed it in his hand, then continued, "I won't be here for Christmas, nor for Paul's wedding...Lidia, I'm just so tired of explaining myself to everyone."

"I understand." Then reflecting for a moment, she said, "I think that doing the doctorate will suit you better. You're a scholar, not a parish priest. I think you'll follow Northrop Frye, publish some enlightened exegesis, make us all proud," she smiled at him, turning-up his collar.

"Well, I can but try," he promised. Then reaching out to grasp her arm, "Lidia, don't you ever want to know –

"Know what? I believe I know all I need to about us, my family, and how to protect them. And that belief protects them," she said.

"Of course, it does. But knowledge and belief are two different things," Frank pointed-out, standing.

Looking up at him, Lidia said, "I never thanked

you, I should have."

"For what?"

"For helping me in my hour of need, I remember the fear and shame, you helped me find my way past it to a new beginning. Now, who will help you?"

"Why, God, of course."

"Of course, 'belief'," Lidia said, with a little smile.

"Yes, even though I've let God down."

"Frank, you let yourself," she countered, then with quiet passion whispered, "We've, let ourselves, down."

He lowered his eyes, then pulled a bag from his pocket. "I've brought you a copy of our book, it's done well," he said, hand trembling, offering now what seemed pathetic.

"Thanks," she replied, tucking it into her valise. "Sorry, but I have to run. Maybe we can talk again before you go?" Lidia pulled her toque over her ears, planted a farewell kiss on his cheek, and turned away, following the crowd out of their dreamy respite, into cold, mundane, reality.

Frank sat down, feeling stupid, ineffectual, with his clumsy declaration of love. Lighting a cigarette, he watched intently as a lone skater cut figures in the ice, and wished he could take it all back, skate away, fast, and free, down a long, frozen river.

Chapter Six

FELIZ NAVIDAD

CHRISTMAS CHAOS WAS in full swing at Javi's house, as he and Lucinda prepared for their first Christmas party. They rose early, no time for more than coffee, so to fortify themselves in the endeavor, they munched on a couple of pan dulce al por mayor, mini versions of panettone, and drank a few goblets of spiced-rum eggnog, which Javi, considering it had eggs, counted as brunch.

"And now for the final touch," Javi said from the step ladder, reaching-up to put the Angel in her triumphant place at the top of their Christmas tree.

"No dad, she's not facing directly out. To the left, okay. Oh no, now she's crooked. Pull her up, dad. No, up! That's it. Now, turn a smidge to the right… perfect," Lucinda exclaimed.

"What a lot of fuss to just shove a Christmas tree up an angel's butt,' Javi said, laughing, climbing down from the ladder.

"Don't be gross, dad," Lucinda frowned.

"Oh, lighten-up Lucy and drink some more egg-nog," he laughed. Then turning to the pile of boxes on the living room floor, "Now, for my surprise."

He lifted a carved wooden chest from a big packing box. Brushing away the excelsior, he offered it to his daughter, helping her to place it carefully on the long, railroad-cart coffee table.

She knelt beside it, opened the heavy lid and reached inside, "Oh wow, this is beautiful, dad," she exclaimed holding-up an intricately carved, polychrome figure of Melchior, one of the 'Three Wise Men', with his long white beard and golden robes. "Oh and here's Balthazar, so grand, with his jewelled turban, and look, his gift of myrrh's in a little enamelled brass urn, its lid even opens!" she said, delighted.

"It was hand-carved in Naples around 1890. That's where the best nativities are made. I'm afraid the other two Wise Men lost their original gifts ages ago, so we substituted two little ring boxes. You know this crèche was from your abue Imelda's family."

"I wish I had known her," Lucinda said thoughtfully, picking-up a figure of the Christ child.

"I do too. She was a very special woman, always on the go, a force of nature, ran dad's business when he was away, ran the family, was a brilliant cook and hostess. She always had time for people. Everyone loved Imelda," he said smiling at the memory.

"But after the stroke, before you were born, she was barely hanging-on to life, not living it, wheelchair bound, struggling to speak, her death was a kindness to her dignity. I never want to linger that way," Javi said, looking down, shaking his head.

"Oh dad, that won't happen!"

"No… of course not. Anyway, does it please you, princess?" Javi said, smiling.

"Oh yes. So, is it mine now?"

"Of course, just be careful with it, okay," he said, as his daughter gave him a loud kiss on the cheek.

"Okay," she agreed, standing up, looking around the room. "Now, where will we put it?"

"Under the tree, that's where they always go."

"No dad, it'll be too crammed with all the presents. I want to put this in a prominent place, and give it some nice lighting," Lucinda countered, pulling-out the sofa table.

"Where are you taking that?"

"To the mirror-wall of the foyer, we'll put the nativity on it, so people can admire it when they arrive."

"Good idea," Javi agreed, "I think we have a string of LED lights for the manger shed somewhere. In the meantime, let's get this table out there, then you set it all up, 'cause I have a suckling pig to tend to."

WHILE LUCINDA WAS occupied with the nativity, fussing over the placements of the rest of the festive décor, and cleaning-up the living room, in the kitchen, Javi went over his eclectic Christmas party menu.

Opening one door of the glass front fridge, he recited, checking-off, "Starters: three kinds of pionono: ham, crab and smoked salmon. Cold collation of shrimp mousse, smoked trout and duck pate. Warm offering: brandade de morue and escalivada. Two wheels of baked brie encroute, one of garlic and rosemary, one of olive tapenade…and a partridge in a pear tree."

"Now, desserts," he continued, opening the opposite door, "one Bailey's crème caramel with chocolate espresso beans, one mango-raspberry trifle, and assorted baba rhum baby cakes. Good, okay now let's see how my little piggy's doing." Javi lifted the handles on the heavy pan and placed it on the counter, then tipped the pan into a bowl in the large apron sink, pouring-off the bourbon, spice and brown sugar brine, to reduce for the glaze. He left it, tilted in the sink to drain completely while he prepared the rub.

Javi picked-up the laminated page containing his mother's hand-written recipe for suckling pig, and holding it arm's length in front of him, squinting, he read the next steps in the instructions:

In a small processor, combine 6 tablespoons of peri-peri spice mix and 2 tablespoons cumin, 2 tablespoons mustard seed, 2 tablespoons dried fennel seeds, 4 tablespoons of coarse fresh black pepper and 3 tablespoons kosher salt, 10 garlic cloves, several handfuls of each of fresh chopped parsley and a bunch of fresh thyme. Process on high, adding 5 tablespoons apple cider vinegar and enough sunflower oil to make a paste.

Scald the pig's skin with boiling water from the kettle. Dry the pig well, then stuff the belly full of the chorizo sausage mixture and sew-up with cotton string.

With sharp box-cutter, make little slashes all over the pig, not deeper than the fat layer, then rub-in paste, getting as much in as possible. Sprinkle the skin lightly with baking powder, so the crackling will bubble and crisp, but not be too hard. Place a wooden block in the mouth to keep it open for the apple later.

Place in preheated 400 convection oven 25

minutes, then turn down heat to 350 and roast for 90 minutes per pound, baste every half hour or so.

At last 60 minutes of roasting, drain off enough pan juice to cover bottom of a roasting pan. Place in fridge to solidify fat. Then, remove excess fat, leaving just a little. Add vegetables, crab apples, season with salt and pepper, turning over everything to coat in juice. Add several sprigs of rosemary, cover, and roast at 375 for 45 minutes, uncover and complete cooking until tender, turning over to brown well.

Okay, mamacita, got it, Javi thought as he pulled out the spice mixes and began preparing the garlic and fresh herbs. While he worked, he sang his own version to the carol streaming from the speakers, "Good King Wencsel's Ass looked-out on the feast of Stephen."

"Dad, do you have to be so crude? It's a Christmas carol, not a bar song," Lucinda shouted.

"What? Since when are you so pious? I'll have you know that creative version is what got Paul and me suspended for a week, giving us more time to goof around and more chance to fail our exams. And we did, some of them anyway. "Can't win 'em all," or so I tried to convince your abue, who wasn't buying it."

"You're supposed to be setting a good example

for me, if I end-up a juvenile delinquent, it's gonna be your fault," she laughed.

"End-up? You've already crossed that line, daughter," Javi retorted. "Now go to the terrace, rearrange the lights, and ornaments we so carefully placed on the boxwoods yesterday, fluff-up some snowflakes, they look like they're flagging. But before you do, pour me a glass of that prosecco in the fridge, my hands are mucky."

Lucinda placed a flute at her father's elbow, saying, "I just want everything to be special, to be perfect my first Christmas party, in my new home," her smile puckering the dimples at the corners of her mouth, her deep violet, half-moon eyes, excited.

"I know. Charlotte and the rest of your friends are coming, right? I hope they can stay for the pig roast."

"They've all r.s.v.p.'d and will definitely stay for the roast, if only because they have to face the dry family turkey Christmas day."

"Good, they'll have a fun time, and I'll behave, I promise," Javi said, taking a sip of wine.

"Thanks, dad…um, I have a favor to ask," she said leaning against the island, "Chris just sent me a Christmas greeting – please don't get mad. I want to invite him over tonight, he'll probably only stay for a drink. I don't see why we can't just be friends. Please dad."

"Well, it's Christmas, goodwill towards men and all that. Okay, just so long as he doesn't try anything with you, got it?" Javi said, sternly.

"Oh, he won't. You scared him well-off last time," Lucinda said, brightening.

"Good, I'm getting the hang of this 'daddy gig', don't you think?" he said grinning, rinsing his hands in the sink.

"Yep, I think this exam is one you pass," Lucinda replied, pulling on a sweater, heading for the terrace.

"Right, now let's see if I can't make this two out of two, eh mamacita. I hope my sewing skills are up to your standard," he mumbled to himself, searching the kitchen drawers for the box-cutter, cotton string and the reading glasses he was usually too vain to wear.

THE PIG WAS sewn-up and roasting away in the oven, when Javi's entry system buzzed for the third time since noon.

"I'll get it," Lucinda yelled, rushing to the console.

"Who is it?" Javi asked.

"It's Nick," she said, opening the door to greet him. "Hi! Gimme your coat, and just go on through.

Dad and Becky are in the kitchen."

Nick made his way around the people from the table service rentals setting-up the bar, and three round pedestal tables in the entertainment area, the two loveseats and occasional chairs rearranged for the purpose.

"Buon Natale, compare!" Javi saluted his friend.

"Feliz Navidad!" Nick exclaimed, in return.

Becky, at the kitchen table, arranging six tall vases of white and red amaryllis, chimed-in with her own Christmas greeting.

Javi handed Nick a glass of prosecco, and asked "What's up?"

"Just wanted to see if you needed any help with the pig roast."

"Uh-huh, and maybe cop a look at Imelda's world-famous recipe?" Javi said, grabbing the laminated sheets, holding them behind his back.

"What 'world famous'? C'mon, it's good, but 'world famous' is stretching it, no disrespect," Nick said taking a sip of wine.

"None taken, but since my dear departed mamacita's recipe's not that great, guess you don't want it anyway. You can do something much better, I expect," Javi said smirking.

"Okay, hands-up. Yes, I'm here for the recipe. It was the best roast pork I've ever had. Like Scrooge, it haunts me, the ghosts of pig roasts past, it stalks my taste buds, invades my every porcine culinary fantasy."

"Yeah, and like Scrooge, you're just as stingy. You've never shared your entire Bolognese recipe, you've always held something back, you snuck-in something even when we made it together, I know 'cause it never tastes the same when I make it."

"Okay, I'll give it to you in the New Year. So, *per favore*, for Christmas? You know Imelda would've wanted me to have it," he implored.

"If Imelda wanted you to have it, she would've given it to you. I'm keeping this in trust for my daughter," Javi declared, shoving it into a nearby drawer.

"Since when is Lucinda interested in cooking?" Nick asked.

"What? I'm a good cook, aren't I dad?" Lucinda defended herself from the hallway.

Nick countered quickly with, "Yes, I hear your 'Toasted Tequila Forman' is quite a hit!"

"Oh, leave the kid alone, Nick. She may be a bit reckless, but at least she tries," Becky remonstrated, carrying a vase to one of the tables, "now, since you're here to help, you can take those two vases to the other tables."

Nick did as he was told, then returned to take a

perch at the kitchen island. As he held out his glass for a refill, Becky said, "Oh no, you haven't earned it yet, come help me with the poinsettia's, they're in the hallway, follow me and I'll show you where they go."

Nick slid off the stool with a groan, reluctantly following her command.

SANTA BABY

AFTER NICK FINISHED floral duty, had a second glass of bubbly and was shooed-off home, the tables were done and Javi could hear Lucinda's shower running, he took Becky's left hand in his, as they sat together on the couch.

"Well, at last a little time to ourselves," Javi said with a sigh, then reaching into his breast pocket, he pulled-out a large Princess-cut diamond ring, slid it onto Becky's third finger and said, holding it up to admire, "Yes, that's perfect. What d'ya think Beck?"

"I think it's perfect too," she said quietly, smiling.

"Good, 'cause I've misplaced the box, so you'll just have to wear it anyway," Javi said, smiling back at her.

"I guess," she said, turning to kiss him. As they embraced with passion, Becky said, "So, 'Santa baby', since the roast doesn't need basting for at least thirty minutes, shall we have a little rest in the bedroom?"

"Oh yes, Mrs. Claus, Santa definitely needs a little rest," Javi agreed, grinning widely.

JINGLE BELLS

THE CHRISTMAS EVE party was well under way and still guests were arriving, swelling the number of revellers to past twenty.

"Hi guys, Feliz Navidad!" Lucinda greeted her friends as they shuffled-in. "Just dump your coats in my room, dirty boots on the mats outside the door."

Then above the heads of the clutch of school friends, she saw Chris. Lucinda tried not to look too pleased, as she wasn't sure if he'd accepted her invitation, an offer she hoped seemed off-hand and casual, to 'drop-by, if you're in the neighborhood'.

He kissed her on both cheeks and handed her a bottle of Dom Perignon.

"Wow, thanks Chris, and it's chilled too. My dad will be pleased, especially if we run low," she said, thinking, *that was a stupid comment, stop blathering idiot, and show him in.*

"My dad won't be pleased, seeing as it's from his

cellar," he laughed, "I thought we could find a quiet spot somewhere, and enjoy it together." Chris leaned-in for a proper kiss.

Lucinda pulled-back reluctantly, "Better not, my dad's got his eagle eye on you."

"Okay then, take my coat, and point me to the bar."

Not wanting to get way-laid by tedious introductions, Chris slid quickly past Lidia and Becky, who stood admiring the decorations.

"It all looks so lovely, Becky, and that blue spruce is gorgeous. The whole place, even the terrace sparkles, with all the lanterns, stars and fairy lights," Lidia mused.

"That's not the only thing that sparkles, girl-friend," Becky said, raising her left hand for Lidia to admire.

"Wow! Now that's some serious bling, needs sunglasses just to see it… So, you're finally engaged, about time too. Hm, could it be that Paul's recent nuptials gave you a nudge?" Lidia said, giving her friend a kiss and a hug.

"Well yes, that, and I thought I'd put him out of his misery, poor guy," Becky laughed.

"Oh right. And you're not a lucky woman?"

"Yes, I am… I hate to admit it, but after I left Paul, I had anxiety that sometimes froze me. I knew I had done the right thing, just not in the right way, I really regret that," she said, looking down at her ring. "You know, things are going so well now, it scares me."

"You're scared? Why?"

"Because deep down, I feel I don't deserve it. I keep thinking, in the back of my mind, what is this happiness going to cost?" Becky said, her eyes glistening.

"Don't ruin this for you and Javi. We've all done shameful things; all have guilty secrets. It doesn't mean we deserve to be punished on and on. Guilt does that to you, it's the whip hand that keeps on punishing," Lidia whispered.

"How would you know? You have a perfect life, solid marriage with a man you adore, that's something you can always count on," Becky said, taking a deep gulp of champagne.

"No one has a perfect life, not me, not anybody. And what we think we can count on…sometimes not even love… Sorry, I'll shut up now and get us more champagne. Ready for a refill?" Lidia said, putting a consoling arm around her friend.

"No, thanks. I'm good for now," Becky said quietly, turning to look-out at the pretty terrace lights piercing the darkness, the sparkling crystal snowflakes drifting down from the sky. She walked over to get a closer view, when, from a corner beyond the doors, she spied a plume of smoke, another, then another, then heard laughter and coughing.

Deciding to investigate, she stepped-out onto the terrace to find a group of young people huddled together, passing a joint and a bottle of champagne. There was Chris, tall, well-built, tousled blonde hair hanging over his blue, sleepy eyes, drawing deeply on a joint, then handing it to the boy next to him, Justin, Charlotte's older brother. Hearing the door open, Lucinda turned around, champagne bottle in hand, to face Becky.

"Oh, uh, I just came out to see how everyone was doing, right Charlotte?"

"Yeah, that's right, I was just coming in, I needed some fresh air," Charlotte replied, pulling her arms around her, making for the door, "c'mon Lucinda." They both exited hastily past Becky.

Chris coughed, and blew out some smoke, "Hey Becky, want to join us? Justin, offer the lady a toke," he said, looking her up and down, elbowing his friend, who extended the joint to Becky, who took it and stubbed it out.

"What did you do that for?" Chris said.

"I think you'd both better get inside and have some food," Becky said coldly.

"Okay, we're going...you know it's practically

legal. Anyway, it will be soon, and hey, it's Fair Trade organic!" Chris said in mock sincerity.

"Yeah, even the unbleached rolling paper is made from flax," Justin giggled, making Chris double-over laughing.

"Right, like I care," Becky smirked, waving them in. Closing the door behind them, she went in search of Lucinda, who found her first.

"Sorry Becky, you won't tell dad will you? Please! It would just spoil the party. I'll make sure they behave, okay?" Lucinda pleaded in a low voice.

"I won't tell him until after, maybe not at all…we'll see. I hope they're not driving."

"No, they took an Uber here…look, sorry but I've got to go see my other friends," she said, spying a waving hand from across the room.

Becky joined Lidia, Nick and Javi at the kitchen island, where Javi was pouring more champagne from his private stock. They were deep in conversation about Frank's decision to quit the priesthood.

"Well, I didn't see that coming, a sabbatical yes. I think he was heading for burn-out, but to pack it all in, that was a shock. And he never said anything to me, we usually confide in each other," Nick said chagrinned.

"I'm in the dark too, although we're not as close as he and Lidia, did he say anything to you about why he needed to run-off so quickly to the 'city of dreaming spires'? I mean he could've at least waited to celebrate a farewell Christmas with us," Javi said, topping-up Lidia's glass.

"Ah, not really, he just said, he's tired of explaining, I guess they put him through a bit of an inquisition in Rome over his decision," she said shrugging.

Becky looked at Lidia and said, "I know he's not much of a talker, but you and he were like brother and sister, kind of soul mates. I'm surprised he kept so much to himself. Anyway, how did he get a visa so quickly?"

"He was born in England, Liverpool, the family immigrated when he was a kid. And we weren't as close as that. Good friends, sure. Why shouldn't he keep such an important decision to himself, I mean from us, when he surely had lots of counsel in Rome. Like I said, he was just, 'all talked-out' about it," Lidia said, shaking her head and sighing.

"Sounds like depression to me," Javi added.

"Maybe," Nick replied, "but I think there's more to it than that. I sense he's keeping a secret, running away from something weighing heavily, hence the flight to Oxford. Anyway, I put him in touch with two of my friends there in Classics; they'll keep an eye on him. There's an Art History conference I might attend at Christ Church in February, I could touch base with him then," Nick said, opening the oven door, checking on the pig roast.

"Oh really? Well, you didn't tell me," Lidia said. "And I can see why Frank fled so quickly, with all this speculation and spying. Why don't you all just leave the poor man alone to live his life?" Lidia exclaimed, banging down her glass, heading towards the powder room.

"Sheesh, she certainly seems touchy about it," Javi said, getting a ladle to baste the roast.

"Hmm, I'd say protective," Becky replied thoughtfully, taking a deep drink of bubbly.

THE REST OF the festivities proceeded smoothly and merrily, the piece-de-resistance, the suckling pig, was paraded out to the banquet table by Javi and Nick, accompanied by revellers blowing plastic horns and cranking tin noisemakers. The beast was served-up in juicy, luscious, crackling portions, occupying the mouths of the hungry guests, the silence of satisfaction descending upon the room.

Nearing twelve o'clock, when everyone was satiated, the hosts gathered their guests on the terrace to countdown to midnight. They shouted-out wishes of love and hope to their city, to their absent friends, to the whole human world. They lit their Roman candles, from one to the other, held them high, sparkling like diamonds, against the darkness.

SHATTERED

CHRISTMAS MORNING IN the Ponti household was an unusually subdued affair. The family, still in pyjamas, after having opened their gifts, were gathered in the kitchen, awaiting the Christmas waffle breakfast, for the first time, cooked by Jesse.

Even the traditional Christmas tree was subdued, Lidia deciding against a floor-to-ceiling tree in favour of a mid-size potted specimen, perched atop the butlers' table, a post which removed its colorful brilliance from the curious reach of Antonio and Pickles.

She reasoned to Nick that they didn't want a replay of their daughter's first Christmas when most of their apprehensive dialogue began with "No, Jesse!". Did they want Antonio's first words to be "No, Antonio"? As it was, he and Pickles were huddled beneath the kitchen table, busily tangling-up ribbons, and ripping-up wrapping, while The

King's College Cambridge Singers were exalting in their moving rendition of 'Once in Royal David's City'.

Lidia was emailing pictures of Antonio and Pickles, grumpily wearing their elf hats askew, to Shelton and Clive on holiday in the Turks and Caicos. Jesse was preparing the batter for the waffles, as Nick blithely sipped his mimosa, humming along to the music, scanning the headlines in the New York Times when he stopped at a report of a drive-by shooting in New Orleans, "Drag Queen Cabaret Performer and Fan Gunned-down in Alley", beneath the headline were pictures of the victims, a young, white man, in drag as Cyndi Lauper, striking a selfie pose and laughing, alongside Lola, as Tina Turner, glamorous and proud.

The exuberant images were made grotesque by the brutal facts of the report beneath them that an unidentified, helmeted motorcyclist pulled-up in an alley beside the stage door of the Blue Angel Cabaret December 23rd, and fired-off a round from a semi-automatic silencer handgun into the crowd of autograph seekers. Several fans were wounded, the one, dressed as Cyndi Lauper, died in hospital, the performer, hit in the head, died where he fell. The police had no suspects.

Nick dropped his paper in disbelief, shaking

Lidia's arm, he shouted, "It's Lo! Lidia, it's Lola."

"What? Don't tell me she's got bad reviews," Lidia said, pulling Antonio up on her lap, who grabbed for the paper as Nick read out the report.

"I can't believe that! I just can't believe it," Lidia started to shake and cry.

Jesse rushed over to the table, saw the pictures and the horrific headline, "Oh my god," she put her hand to her mouth.

Lidia looked up at her distraught husband, and cried, "She never made it home, Nick. She'd never make it home now, to her mom…now she'll never make it home!"

Nick grabbed hold of her, and Jesse took Antonio.

When Lidia was calmer, he turned to a sobbing Jesse, "Someone has to tell Aldo."

"I'll do it dad, I promised to Skype him this morning," she said, wiping her tears with the back of her hand. Lidia put her arms up for Antonio.

"Are you sure?" Lidia said.

"Yes, mom. I'll be okay. In fact, I need to call him now," Jesse said checking the kitchen clock.

"I'll go with you," Nick said, rising as Jesse went to the den to make the call.

He stood behind her, hands on her shoulders, as she waited for Aldo to pick-up.

"Hey, Buon Natale, pussycat! Look what I just got," he held-up a publicity shot of Lola as Tina with a red lipstick lip-print above the greeting, "Merry Christmas to my Italian Stallion, love Tina". In the other hand he dangled a metal Statue of Liberty key-fob. "I wish I could've seen the show. She's coming here in June, so, if you're still here you'll have to share a bathroom. How's the weather there? It's good here, mild, around fourteen Celsius, sunny but too cold for –

"Nonno, please! I have some news, really bad news. Lo's been shot… she's dead nonno," Jesse lost control and began crying again.

"Shot? Shot where? Who? Who shot her?" Aldo shouted.

Nick took over, "She was shot in New Orleans, outside the theatre, we don't know who it was, they were on a motorcycle, helmet down, sprayed some shots, then just sped off," he recounted, still incredulous.

Aldo listened silently to the details of Lola's murder, his jaw clenched, the tendons in his neck straining, choking off his sobs. His grip tightened around the metal fob, biting into his palm. He turned his face away from the screen. There was nothing more to say.

Nick and Jesse returned to the kitchen to find

Lidia, tears streaming, re-reading the newspaper account. "We have to call them," she said to Nick, who passed her some tissues.

"Who?"

"Lo's family, we have to call them."

"We don't have their number do we? I mean his mom's number, we don't even know her name," Nick said, suddenly anxious.

"They must have his cell phone, we can call that, maybe they'll pick-up. I need to talk to his mom; she needs to hear from us. Take Antonio, I'm going to try to call her now, and Nick, her name's Delphine Dupré," Lidia said, calling the number.

Lola's uncle Nate answered, Lidia explained who she was, and extended her condolence to the family, sobbing when she talked of Lola's mother and how she so looked forward to coming home for Christmas.

Meagre comfort is offering condolences for such a loss, but a gesture that must be made, nonetheless. He thanked her, told her where she could send flowers and said he'd be in touch later, regarding his nephew's personal effects.

That night, as he lay in bed beside an emotionally exhausted Lidia, Nick couldn't stop the anger rising within him, replacing disbelief and sadness. He was indignant at the cruelty of Lola's death; that with one craven bullet, she'd never get to be who she wanted to be. Her dreams shattered, her mother's privacy, shattered. All of it exposed in the papers, and what little remained of their friend, lay bare and shattered too, on a mortuary slab.

A WEEK LATER, Nick was in Lola's apartment ready to tape-up the last box to be sent to her mother, when Lidia came down to ask, "How are you doing? Are you okay?"

"Yeah, not too bad, sad...I hate doing this." Sweeping his arm across the room, Nick observed, "She didn't leave much here, mostly clothes, it's all going to Value Village. I'm sure they'll think it's quite a treasure trove. Do you want something? A momento? I'm sure no one would mind."

Lidia gently pulled-out a long silk scarf from the rack, it was a soft coral, with blue and yellow watercolor butterflies, fluttering along its luminous length. She held it up to her face and breathed-in deeply, exalting in the heady scents of jasmine and tobacco. So 'Lo', that it made her want to cry, but she stifled her tears in the soft comfort of the silk.

"Lo certainly loved her clothes," Nick said.

"Oh yes, lots of color. She used to say, 'Always

dress your best and not like the rest.' Lo had an original sense of style, flamboyant, but she could carry it off. I think she despaired of my muted tones," Lidia reflected, draping the scarf around her neck.

Nick picked-up a pair of sapphire sequined sling-backs from the closet, "There was nothing muted about Lo. And she loved fancy shoes, must've spent a fortune on them. Could give Imelda Marcos a run for her money," Nick said, with a wan smile.

Lidia took an envelope from her back pocket, "Nick, I've written a letter to Lo's mom, from all of us. I just wanted her to know how we felt about her son, how he was like family, and that he taught me her lullaby, for my son," Lidia started tearing-up.

"Oh cara, c'mon please, no more tears," Nick put his arm around her.

"I called her Darnell, in the letter, not Lola, do you think that's okay?"

"It's fine, you've done the right thing, that's the name she knew him by, the name she gave him, let's not take that away from her too," Nick said. "Here, I'll put it in his bible, okay? I'm sure she'll find it there."

"Can I?" Lidia put out her hand for the bible.

"Sure, you choose where you want," he said, handing it to Lidia. She turned the pages to the testament of Luke 15:11, to the account of The Lost Son, and gently placed the letter there.

DECEMBER 31ST, TORONTO'S streets and sidewalks were nearly impassable from the effects of a forty-eight-hour blizzard that choked the city. The roar of giant snowplows echoed down the main streets; parked cars caught in the storm were buried beneath an avalanche of snowbanks that made virtual half-pipes of sidewalks. Some enterprising citizens ditched walking and public transport for cross-country skis, the rest, struggled, slipped, and grumbled their way to their destinations. Most offices were closed, only a few brave retailers managed to open, mainly pharmacies and convenience stores.

Jesse stood at the counter of The Dep, ready to serve custom, as they were the only store open in the neighborhood, even though their shelves were starting to look pretty empty, as the storm that barreled across the Great Lakes stopped their supply chain.

"Well, what do you think, Jess?" Josh asked as he

opened their last box of bathroom tissue six-packs and stacked them on the shelf.

"I dunno, was this Miriam's idea?" she asked thoughtfully.

"Yes, I told you already, not that you were listening. Mom has a good solution to my cash-flow problem, turn this business into a co-op, sell shares, not in the bricks and mortar, but in the business of purveying artisan, sustainable products; every shareholder gets an annual dividend and a vote. It's not that different from crowd-funding, except the shareholders will hopefully be life-long stake-holders in growing this business."

"Where'd she get the idea from?"

"From the hippie co-ops in the sixties, but it actually goes back to the Industrial Revolution. It's a great idea, I don't have to go to the bank for a second mortgage at Mafia rates, but I'll have to rent out the apartment."

"Why? We just moved-in!"

"Because, Jesse, you just moved-out, and now that I've renovated it, I can rent that three-bedroom out for four times what Black Jack was paying. Jess, I need the cash-flow, understand?"

"I guess…it's just that it was such a nice place, my first home away from home," she said sighing, scratching-off the squares on a Super Bingo card.

"I know," Josh said, breaking-up the packing box, then carrying it to the back, passing Jesse, he asked, "Any luck?"

"Naw, not one number, or letter. This is no fun," Jesse said, looking down at the promo that promised endless jollity.

Returning from the back room, Josh put his arms around her waist and whispered in her ear, "Well, I can tell you what will be fun…closing the shop and cuddling upstairs with a box-set of Game of Thrones, season five, and a stack of frozen pizzas and chicken wings, just past their sell-by, what d'ya say?" he said, nibbling on her earlobe.

"Are you sure? No pressure?"

"No pressure, just sex," he laughed. "Look, I know you're going to Corfu in a couple of days, I now think that'll be good for you. But I'm glad you stuck around for New Year's; I didn't want you to leave on a sour note. We can be good together, Jess. You just have to sort yourself out. New year, new leaf; no lies, no assumptions, okay?"

"Okay! So, go turn that sign over."

JAVI'S LIVING ROOM was cluttered with packing boxes, as Lucinda and Kate, kneeling on the floor, marked their contents.

"Well, this should make next year's decorating easier, now we'll know where everything is," Lucinda said, satisfied with her new system.

"Yep, even listed the colors, your dad'll be impressed," Kate confirmed, standing up, snapping the cap back on her sharpie. "I always get sad taking down the decorations, all the magic gone, sleeping in a box 'til next year. And the tree looks so awkward, just standing there naked, waiting to be taken to the garbage."

"It's still in good shape though," Lucinda said, passing her hand along a still fresh and supple bow. "Maybe I could get a can of fake snow next week and make it look like a little corner of the forest, but inside."

"And birch logs stacked around, a few fake, feather birds, red berry clusters, big sugar pinecones in a basket and some moss balls. All of it'll be on sale too.

"Ha! There could be a trend in this; I mean why throw away a perfectly pretty tree, especially specimens like this giant blue spruce, looks like something out of a Currier and Ives print," Kate said, hands on hips appraising it. "How much is this worth?"

"I think Dad paid about three-fifty for it, delivered," Lucinda said.

"See, this is way too good, and expensive, to waste. I guess your dad's just going to pitch it when he and mom get back from Palm Beach. Oh well, maybe next year we can do a little winter vignette and post it on Pinterest, Instagram, and Twitter too, see if it gets likes and retweets."

"Sounds good, if we remember," Lucinda said, laughing.

"Okay now, let's get these boxes to the storage room," Kate declared, pushing-up her sleeves.

"Leave it Kate, Charlotte will help me with them later. You've done enough, want a beer?"

"I'll take a white wine if you have it," Kate said flopping down on the couch.

"Coming up," Lucinda said, putting two glasses, a half-bottle of chardonnay and a bowl of chips on a tray.

As Lucinda poured their drinks, Kate munched on the chips, "Mm salt and vinegar, my fave, but not too 'wine friendly'. That's okay though, I'll adjust," she said, taking her glass.

"Thanks for all your help," Lucinda said raising her glass.

"No problem, just doing my guardian duty. You do realize that you, me, and the twins, will be stepsisters?" Kate said taking a sip of wine.

"I know, how are Danielle and Monique taking it? I don't see them much, so I don't really know them, but they seem very nice."

"My sisters are good people, mostly we get along, and they're pretty easy-going, as long as both mom and dad are happy, and they leave us to live our own lives, too."

"It seems like everyone's in blended families now. I had a stepdad, Hans; he has a son, Andreas, in university in the States, but we only met once at the wedding. Now Hans and mom have split. Just before Christmas, he walked out, went back to Germany. Now, I'll have a stepmom, and I'm really glad that I'll have sisters. I hate being an only child," Lucinda said, taking another sip of wine.

"Ironically, that's exactly what I dreamed of being when the twins were younger, how I envied Jesse. But one thing's for sure, Lucinda, you won't be 'only or lonely' in our family. I mean it's huge! We have eighteen cousins on dad's side alone, and some of them are pretty good looking, but still, you know, cousins," Kate sighed.

"Ha! But not for me, only nominally, not really blood, right?"

"Right! So, Lucinda, you've hit the jackpot, cool sisters and handsome cousins too," Kate fist-bumped her future step-sister.

"And your mom's side?"

"Hmm. Very 'rustic', a bit inbred, but don't tell her I said that." Kate smirked, popping a chip in her mouth.

Lucinda laughed, "Your secret's safe with me. Speaking of which, I have a little secret of my own."

"And that is?" Kate asked warily, taking some more chips.

"Well, I told my dad I was going to stay over at Charlotte's for New Year's..." Lucinda's voice rose slightly, looking knowingly at Kate.

"Yes, that's what he told me, so I didn't need to stay here," Kate anticipated what was to come. "I have plans! I actually have a date with a hot chef, some steamed lobsters, and a cool martini or two at his place. Please don't tell me I need to cancel!" Kate slid down in the couch, holding her glass out for a refill.

"No, no! Of course not," Lucinda assured her, topping them both up. "I don't need baby-sitting, for god sakes, I'll be seventeen soon. Anyway, it's just that Charlotte's parents are having their own get together with the old cronies on their condo board, so it'll be boring and crowded there and since this place'll be empty, why not move our New Year's party here?"

"Why not, indeed?" Kate said, arching a brow. "And just who and how many are on the guest list? I'm warning you right now, it better not be that Chris, mom and Javi were strict on that."

"Oh no, no Chris, I haven't even heard from him since Christmas eve. This party is strictly hens, no roosters. Just Charlotte, and three other girls from the soccer team and one from the equestrian club. That's if they all show-up, the weather's pretty crummy, but most of them are only a few subway stops away, two live further out. I thought we could have a pyjama party, there's lot's of room here to crash, lots of food and Netflix, so we can have a blast," Lucinda said, taking a handful of chips.

"Uh-huh, so you're sure no Chris? Cross your heart and hope to get zits?"

"Cross my heart and hope to get zits, NO CHRIS!" Lucinda shouted, laughing.

"Really? Well, as your 'Guardian Angel', it's my duty to give you some life lessons: No drinking alcohol, but since I noticed you already are, on my watch, heed the following rules; never on an empty stomach, always down a big glass of milk before a party and never EVER, mix grain and grape, or hops and grape, or weed with any of the above, okay?"

"Okay, got it,"

"And never, ever let a guy put his tongue down your throat, his hands up your top or down your pants unless you really want him to, and one of you has a 'rubber', which is nearly the most important part," Kate said, draining her glass.

"What's 'a rubber'?"

"A condom, always protect yourself, never assume he will,"

"Okay."

"And always be firm and vocal about 'NO! No means, 'no', give the guy a break, he's not a mind reader, got it?'

"Got it."

"And even if you've got protection, don't swallow, it tastes like crap and it's still risky, STD wise."

"Oh, I would never…you know, swallow," Lucinda said bewildered, sticking her tongue out in disgust.

"And don't give it up in a drunken fumble on some rec room couch, back seat of a car, or worse, vertical, too uncomfortable, more fun for him than you. I'm assuming you're a virgin?"

"Yep."

"So, for your first time, wait for someone you actually have a relationship with, then be prepared to have it break-up later."

"Break-up, why?"

"Cause life's a buffet, Lucinda. Don't settle for the first thing that lands on your plate!"

Lucinda looked solemn and poured them both more wine.

"So, to recap, what have we learned so far?" Kate asked.

"Ah, drink lots of milk, don't mix drinks or weed, and don't have your back against a wall. Say, 'No!' and mean it. Anyway, you'll break-up later even if you don't mean it, and never swallow crap, it can have STDs, use a rubber and never load-up on the first dish on a buffet. Right?'

"Right, so my work here is done. Have a nice, safe party, and a Happy New Year… and don't forget, I'll be calling you throughout the evening, at random, so don't let it go to voice mail. I have a key, don't make me use it, I won't be pleased, okay?" she said, pulling-on her coat and boots.

"Okay thanks, and Happy New Year to you too…oh, and Kate, no offence, but you are so like your mother."

"Yeah, I've been told. Makes me wonder how dad and I get along so well…Ta-ta, and I'll be calling!" Kate said as she waved good-bye from the door.

JUST AFTER MIDNIGHT, and Kate's last, slightly giddy call; Lucinda, Charlotte, Tibby, Michaela and Kerry were winding down from the hilarity of a couple of rounds of Twister and binge-watching Buffy the Vampire Slayer. All five were feeling the effects of three bottles of chardonnay, spicy chicken wings, a big plate of nachos, and a bowl of hot-buttered popcorn.

Deciding to call it a night, they went to their assigned sleeping quarters, Tibby and Charlotte to Lucinda's room, Michaela and Kerry to the roll-out in the den and Lucinda to her dad's room, where, climbing into bed, she saw there was a text from Chris, who was in the lobby, could he come up?

She quickly pulled-on her yoga pants and a loose, low-cut jersey, brushed her hair and put on some mascara and lipstick. She just made it to the door as he knocked.

"Happy New Year, sweet little Lucy," he said, grabbing her close and kissing her long and hard. Then looking around, "Hey, where's the party? Justin said you were throwing a party."

Lucinda recovered herself, and said, "Well, I was, but my friends have all turned in for the night…light-weights."

"That's okay, you and I can have a better time on our own. Wadda ya say, sweetness?" he chucked her under the chin then sauntered over to the kitchen.

"Have you been drinking?" Lucinda, following him, asked.

"Sure, but not enough. How about you?"

"I've had some white wine," she shrugged.

"Oh, don't tell me all you have is that girly piss," he said, annoyed, opening the fridge door, then the freezer, "Ah-ha! There you are, my pretty, daddy's stash of Stoli!" he laughed triumphantly holding-up a frosted bottle of premium vodka.

"I don't think you should Chris, that's my dad's favorite, he'll notice it's down."

"Oh c'mon, it's New Year's Eve! Time to turn over a new leaf little girl, stop being afraid of 'daddy', grow-up, be a woman!" he challenged her. "Now go get us some shot glasses, and some matches." He flung his jacket onto the kitchen chair and pulled-out a pipe and a foil packet from his shirt pocket.

"What's that?" Lucinda asked as she set out the glasses and handed him a box of matches.

"It's a hash pipe, silly, and this," he said unfolding the packet, releasing an exotic, pungent aroma, "is the best Kashmiri hash there is, a veritable 'trip to the moon'… you ready for a trip to the moon?" he asked, passing it beneath her nose, as she inhaled its fragrance.

"Mm, sounds good to me," she said as he poured their shots, she followed his example, downing hers quickly, another, and then another, she was beginning to feel drunk.

"Now, draw-in deeply," he said passing her the pipe, after taking several tokes himself, and releasing them with dramatic satisfaction.

She did as she was told, and after the second draw, her head began to throb, she felt as if she was floating, her sight was blurred, and the room was moving around her. Then Chris's lips were on hers, then on her breasts, his hands around her waist, crouching, he pressed a cheek into her warm, smooth belly, she was aroused and yearning.

He rolled down her pants, grasped her buttocks, and hoisted her up on the counter. Opening his fly, he pushed her back on her elbows, and thrust hard into her, moaning, and it seemed to her, in another place, beyond recall.

Lucinda stiffened with pain and fear, sobbing as he thrust again, and again, and again, until suddenly, it was over. He let her down and leaned, head hung between his arms, facing the counter, breathing hard. Trembling, Lucinda picked-up her pants, and ran to the bathroom, where she crumbled to the floor, crying, praying none of her friends would wake-up and find her like this.

By the time she made it back to the kitchen, Chris, and the bottle of vodka, were gone. Everything was cold and quiet, her friends, thankfully still asleep. She curled-up on the couch, pushed her face into a pillow, stifling her cries, pulled the throw tightly around her, and passed-out until morning.

❧

CHRIS FLOPPED-DOWN ON the frat-house common-room couch, joining his two friends, Justin, and Pete.

"Wow, man you look rough," laughed Pete as he took a swig from Chris' vodka, passing it on to Justin.

"Yeah, where've you been? You slunk-off before I could win another hand from you, you pussy," Justin said.

"Uh, I've been up to some foolishness…with Lucinda, and I think I might be in trouble," he said, feeling depressingly sober, having just walked several blocks in from the cold.

"Oh? Is she legal now?" Pete asked.

"She's nearly seventeen," he said, annoyed at the inference.

"Oh, as old as that eh?' Justin chimed-in, snickering.

"Yeah, as old as that, and it turns out, still a virgin, or was, 'til tonight," he said sullenly, taking a swig from the bottle as it passed around.

"You idiot! What were you thinking?' Justin said, leaning over, concerned.

"I guess I was thinking how fucking beautiful she is, how gorgeous and big her tits are…" Chris trailed off.

"And how long her legs are, they go all the way up to…" Justin said, mocking him.

"Oh, shut the fuck up, you pedo," Chris yelled, angry.

"Pedo? I'm not the one playing around in the sandbox buddy. And if you ever lay a hand on my sister, you're a dead man," Justin snarled, grabbing his collar.

Stop it," Chris brushed his hand away, "I could be in real trouble here. I thought she knew the score, understood what was going to happen. I didn't know it was her first time. I mean, who's nearly seventeen and still a virgin?" he said his voice rising.

"I know, kids today, eh?" Pete said chuckling.

"It *was* consensual, right?" Justin asked warily.

"I thought so, she seemed into it. But now I'm not so sure, from her perspective, I mean. From mine, yeah, definitely consensual."

"So, she never said, 'no', or pushed you away?" Pete asked.

"Nope, just started to cry a bit, while I was, you know…look I was too far into it to stop, and I was stoned. Anyway, I finished quickly," Chris said, taking a deep swig of vodka.

"I think you watch too much porn, amigo," Pete added.

"Uh-huh, so Chris, it's more of a 'Wham, bam, thank-you, ma'am' situation, then?" Justin pondered.

"Guess so. It's just that she might not see it that way, she seemed pretty upset," he said shrugging.

"And what did you do to console her? Nothing I hope that's incriminating," asked Justin.

"I didn't say or do anything, I just ran out."

"Ooh, that's not good, running from the scene. Now you have a hurt, possibly very angry girl on your hands," Justin said.

"Oh yeah, 'hell hath no fury', Chris," Pete warned.

"Shit! What do I do now?"

Justin thought about it for a minute, while Pete got up to use the john.

"First, were you protected, or unprotected?" Justin asked.

"Unprotected."

"Oh, this just gets better and better, now we have the possibility of pregnancy, assuming she's not on the pill."

"Don't know, I assumed she was, but now, I don't know," Chris said rubbing his eyes, trying to stay focussed.

Justin began to pace. "What I suggest you do is text her, an apologetic, yet non-committal statement. Something like, 'I'm sorry I left, I really wanted to talk, but thought you wanted to be alone… not sure why you were upset. Really sorry if I hurt you in some way, but please, let's talk, if you're up to it.' Got it?" he said, grabbing the bottle from Chris.

As Pete returned, overhearing Justin's advice, he added, "And send flowers, that'll cheer her up."

"What? I don't think this is a floral situation, asshole. I mean do you really think FTD makes an 'Oops! Sorry I popped your cherry' bouquet?"

"Alright, I just know my mom likes it when she gets some," Pete said, laughing.

Justin looked over at Chris, who was nodding asleep, and shook him. "Text her now, so you can get a grip on the situation before it gets out of hand, understand?"

"Yeah, yeah, got it. Just lemme go to the can, splash some cold water on my face, then I'm on it," he said, stumbling off toward the bathroom.

BY ELEVEN O'CLOCK, New Year's Day, Lucinda's guests had dressed and quietly snuck out, heading to their parental homes, hot showers, and celebratory lunches, leaving their unresponsive hostess to 'sleep it off' on the couch.

Shortly thereafter, Kate let herself in, to check that all was in order, gather Lucinda to take over to her dad's New Year's luncheon and mooch a few bottles of wine. Walking into the kitchen, she waved a hand in front of her nose, exclaiming, "God! It smells like an opium den in here!' then shouted, "Hey! Lucinda, wakey-wakey!"

She looked-in to her bedroom, the den and the master suite, to find only rumpled bedding and general chaos. Then, hearing some groaning coming from the living room, Kate turned quickly, went over to the couch, where Lucinda struggled to sit upright.

"Wow, looks like you've been partying all week. Tsk, tsk," she admonished playfully, wagging a finger at her. When she failed to smile, Kate worried, "Hey, what's up? Are you sick?" she felt her forehead and checked beneath her jaw for swelling. "You really do look awful."

Lucinda began to cry and pulled the throw over her face, "Don't look at me, leave me be, please, just go away."

Kate put her arm around her and gently pulled

the cover from her face, "Hey now, what's the matter? Did you have a fight with your friends?"

"No, no fights…"

"What then? Oh, you're really shaking, should I call a Home Service Doctor?"

"No! Please, no doctor. I'm not sick, just upset, with Chris," Lucinda said, looking-up at Kate timidly, expecting a rebuke.

"Chris? Shit, don't tell me he was here! I trusted you! You played me,"

Kate said angrily, getting up.

"No, please Kate, I didn't. He just showed-up, after midnight, everyone was asleep, and I was going to bed too."

"So, you just had to let him in? That guy's trouble with a capital T. I don't like him, neither does your dad, or my mom. So, what did he do? And you better tell me the truth," she said sitting back down beside Lucinda.

"He brought some hash; I've never had hash before. It was really strong, and the room was spinning, and he was all over me, he pulled my pants…" Lucinda began to cry uncontrollably and couldn't continue.

"Oh my god, did he rape you? Did he force himself on you? Lucinda, you have to tell me," Kate took her in her arms to quiet her down. Then said softly,

"Try to stop crying for a minute, and speak to me. I want to help you, but I have to know what happened, okay?"

When Lucinda's torrent of tears finally trickled into little sobs, she tried to relate her story, "He pulled my pants off, put me on the counter, then he started. It hurt, it scared me, I started to cry a little, and then, he finished. It was like I wasn't even there!

"He just used me like a thing, to jack-off in, I hate him!" Lucinda's eyes lit-up with anger, her voice rose, "I hate his pigging guts! I never want to see him again, ever!"

"Okay, okay, you don't ever have to see him again. But I need to know if he forced you. Lucinda, look at me," Kate said, putting her hand beneath her chin, "Did he force you?"

"I, I'm not sure. I mean, I don't know, it was so fast. It's not the way I thought it would be. I didn't push him away, I was too scared. I guess, at first, I wanted to let him do it, for him to love me, like I loved him, but not like that. He treated me like shit, he didn't even try to make it up when he saw I was upset. I ran away to the bathroom, then he left, just like that, like he was through, had no more use for me."

"Did he use a condom?"

"No."

"Well, has he tried to contact you since? Where's your phone?"

"Over there, on the counter," she gestured towards the kitchen.

Kate picked it up, looks like you've got a text from him, early this morning, around three. Here, have a look," she handed Lucinda her phone.

"Oh, no way!" Lucinda shouted.

"What? What'd he say?"

"That he didn't know why I was so upset, but he's sorry anyway, and wants to meet with me," she said, in a mocking whiny voice. "No fucking way am I ever being in the same room, or even talk to him again, ever!" she deleted the message and threw the phone on the coffee table.

"You should talk to him; I'll be there to support you. It'll clear the air, hear his side of it, perhaps he ran out because he was as stoned and as scared as you were?"

"Scared alright, probably scared about me telling my dad. As usual, he's only thinking about himself, Kate,"

"Well maybe later when you feel better. Anyway, he's not my priority right now, you are," she said texting Paul.

"Who're you texting?" Lucinda asked warily.

"My dad, he's having a family New Year's luncheon at Ramona's, I was supposed to get you and some wine and go over. He and Ramona are dry these days, but I guess the twins will just have to go it sober.

"I'm staying here with you. I just said you've come down with a nasty bug, and I shouldn't leave you alone. So, you get into a nice hot bath, I'll make us some breakfast, and then I need to find a pharmacy that's open,"

"A pharmacy? Why?"

"Because you need a 'morning after' pill."

THREE WEEKS LATER, Kate and Lucinda were having pastries and coffee at La Sem Patisserie on St. Clair. They had just finished their cannoli and cappuccino when Lucinda asked for the bill and put a little ribboned packet in front of Kate.

"Oh, what's this?" she said, unwrapping it, to find a crystal pin.

"It's an Angel pin, I got it to thank-you for being my 'Guardian Angel'," she said, smiling.

"It's so pretty! I love it," Kate said, pinning it to her sweater, "Here, since it's coming up to your seventeenth birthday, I got you something too," she said, reaching into her bag for a paperback.

Lucinda turned over the cover, and read aloud, 'One of the most important and influential books written in the past half-century, Robert M. Pirsig's, *Zen and the Art of Motorcycle Maintenance*, is an unforgettable saga of a summer motorcycle trip across America's Northwest, undertaken by a father and his young son'. She looked at Kate, puzzled.

"It's regarded as the book that transformed a generation. It was first published in the early seventies. My dad read it when he was at a turning point in his youth, then, when I turned sixteen and was being a real pain in the butt, angry at everyone, but really with myself, he gave it to me. I've read it at least three times. It's transformative, it grows with you in its wisdom about how to live a better life, and you, if you take it to heart, grow with it. The motor-cycle journey is just a metaphor, as I'm sure you guessed. It's got a lot of psychological references in it, which you won't understand yet, but just stick with it, and you'll take from this first reading, what you need to lead your best life now. Okay?" Kate smiled at her reassuringly.

"Okay. But I do think I've already sorted some of that out for myself. I don't care anymore what losers like Chris think of me. I only care what I think of me, and I told him so." Lucinda grinned.

"So, you finally agreed to talk to him?"

"Yep, I let him call to apologize, I really wanted to stay calm and collected, like I didn't care. But I lost it, I let loose, all my anger, I just poured it out on him, where it belonged. I felt better; but then, I felt sorry," she said, putting down change for the tip.

"What? You're sorry? What for? Like you said, he's a loser."

"Yes, but a really down-and-out, loser. He failed his exams, so law school expelled him, he blew his bursary on partying, drugs and drinking, so he's had to move back with his parents, they'll only let him stay as long as he's working and in counselling."

"And you believe him, about the counselling, I mean,"

"Maybe." Lucinda shrugged. "It's not my problem. He's caused me a lot of pain, which I'm over, but I don't think I can forgive him yet," she said, putting her gift in her purse. "I'm going to Mendoza for March break; my mom's having a tough time herself, I want to be there for her. And I'm kind of missing home and my family, my uncles are getting older, and I want to spend some time with them too," she said, looking off into the distance.

"I guess the warm weather and sunshine won't hurt either, after this miserable Canadian winter," Kate said, putting on her coat.

"Oh yeah, it'll be so nice to get out of the cold."

NICK HAD TWO days left before second term convened at the college, and since Lidia and Antonio were recovering from colds, Lidia charged Nick with an errand to St. Edward's rectory, to fetch a box of promotional copies of their cookbook Frank had left for her.

Father Ambrose, Frank's replacement, was out, but left a note on the door to go to the church and see Mrs. McNamara, the cleaner, she'd get it for him. Finding the church empty, he followed the front passage to the meeting room, from where he heard voices, and Frank's name mentioned. Curious, he stopped just outside the entrance, where Mrs. McNamara, and the caretaker, were deep in conversation over tea and biscuits.

"Well, I for one, miss Father Frank. He was always there for us parishioners, visited mom all the time in the home, then nearly every day for my brother, at the hospice, towards the end," caretaker Graham said, dipping his Digestive into his tea.

"Oh yes, he was there for his flock alright, too much so, as far as I'm concerned. That was his problem," Mrs. McNamara replied, pouring herself another cup.

"You mean why he left the parish?"

"Left? More like kicked-out."

"What?" Graham exclaimed, putting down his mug before taking a sip.

"Oh c'mon, don't be so daft, why d'ya think he was hauled off to Rome…to answer for his wanton ways!"

"What do you mean, woman?"

"Woman is at the heart of the matter, a blonde, blue-eyed woman, meant to be a devout Catholic, 'helping' him with that book. They were always at it at the rectory, every time she was to come, he was always for letting me go early, one Friday he practically threw me out the door. I got half-way to the bus stop, when I realized I'd left my phone in the kitchen," she said, pausing to take a sip of tea.

"And?… c'mon Mary Margaret, don't kill us with suspense."

"And I let myself in, then what do I see through the crack between the living room doors, those pocket doors never closed proper, even though 'father all thumbs' tried to fix them. Anyway, what do I see, but those two in a clinch!"

"No!" Graham's eyes widened, then he thought, "Perhaps he was just, you know, consoling her?"

"Oh, is that what you'd call it? Well, they were too familiar. On the few occasions I'd still be there, finishing-up, he was always touching her, putting his hand on the back of her neck, or the small of her back, or rubbing her arm, it was altogether too familiar for my liking."

"So what? A little cuddle, inappropriate, but not really enough to defrock the man, surely."

"Oh no, there's more to it than that, Graham. Well before he left, who shows-up with a swollen belly? On two occasions, once in the rectory and once for confession, much needed, no doubt," she said indignantly.

"No!"

"Oh yes," she nodded with knowing satisfaction.

"Mary Margaret, you can't know it's his for sure, the woman may be married, could be her husband's."

"Alright Graham, it could be, and it could've just been the fairies, or the baby 'could've' just been found in that cabbage patch he always grew," she scoffed.

"Hmm," Graham said.

"Any road, I never trusted him, far too handsome for a priest,"

"Oh, Mary Margaret," Graham sighed.

Nick turned to walk away, hesitated, then

knocked lightly on the doorjamb instead.

"Yes, dear?" Mrs. McNamara said, looking up from her tea.

"I'm Nick Ponti, I'm here to collect some books."

"DID YOU GET them?" Lidia shouted from the kitchen, hearing Nick in the front hall.

"Yep," he said, putting down the box, hanging-up his coat, as Pickles and an exuberant Antonio in his walker, came scrambling down the hallway to greet him.

"Hey, watch it little man, there's a speed limit here!" he said, smiling.

Lidia was following close behind. "Guess what he's been up to today."

"Oh, another surprise," Nick exhaled deeply, "So, what now?"

Lidia bent down and half-whispered in Antonio's ear, he gurgled, pointed a finger at Nick and shouted, "Da! Da!"

Nick looked unimpressed.

"His first words, Nick! He's saying Daddy!"

"How'd you know it's 'daddy'?"

"Because he's pointing at you, you idiot! And he just kept saying it earlier, when he was playing around with your slippers, he's saying daddy!" Lidia insisted, exasperated, now Nick had taken the joy out of her surprise.

"Da! Da!" Antonio shouted again, pointing at Nick, drooling, sticking his fingers in his mouth.

Nick picked him up from the walker, and held him close, "So you think I'm your daddy, eh?"

Antonio, affirmed with another 'Da! Da!" patting Nick's face with his fat, dimpled hand.

"Oh, is that so?" Nick gave him a kiss and said, "That's right, I'm your daddy and you, you little chubster," he pinched his cheek, "I guess that makes you, my sweet baby boy."

Putting his son back in the walker, turning it towards the kitchen, he exhorted, "Now go, little man, go!"

Nick and Lidia laughed, as Pickles jumped-up on Nick's pant legs. He rubbed him behind the ears, shooed him off and chased Antonio down the hall.

Lidia picked-up her box of books and followed. She set the box on the table and remarked, "Huh, this has been opened," as she dipped her hand in and took out the top copies.

"Opened? So what? What're you looking for?" Nick asked, opening the fridge.

"Nothing, it's just that these came directly from the publisher, all ten copies for my promotion, no need to open it. I just thought then, there must be a note from Frank."

"And is there?" Nick said, searching the crisper, getting an onion, some mushrooms, and thyme.

"No, just the packing slip," she sighed, tossing it aside, repacking the box.

"Likely Ambrose opened it by mistake. Anyway, does it really matter?"

"No, not really. Oh, before I forget, Jesse Skyped, thanks us for her birthday 'bursary'. Says Corfu is cool, rainy, and boring in the off-season, so she's using the money to tour some other islands, then visit Athens."

"That's nice," Nick said, measuring-out some rice.

"She's hooking-up with a high school friend who's a marine archaeologist in Crete; Tyler 'somebody', she worked with him on the Yearbook Committee."

"I almost envy her right now. How's she and Aldo? Is he behaving himself?"

"Seems so," Lidia said, handing Antonio his teething ring, "but she said he's quiet, and grumpy, since Lo's death. Said Voula's keeping an eye on him. You know she's back in the picture, full-time now?"

"So?"

"So nothing, it's just that I think she's using him

as a fall-back."

Nick, scrubbing the mushrooms, observed, "Aldo can take care of himself. He wouldn't have her back if it didn't suit him." He turned to look at her. "You're a lot like that too."

"What do you mean?"

"You take care of yourself, always arranging your life and the people in it to suit you," he said, turning back to his task.

"Doesn't everyone?" Lidia said, shrugging. "You're in a funny mood. What's up?" she asked, her eyes narrowing.

"Nothing, I'm just hungry and want to get on with this risotto. Pour us some wine?"

"Sure," she got up, reached for the carafe and two glasses from the sideboard. "I've checked the osso buco; it was done, so I basted it, then turned the oven off."

"Good," Nick said, taking a sip of his wine.

Lidia stood beside him, glass in hand, looking pensive. "I've been pondering Voula and her astrology. Dad acts the skeptic, but I'm not so sure she doesn't influence him with it.

"What do you think, Nick? Is it nonsense, or just possible that influences above determine our lives, as influences below? Here on earth?

"I mean, the circumstances of our birth, cultural,

temporal and geographic, shape our lives to a degree, so is it possible planetary influences do the same?" She took a few sips of wine, waiting for his response.

"Possible? Anything's possible. What's probable vexes me. Ultimately, it's probable that 'The fault, dear Brutus, is not in our stars, but in ourselves,'" Nick quoted from *Julius Caesar*, as he tore the skin from the onion.

"But how does Shakespeare square that with the prophecy of the soothsayer, 'Beware the Ides of March'? The prophecy was true, the treachery was real, Caesar *was* stabbed in the back!" Lidia said, triumphant.

"The answer to your question, dear Lidia, is that some of us are destined to be betrayed, and others are born traitors." His eyes teared, as he continued to chop the bulb, into pieces.

THE TRUTH AND EVERYTHING BUT

NICK'S FLIGHT TO the Oxford conference was surprisingly comfortable, as the seat next to him was empty, the train from Heathrow to Oxford, punctual, and the February weather, clement. All of which should've lightened Nick's mood. Instead, he sat brooding into his scotch in Marco Baldassare's book-stuffed, oak-panelled study. Baldassare was his old thesis supervisor, now Professor Emeritus of Renaissance Studies, and friend. Nick sat patiently across from him, while the professor riffled through a stack of papers on his desk.

"Damn and blast! Now, where did I put the stupid thing?" he cursed, searching for the program of speakers for the conference.

His wife, Claire, rushed in, hearing him bellowing from the hall. "What's wrong now? What've you misplaced? Not your will I hope," she chuckled.

"Why? You're not in it. I'm looking for the itinerary of speakers, and the whole damn program's folio," he said, his face reddening. "You've been tidying-up here again, haven't you woman!" He fixed her with a fierce stare.

"Don't be absurd, I never touch your awful papers, and neither does the housekeeper," she answered, unperturbed. "Nick, would you like me to freshen that, I think I'll pour myself one too," she said, taking his glass, heading for the drinks' cabinet.

"Ah! Here it is! Just where I knew it would be," Marco said, triumphantly waving the sheaf of papers in the air.

"Yes! What a surprise, in the file drawer, in a folder labelled 'conference'," Claire teased, looking up at him from the rim of her glass.

"Never mind that. Now, I've to get on the blower, try to reach Reese McLaren, see if I can bump him up to take Fennimore's place as first speaker. Reese's a windbag always goes well over-time, so there won't be a gap afterward.

"Then I'll slot you, young Nick, in at the end of day one, instead of at the top of day three, where I'll stick Fennimore. That is, if he ever gets that ridiculous old Aston Martin to run.

"Did I tell you he's stuck in the Midlands in that rattle trap? He thinks women admire him, the jackass. You should see him, top down, in his tweed cap, aviator sunglasses and precious driving gloves." The professor scowled in disgust.

"Well, I think he looks dashing," Claire said, grinning impishly.

"Oh, you would. You have such peculiar taste," he retorted, dialling McLaren's number.

"Explains my marrying you, I guess." Then turning to Nick, "How's Lidia and your new baby…Antonio, is it?"

"Yes, that's right. He's well, just cut his first teeth, uttered his first words. Lidia's well too, although itching to get back to work, I expect," Nick said glumly, taking another swig of scotch, before offering his phone to show her a picture of them together.

"Lovely…I'm so pleased for you both," she said admiring mother and child, "Oh and before I forget, I put a little present for Antonio in your room, so don't forget to pack it when you leave."

"Thanks Claire, that's very thoughtful of you."

"Oh, it's not much, just a small stuffed bear named Pooh and a book, 'The Magical Pop-up World of Winnie the Pooh', she recited, smiling, pleased with herself.

"Oh Pooh, and not Paddington? Paddington's the only bear I can bear," laughed Nick.

"Not me, I can't be doing with that simp, although my children favored him, must take after their father."

"I've got Antonio started on Freddy, which he loves."

"Well Freddy; all a young chap needs to know about getting along in the world, having adventures, being a poet, a philosopher and a bon vivant, he can learn from Freddy, the most erudite pig." Claire smiled, fondly remembering her children's nursery time.

Then turning to more mundane matters she said, "Now, I hope you don't mind, but we've invited a few of your old friends from Classics for dinner tomorrow. I trust you won't be too tired for a bit of company?"

"No, no, not at all, it'll be great to see them. I haven't much time during the conference, so it'll be a nice opportunity for a proper catch-up," Nick said, brightening.

"Good! I'll make your favorite, standing rib roast with Yorkshire puddings, asparagus with hollandaise, and crème brûlée to finish."

"You remembered, thank-you," he said, eyes lighting-up, licking his lips. "I can taste it all now, you made the highest, lightest Yorkshires and the velvetiest Hollandaise."

"Course I remembered. You were a lanky young man then, with a surprising appetite," she said, appraising his present girth.

"Yes, and you graciously invited me and various other hungry strays for your Sunday roast dinners," he said smiling fondly.

"Speaking of dinner, I'd better crack-on, see how Saadri's making-out in the kitchen. And don't let him drink too much, he'll only get bellicose," she advised, pointing at her husband.

Marco concluded his call, as Claire left the room. "Well, that's sorted," he said, rubbing his large, mottled hands together. "So, you're up to bat tomorrow, but not until the end, where it won't matter, as no one will be listening by that time, much less inclined to ask questions."

"Oh, thanks a lot Marco, that's reassuring," Nick said.

"Don't take it personally, young Nicholas, it's just that by then, everyone'll be ready to belly-up to the bar, not quiz you on…let's see," he referred to his program, "Ah yes, *'Goddesses, Mistresses, Maidens and Madonnas; Botticelli's Women'…* gripping stuff," he looked-up from his reading glasses and smiled.

"I thought so. Anyway, that's not really uppermost in my mind at the moment." Nick drained the last of his scotch.

"Oh, what else then, is churning your little grey cells?" Marco asked, rising to refresh his drink and pour Nick another, which he declined.

"A dilemma, a moral dilemma, one featuring a good friend of mine."

"I see, and is he the kind of person who likes burdening his friends with his problems?"

"No, not especially. But you could help me, help him."

"Then glad to be of service. I like a moral dilemma, a philosophical debate. So, of what does this dilemma consist?" Marco said, sitting back down at his desk, drink in hand, his attitude attentive.

Nick reflected for a moment, then said, "I suppose at the heart of the matter is the issue of truth.

How much truth do we need in our lives? To be able to live them peacefully, decently, I mean."

"At the risk of prying, I'll need a little more detail than that, like what's this truth about? Is your friend seeking it, or avoiding it? Holding it to cover it up, or is someone trying to conceal it from him? To spare his feelings perhaps?" Marco raised a querying eyebrow.

"He's not sure… There's no clarity as to whether or not there's truth to be revealed, or a truth being concealed. So, if he doesn't know, how can he be said to be avoiding it, when 'it' may not even exist, outside his imagination, of course," Nick responded with consternation.

The professor took a long draught of liquor, then dabbling his mouth with his fingers, replied, "The imagination is a cloudy mirror, what we imagine says as much about ourselves, our insecurities and fears as it does the chimera we perceive. As for 'The Truth', there isn't any one truth outside of observable, tangible facts.

"Out of these we create our own truths; the stories we tell ourselves about our lives, the play we cast, the roles we assign to ourselves and our fellows. Each in turn, with their varying 'truths', derived, ironically, from the same set of facts."

"What does that mean, Marco?" Nick scowled.

"Tell your friend, the sword of truth is double-edged; tell him to ask himself, "Will discovering the truth help me live my life with a better story, or a worse one?" If he decides, 'a better one', then I say, poke that hornets' nest, turn-over that mossy stone and expose the pestilence. But if the answer, is 'a worse one', then he should jog-on, leave well enough alone, and be happy with his life and the story he's created for it; a cotton wool to wrap around fragile happiness," Marco said, leaning back in his chair, satisfied with his explanation.

Just then, the dinner gong sounded, a quaint domestic custom the hostess always performed when they had guests. Nick was startled out of his sullen contemplation, and before rising to follow Marco to the dining room, asked, "But, what about morality? Surely truth plays a part in discerning what's right, from what's wrong?"

"Aristotle in his *Nichomachean Ethics* asserts, 'Happiness, living well, is the highest virtue.' So, should we pursue truth at the expense of our happiness; No!"

"Then, ignorance is bliss?"

"Well, if you must reduce it to a tired, but useful cliché: Yes! Ignorance, in matters of the heart, is bliss."

"I didn't say anything about 'matters of the

heart'," Nick protested.

"You didn't have to. Now let's go in to dinner, the aroma of Saadri's lamb curry, calls."

THE NEXT MORNING was an early and busy one for Nick, who helped Marco attend to the last-minute details and technological glitches that inevitably arose the first day of a conference. After his go-fer duties were done, he settled-in to listen to the lectures and presentations his colleagues in Renaissance Studies gave.

Some were enlightening, even stimulating, others tedious. His own offering, at the bottom of the bill, was well-received, and contrary to Marco's prediction, raised interest and provoked several questions from the mixed audience of academics and students. It was a packed hall, but sitting in the aisle near the back, he spied Frank.

He should've felt grateful that his once close friend had come to listen to him present his paper. Instead, he felt hostility and resentment upon seeing his stupid face grinning directly at him from amongst the crowd. Nick looked down, *God, do I really want to see him? Or is my ego just itching for confrontation?*

Either way, after his talk, he found himself huddled reluctantly in a corner, drink in hand, with Frank. And before he could make up his mind about how he felt, Marco jumped-in between them, both feet in his mouth, inviting Frank to dinner. An invitation he begged-off, despite Marco's hearty insistence.

After several banal exchanges, and congratulations to Nick on his work, Frank finished his drink, and there stood between them an awkward silence. Refusing a second beverage, Frank urged Nick to come to his rooms at St. Benet's Hall, before catching his flight home, then he made his excuses and bid a hasty retreat. Nick, not being able to find a reason to refuse, felt uneasy and unsure of whether or not he should actually fulfill his promise, and his mission.

THE NEXT THREE days of the conference proceeded quickly for Nick, filled as it was with meetings and meals with other foreign delegates whose work interested him, and liaising with his opposite numbers in Renaissance studies at Oxford. He received a few chatty emails from Lidia, to which he gave terse replies, not feeling very communicative or homesick.

Then, on the last day, she sent a very sad one telling him of Ramona's miscarriage. He called Paul, expressed his condolences to them both, promising they'd get together when he got back.

On the third evening, the second last day of his trip, he and his hosts went to a performance of *Othello* at the Oxford Playhouse. Before the show, Nick took them to dine at The Randolph, where the renowned roast halibut did not disappoint, and so all were in an amiable, and sanguine mood. The production was good, the seats well-situated and comfortable.

When Act V opened, the expectation of the audience was high. But as the scene progressed to when Othello enters the bedchamber, confronts Desdemona with her adultery, and she pleads with him for her life, Nick broke-out in a cold sweat and began to feel anxious.

He gripped the arm-rests tightly as Othello started to smother his wife, then turning on her again, to finish the job, Nick muttered "*No*," then blurted out louder, "*No*". People shushed, and Claire put her hand over his, regarding him with concern. He squeezed his eyes closed until the blood in his temples pounded. He realized he couldn't go on this way with Lidia, the burning devil of suspicion and jealousy between them day and night. It was then he made-up his mind what he had to do.

On the day of Nick's departure, Frank waited by the window in his rooms for his friend to stop by on the way to the airport. Seeing Marco's car pull-up, he rushed-out to help Nick with his things. Then he settled him into one of the two chairs in his modest accommodation and put on some coffee.

"Still black?" Frank said, handing Nick a mug.

"Yes, still black. And you, you still like that extra sweetener, don't you?" Nick observed pointedly.

"Yes. I'm afraid I just can't handle bitterness very well." Frank sighed, sitting down with his fragrant brew.

"Unlike those of us who just have to get used to it," Nick said, taking a sip.

"Alright Nick, looks like you're working-up to a theme here. Trying to tell me how bitter my friends are about me? About me leaving so abruptly. I get it, alright?" Frank said brusquely, putting his mug down heavily on the coffee table.

"A guilty conscience needs no accuser, Frank. And what I don't get, is why you're annoyed at your long-time friends feeling betrayed, to say nothing of your parishioners," Nick said, heatedly.

"Parishioners? How do you know anything about my parishioners? Have they been gossiping to Lidia?" he asked, warily.

"Maybe, how should I know?" Nick shrugged insouciantly, "Their long-time, devoted priest suddenly deserts them, and who knows what they're liable to think?

"I mean just look at this," Nick held-out the current copy of *The Guardian* he had tucked in his pocket. It was opened on a piece titled, *Special Privileges for Philandering Priests*, "Ha! I wouldn't blame them if they reckoned you'd got this special treatment, shuttled-off to a cozy monastery in Oxford, where you can pursue your bookish ways…maybe wanton ways too?" Nick insinuated.

Frank's color rose with his anxiety at the turn the conversation was taking, "That's beneath you. I came here because I needed to be here, to pursue a long-lost vocation, and a long-lost self… The friend who has needs! Yes, that's right, Nick, little 'ol harmless, saintly me, having needs. I'm a human being, just like you. So, leave parish gossip and lewd innuendo out of it."

"Alright, fair enough," Nick conceded. "But we all feel betrayed. You were, for some of us, a confessor, for all of us a trusted and valued friend. Then you literally vanish to Rome, then off to Oxford. No explanation, no heart-to-heart. Paul is especially hurt that you wouldn't stay for his nuptials, and did you know Ramona just lost the baby?" Nick said, indignant, pulling-out his phone to summon a cab.

"No, no. I didn't know about their loss. He hasn't been in touch," Frank said, looking down at his lap, admonished.

"No wonder. And Javi? Do you know he and Becky are engaged?"

"No, but I'm very happy for them, Javi's come a long way."

"Ha, you called that one wrong, now didn't you. You thought she'd go back to Paul," Nick smirked.

"Yes, I guess I did. Unlike the pope, I am not infallible," Frank countered.

"Well, congratulations to Javi and Becky, and sympathy to Paul would be appreciated by them, I'm sure. Now, I think I'd better go, my taxi will be here any minute."

Nick stood by the cab as the driver took his luggage to the trunk. Frank handed him his briefcase, opening his palm for a shake. Nick thrust an envelope in it. An unopened, sealed envelope, the one Frank addressed to Lidia and left in the box of books.

Then Nick said, coldly, "Good-bye," with a finality that startled his friend.

As the car left the rows of houses and shops behind for the open highway, Nick looked-out with resolve, thinking, *Antonio is mine, Lidia is mine.* He had no cuckoos in his nest. His life story was his as he created it, and no fallen angel, no dissembling Iago, no Frank Kelley, would take it from him.

ABOUT THE AUTHOR

Loretta Gatto-White is a former food columnist, freelance journalist, and anthologist. Her essays, and poetry have appeared in literary anthologies, journals, and magazines. Her stories have been translated into Italian, published online and in print. The books comprising, *A Pinch of Coriander trilogy* are her first novels.

Website: www.gattowhitewrites.com

Available now in paperback and eBook:

A PINCH OF CORIANDER
TRILOGY
Book One: *Time Will tell*
Book Two: *The Truth About Secrets*
Book Three: *Long Way Home*